WINGSTROKE BY WINGSTROKE,
I BEGAN TO CLIMB . . .

The wind jerked and twisted, screaming in my ears until I screamed back at it, cursing its fey power. My s'olel saw chunks of glass, spires and spikes and monstrous mountainsides, jump out at me tauntingly, only to disappear again, in a malevolent game of Blind Bluff. My vague intention of seeking out a spot to endure the storm evaporated into panic at the dangers of the cruel glass. I continued to climb my invisible path upward, out of the gorge, vaguely astonished at the continuing clarity of the wind map I had drawn in my mind.

Sudden downpours soaked me to the skin and chilled me to the bone. Through wind and storm and cloud I flew heavily upward, the mountainsides drawing slowly back until I could sense them no longer. My breath groaned and gasped in my ears. Suddenly, lightning danced across the surface of the earth, and for the fraction of a moment I saw the mountains and valleys outlined with stark blue light below me. Shivering violently with cold and terror, I tried to shift my direction away from the lightning, but it erupted all around me, flickering and dancing eerily among the heavy clouds.

I entered the damp, roiling center of a stormcloud, and struggled there like an insect caught in a puddle of treacle. After a time the length of a nightmare, I saw the mists fray away above me, to reveal glimpses of three ghostly moons, and a thousand brilliant stars. In an ecstasy of hope, I used the last of my strength to drive myself up out of the clouds.

LAURIE J. MARKS
in DAW Books:

THE CHILDREN OF TRIAD

DELAN THE MISLAID (Book 1)
THE MOONBANE MAGE (Book 2)

THE MOONBANE MAGE

LAURIE J. MARKS

DAW BOOKS, INC.
DONALD A. WOLLHEIM, PUBLISHER

375 Hudson Street, New York, NY 10014

First Printing, April 1990

1 2 3 4 5 6 7 8 9

PRINTED IN THE U.S.A.

For Sara

From the Historical Archives of the t'Cwa Library
Historical Note
to Preface This Personal Account
Written by Ishta Laril
Now Taiseoch of t'Cwa

Ours is a small world, which must be somehow shared by several races. No two have ever seemed more likely to destroy each other than the Aeyrie inhabitants of the glasslands, whose traditional realm is the air and the intellect, and the Walker inhabitants of the lowlands, whose traditional realm is the earth and physical labor.

Yet four visionaries, the Walker Lian of Troyis, the Aeyrie mage Pehtal and ids lover A'bel, and Lian's lover and telepathic partner, the Mer called Pilgrim, were the first to learn that the members of the different races are not so far different from each other as we seem. It was these four who founded the Community of Triad, the one place on earth where members of all races strive to live together as one people.

The peace movement, also called by both Walkers and Aeyries the "h'loa p'rlea," originated in Triad, in the heart of the movement's Aeyrie leader, Malal Tefan Eia. A h'loa p'rlea is a movement of warm air, the first soft wind of spring which bears the spores of the sucker plants that will once again cover the bare mountains with greenery. So, because of the vision of

Triad and the energy of Eia, the Aeyrie and Walker people were learning to invest the vocabulary of peace with the words of hope.

But there was a time that the h'loa p'rlea was only a young Aeyrie's dream, and the community of Triad was only an aberration in the long tradition of separate and hostile peoples. In that time, Eia met by chance a youngster named Delan, who had been raised a Walker and did not know that id was in fact an Aeyrie. Id had fallen into the hands of an old enemy of the Aeyrie people, a Walker sorcerer named Teksan Lafall.

In *Delan The Mislaid*, Delan has recounted ids role in the conflict which came to be known as Teksan's War. The tale of how Delan, an onfrit named Ch'ta, and an Orchth known as Och, managed to avert the war has all but overshadowed ids later fame as a painter, seer, and as the chosen taiseoch of the Triad community.

Twenty years after that war, the usual trade of food for ideas between the Walkers and the Aeyries had been expanded to include another much more tentative trade, the trade of trust. But the achievement of the goal of lasting harmony still largely depended on the continuing efforts of Eia, Delan, and the Triad community. The peace between Walker and Aeyrie remained a fragile peace, and all it might take to disrupt it again was one disaffected meddler.

Chapter 1

The night before my banishment, I danced in the mountain's belly. I remember the shadows jerking across the floor like supernatural puppets, growing and shrinking with the flickering of the air lamp's flame. I remember my opponent's golden wings spreading a shroud of shadow across the light refracting through my blade. The sharp breeze as those powerful wings snapped through the still air; the crystalline chiming of glass upon glass ringing in my ears like shattering icicles; the lamplight firing with ruby the blood veins in my own spread wings; these things too I remember.

Jachim danced arrogance, but I danced rage and hunger. Fierce and graceful as a flame, Jachim struck and parried, but it was I who first drew blood. Even as Jachim drew back, hissing and disconcerted, a blotch of red staining the fire of ids golden fur, I struck again. The needle tip of my blade slid into Jachim's wing membrane, and I sliced it through like a piece of cloth.

Blood spraying from the severed veins spattered a hot crescent across my cheek. Jachim's mouth gaped open with surprise as ids falling blade rang against the uneven floor and ids hands fumbled for the ragged edges of ids tattered wing. Out of ids gaping mouth a thin cry, like an infant's wail, ended with a choking sob.

Wand cackled like a demon in ids hiding place partway up the spiral stairs. I laughed also, challenging with my voice the vast silence and brooding darkness of the Well. The mountain snatched our voices away, then flung our voices back at us, the laughter mixed together with Jachim's choking cries, until our three voices seemed one sound, the voice of a lunatic, crying out in hysterical pain.

When I awoke in the morning, I lay without moving, breathing in the familiar scents of sweat, musk, and kipswool. A band of sunlight, slipping in through a broken shutter, drew a line of warmth across my hand. Dust motes swam in the molten gold, sweeping back and forth with the tides of my breath. Idly, I tried to gather a handful of glowing dust, but I could not close my fingers, and the palm of my hand ached as if bruised by repeatedly absorbing the impact of another's attacking blade.

But it had been a dream. The disconcerting vividness of the self-righteous vision tricked me into thinking of it as a memory. But the fierce pain knifing through my forehead, 'achea's only predictable effect on me, proved otherwise. Once again, I had smoked too much of Wand's apparently limitless supply of 'achea, and had awakened exhausted from my night's sleep, the restfulness having been stolen away by dreams.

To remember the vision apalled me. My small hurt and anger at Jachim had been transformed by the drug into a monstrous, careless rage, that casually violated community law and custom, cruelly delivered a crippling wound, and then laughed mockingly. I remembered that as we smoked, Wand and I had spoken of this small hurt, for my lover Lelis had recently chosen Jachim's bed over mine, having been long and determinedly wooed. As if the conversation were a sorcerer's chat, my commonplace hurt grew into a monstrous insult, and then into a wrong as deep and permanent as a deadly wound. And it began to seem that it was not Lelis who had hurt me, but Jachim, by courting and stealing away something which had been mine. So I had challenged Jachim to a duel in the Well—but no, that must have been part of the dream.

Tossing aside my blankets, I rose from my pallet, for the angle of the shadows on my floor told me the morning had already advanced halfway toward noon. I limped stiffly to the mirror. I remembered the duel in the Well so vividly that I had to check to see if specks of black blood had dried in my silver fur, just to reassure myself once again that it had been a drug dream, nothing more.

When I saw the strangely decorative crescent of droplets spattered across my cheek, I stared and would not believe what my eyes saw.

"But it was a dream," I protested, and turned my back on the mirror. I strode hastily to a window and opened the shutters, to let fresh air into the sweat-musty room and clear away the remainder of the night's visions. "A dream," I said again, as the wind-bells and clattering of windmills and the sound of voices flowed into my room, drowning out the thunder of my panicky heart. "It was only a dream."

When a mage makes the motions of the impossible, the impossible happens. In a vain attempt to work the same sort of magic, I made the motions of normalcy. I scrubbed the blood and sticky sweat out of my fur in the baths, ate some bread and fruit left over from breakfast, and hurried to the h'shal Quai-du, even as the time bell was ringing, to take my place opposite my usual partner for the shadrale l'shil. Almost immediately, as if id had been given orders to wait for me to appear, a l'shan came in, bearing an imperious summons from the taiseoch Ishta, my parent.

As Ishta had scarcely set eyes on me since autumn, no doubt hoping to wait out my l'shil year with as little conflict as possible, I could not doubt the reason for the summons. Under the solemn-faced examination of the other winglings, I casually shrugged my wings into order, patted absently the blade strapped to my thigh, and turned to the Quai-du master to excuse myself.

The look on ids face dug under my fur like a summertime drillfly. So. The gossip-mongers had been busy while I slept late this morning.

I turned my back without speaking, and left the h'shal, neglecting the traditional bow of respect, and permitting the door to slap noisily shut behind me.

Where id often met me after Quai-du training, Wand the Red waited in the hallway, rumpled and tangle-haired as always, red-eyed from last night's debauchery, but sleek and hard beneath ids soft fur. Wand and I had become friends soon after id arrived at t'Cwa. Having been banished in the same year from both t'Fon and t'Han, t'Cwa was ids last option before utter exile into a harsh and food-scarce world. Both in t'Han and t'Fon, Wand told me, the community, set on edge by ids rebellious nature, had been quick to act on minor offenses that would have been overlooked in anyone else.

We had met for the first time on the Quai-du floor, where I, still clumsy in my new body and wings, doggedly practiced the basic forms, while all around me the more advanced Quai-du-dre leapt and sparred. Wand's demented brilliance on the fighting floor had already won my admiration when id came up to me on dancing feet to compliment me extravagantly on my own humble work.

Within days, Wand had drawn blood on the Quai-du floor, and had been forbidden to return there. Id continued to practice in secret with friends, myself among them. I had learned more from my secret teacher in one season that I could have learned from the sh'man Quai-du in four.

Yet, something in me shrank away as Wand danced up to me this morning, weapon in hand in casual violation of community law, saying cheerfully, "There you are, Laril! Have you heard that Jachim may never fly again?"

It was the worst of news. I replied nonchalantly, "So? Some flyers only foul the air."

Wand laughed, menacing me with ids blue blade. More than one Aeyrie's blood had blackened that well-tended edge, some of it mine. A fight without blood was like a seduction without a bedding, Wand often said.

I waved off ids playful assault, saying, "Not now, Ishta has summoned me."

"Give the taiseoch a message for me," said Wand, and made a crude gesture.

"Like this?" I repeated ids gesture several times as if to make certain I was repeating the message correctly. But in my belly lay a frozen thing that watched and did not laugh.

I already knew what Ishta would say to me, for I had been hearing the same speech for years: "You are the child of my old age, a miracle child, hatched when I had lost all hope of an heir," the taiseoch would intone. "I have indulged you, I have given you the wing space that a wild child needs, I have not overly punished you. Perhaps I have wronged you with my patience."

Then id would take a deep breath, and look very resolved. "But you are nearing maturity, and it is time to cease treating you as a child. Therefore you will suffer the consequences of your irresponsibility."

Then punishment would follow, the loss of a privilege or the order to make amends. I would apologize gracefully and explain that it had been an accident and I did not know what had come over me. Ishta would beam fondly on me once more, and it would be over, until the next time.

But how could this often-repeated ritual suffice to counteract the nightmarish memory that haunted me, even in the prosaically busy hallways of the lower tier? I could not explain what had happened, and I could not depend on Ishta, after having been subjected to twenty years of disrespect and outrageous pranks, to even attempt to understand.

In the many common rooms which occupied the lower tier of the Ula, scholarly voices murmured, written papers and the pages of books rustled like the rattling of dry leaves, and pens scraped busily. We passed a small group of students clustered around a collection of crystal fragments while their sh'man discussed the reasons for their various pigments. We passed a noisy, busy workroom, where budding inventors pounded, scraped, and clattered their tools. We passed the closed door of the mages' room, and squeezed past a group of earnest young healers following their sh'man on ids rounds.

As long as I could remember, I had been surrounded by the questioning, discussing, arguing, and learning of the University. Most of my childhood bookdays I had spent in these rooms, under the tutelage of one or another passionate sh'man. But since my winging, I had never returned.

No doubt, like everything else I did of my own will, my decision to devote all my attention to Quai-du rather than to mastery of a scholarly subject was a great disappointment to my parent. Walking down the noisy corridor, with Wand commenting sardonically on everything we passed, I tapped my resentment like a windmill tapping the wind. I would be needing it for this confrontation.

The l'shan at the door admitted me without a word. Wand stood back in the hallway, gesturing to remind me again of the message I was to convey to Ishta. Within, the usual muted chaos seemed oddly stilled. Ishta sat at a writing desk, pen in hand, looking vacantly at the paper. Above idre, on the wall, hung a priceless painting by the artist Delan. I had often studied the strange, disturbingly ambiguous depiction of Aeyries and Walkers together, which at times seemed a battle scene and at other times seemed a complicated, beautiful dance. Under a black sky, fire vividly illuminated the shadowed figures—a celebratory bonfire, or a pyre? The Walkers on the ground, and the Aeyries in flight, encountered each other hand to hand in motions which might have been blows of violence, and might have been the intricate gestures of dance.

The door shut behind me. Ishta looked up at the sound, ids weary face framed by a rare disarray of tangled mane, once silver, now nearly white with age. "Laril," id said heavily.

I had worked myself into such a foul mood that I did not wait for my parent to launch into ids rote speech, as was the custom, but said angrily, "Quai-du is the only training I have chosen freely to engage in. Why could you not wait until after my lesson?"

"As of this moment, Quai-du is forbidden to you."

Ishta's words came out of id's mouth like a weary flyer coming out of a storm, landing heavily and sprawling on the flight deck, too exhausted to even stand.

I looked around myself as if seeking some ally to help me stand firm before those frosted stone eyes. The only other people in the room were some of Ishta's advisors, sh'mans and em'ans, whose presence, like the presence of three onfrits in the corner, meant nothing except that they happened to be there. The stone in my belly grew heavier still.

Ishta said, "I had just lain down to sleep last night when Sh'man Prinea came to my room with the news that Jachim had been badly hurt down in the Well, fighting a duel with a l'shil. That l'shil, the healer told me, was my own child."

"It is true," I admitted, but hesitated over the rest of the truth. How could I explain without sounding as if I were making excuses, or without asking myself the same questions that Ishta, and every other Aeyrie in the Ula was probably asking? Where was the sense in such a duel? Why should I fight a forbidden duel over a lover who had every right to sleep with whomever id chose? Why should I violate the code of honor which bound every Quai-du-dre, to which I myself had sworn before I was allowed to carry the blade I had painstakingly crafted? It was too easy to blame my folly on Wand, or on the 'achea I had smoked earlier under Wand's urging. It was too maudlin to explain that in the morning I had remembered what I had done with a kind of dull surprise, as if I were witnessing the idiot behavior of a stranger. To what purpose all these excuses? I had done what I had done, and the responsibility was mine.

Jachim might never fly again. Perhaps next time id

would hesitate to offend me. I said to myself these words, which were what Wand would say, but still, in my belly, the frozen stone lay.

"You may leave your weapon here. I do not wish to see your face again until you have somehow made amends to Jachim. Do you understand?"

"Quai-du is the only thing I love," I protested, then belatedly remembered that to tell Ishta this was to hand idre power over me.

"Jachim was an air dancer," Ishta reminded me wearily.

"Id has other talents," I said, as if I did not myself cringe at the terrible knowledge of how fragile was this gift I had so long awaited, the ability to fly.

Perhaps I hoped my callous words would goad Ishta into challenging me, to force me to admit the truth of this anguish frozen inside of me, so that at last I could ask for help. But again, those frosted stone eyes, the eyes of a stranger, looked at me across the distance that separated us. Ishta only said again, "You may leave your weapon here."

Wand was waiting outside the door. Without my blade, how could I stand before ids scorn? And what would I do with myself, without Quai-du? My entire life stretched before me; should I return to the everyday tedium of the University, and allow study to eat up my heart? "No," I said to Ishta.

All the sh'mans and em'ans, who had all managed up until now to seem preoccupied with books or papers, abruptly turned their faces to Ishta. My parent bowed ids head into that silence, as if we were at a funeral burning, not in the room where we had enacted this same dull drama many times before.

That silence frightened me. It was time to bargain. "I am truly sorry Jachim was hurt. I would be glad to make amends, however I can. Perhaps I could fly to Triad, to convince one of the healers there—''

Ishta said, ''Either give up your weapon, or remove yourself from t'Cwa.''

''What?''

Ishta only looked at me.

''Then I will leave t'Cwa,'' I said, certain that Ishta would never let me go.

My parent stood up from the beautifully carved binewood stool that had been a gift from ids l'per. ''Go, then,'' id said heavily, and turned ids back on me.

As a l'shan I had been a prankster, a disrupter of solemn occasions, in love with play, but rebellious in my studies and undisciplined in my arts. As a l'shil I had rejected the Companion my parent had carefully chosen for me, and embarked on a rambunctious series of love affairs that scandalized even the open-minded Aeyries. I could not be completely oblivious to the concern of my fellow Ula-dre, many of whom doubted my suitability for the role of taiseoch. Yet I had always been certain of Ishta's love, however mixed it might be with exasperation. To learn that in my parent's heart I stood second to the Ula was a cruel shock.

I slammed out of the h'shal, going out the back way to avoid Wand, and stormed through the narrow hallways in a rage. More than one crafter, wings and burdens knocked askew by my heedless passage, shouted after me angrily, ''Watch your ways! Who do you think you are?''

I told myself that I would leave t'Cwa at once, and fly to Ula t'Fon, to study Quai-du there with the taiseoch Hana. On ids few visits to t'Cwa, Hana had always been a sympathetic friend, and had regaled me with tales of ids own feckless childhood. Ishta would certainly send for me soon enough, for id needed me, and I was ids only heir. Meanwhile, it was about time I saw a little of the world. With these words I tried to soothe myself, as I rushed wildly toward the upper tiers, yet all the while I felt that weight in my belly.

I edged past the ladders and toolboxes of a pair of carpenters who had stripped away a section of the paneled wall, exposing the supports dug into the glass behind it. "Fine day," said one of the carpenters politely.

"For some," I replied.

Breathing heavily from careening up multiple flights of stairs, I walked down the curving hall which encircles the mountaintop, then turned down one of the passages that radiates out from the center toward the perimeter of the Ula. I had chosen one of the most remote rooms of t'Cwa, for the sake of its three windows looking out on the windmills below, and, beyond that, the vast, stark wilderness of the Glass Mountains. Through the window I had opened earlier, a cold wind blew through my room, setting the shutter to banging rhythmically.

Faint voices shouted outside. I stuck my head out the window and looked up, where the water tower loomed. Two people clung to the tower ladders, working with pots of black tar to seal the leaks that had dribbled water or ice down the side of the tower all winter. The wind buffeted their remote, slender bodies, but they laughed as they worked.

Below me, a flyer prepared to land on one of the flight platforms, spreading wings like sails and swinging legs forward to stall. Beyond idre spread the apalling wilderness of the Glass Mountains, a waste of mammoth standing crystals, some of which sliced through the upper atmosphere, beyond the reach of even the highest flying Aeyrie, into the perpetual lifeless winter which is the habitation of the moons. Between these massive, upthrusting shards flowed the ever-changing currents of the wind, upon which we Aeyries fling our passion, our poetry, and our very lives.

Because it was springtime, the lower hills which had been bare all season, except for an occasional icing of hoarfrost or snow, were scattered once more with the pale green of new growth nourished by the warm sun. Overhead, the greenery gave way to barren glass, ranging through shades of gold and orange to occasional startling patches of red. Twice a day, the sun shot the mountains through with fire, a glory of light so brilliant that the Walkers had to turn away their faces from it. All my life, I had looked at those mountains, longing to follow the windways to the lands I had never seen. But I had always imagined that Ishta would send me on my way proudly, calling after me to remember to eat regularly, as I had seen so many other parents do. That I might leave in disgrace, with a scandal to delight the gossips in any town I sheltered in, even now seemed unimaginable.

My only article of clothing lay tossed over a stool, for I had meant to launder it this afternoon. I took off my knife and picked up my flightsuit to put it on, but let the mirror distract me. Only two seasons ago I had been wingless and shapeless, clumsy with fat. Like all l'shils, I could never resist the fascination of my own transformation.

Most Aeyries are black, red, brown, or gold. But my nearly white underfur was tipped with a silver-gray the color of springtime rainclouds. I wore the longer, charcoal-tipped hair of my mane loose and uncut, tying it up with a string or braiding it only for Quai-du. For a l'shil, my torsal muscles had already built up substantially, strengthened both by my early metamorphosis, which had allowed me to fly freely for a season before the bad weather set in, and by my passion for Quai-du. Already, the distinctive, willowy look of the l'shil was giving way in me to the inverted triangular shape of a mature Aeyrie, hooding wings and muscular torso resting above slender, lightly muscled legs.

My coloring was rare enough: only a handful of Silvers, all of us related to each other, still survived. But it was my white wings which turned heads as I passed. Ishta's wings were a soft, pale gray, as were the wings of my egg-parent, a remote cousin who had chosen to forego the role of l'per.

Mairli the inventor, long Ishta's lover, had been a white-winged silver, according to the old Aeyries who remembered idre fondly, but Mairli had disappeared some thirty years ago. If there were any others in the world, I had never heard of them.

I fastened my garment, strapped my knife back into its place, and took up my flight vest to put on later. Perhaps it was springtime, but in the upper atmosphere it would still be cold, and I would need the protection against hypothermia, I closed the window of my room and stripped the blankets off the bed, carrying them back down the hall to a storage closet. In the lower tier I would fill a pouch with c'duni and sh'duni to fuel my journey, claim a couple of travel blankets, and possibly ask an onfrit to keep me company.

On the stairs between the second and third tier, Wand found me. "Slipped out the back door of the h'shal? Are you trying to avoid me?" id said accusingly, but did not await a reply. "Jachim's friends are looking for you. Lelis is with them." Wand's eyes were bright with anticipation of another fight, this one even more exciting than the last.

"Where did you see them?" I asked.

"At the h'shal taiseoch—Ishta invited them in; that's how I knew you weren't there any more. While they were waiting, they asked me where you were. I told them you were looking for them."

"You did?"

"You can't say they aren't hoping for a fight!"

Paused on the stairs, groping with one foot for the next step down, looking at Wand's feverishly bright face, the truth came to me like a tinderstick to an air lamp.

"They certainly are," I said. Wand's face brightened even more, as if I were blowing on a smoldering coal. "Why don't you go find Kiris and Sandil, and I'll meet you in the h'shal Tela with Peni and Andu."

Wand hurried away as eagerly as a child on a festival day, to fetch the other wildlings of our much disapproved of crowd. But I stood for a long time in stunned shock, with my foot suspended over the next step down, marveling at my stupidity. Like a puppet on a string I had danced for Wand, feeding ids monstrous hunger, taking risks that id could no longer afford to take, until I had become like Wand, sharing ids hunger, sharing ids emptiness, but paying the price alone. No friendship this, but something else, a thing for which I had no name.

Despite my arms clutching around my belly, a single sob escaped me, and I had to lean on the handrail, blinking painful tears out of my eyes. There was no time for weeping. I had to leave t'Cwa, and quickly, before Wand could embroil me yet again in a battle I truly did not want.

As Wand vainly awaited me in the h'shal Tela, I stood on a windy flight platform, holding onto the overgrab for stability as I checked all my buckles and

straps one last time, and chanted under my breath,
"Food, flight vest, knife, tinderstick, weather?" I
checked the horizon. White clouds billowed above the
mountains in the south. The last thing I wanted to do
was to climb back inside and search out the weathermaster, who at this time of day could be almost anywhere. I decided not to worry about the weather.
"Map, back-up," I finished automatically. But I could
not secure a map without telling someone where I was
going, and so I had done neither.

I walked to the edge of the platform, where a bright-
eyed onfrit teetered expectantly, and spread my wings
to test the wind. The usual strong updraft swept up the
mountainside. If I managed to avoid flying into the
various windmills, water towers, and other parapher-
nalia decorating the mountaintop above me, I could
ride that updraft to soaring height. The farther out I
leapt from the platform, the less likely I was to have
any potentially fatal accidents.

Far below me, a circle of l'shans played near the
Well door, as tiny as nits. Down a distant ravine, a
line of Walker trade wagons crept down a treacherous
slope, the Walker drivers no doubt covering their eyes
and trembling fearfully at the height.

I curled my toes around the edge of the platform,
let go of the overgrab, and leapt joylessly across the
empty air, onto the back of the wind.

Chapter 2

The onfrit who had offered to accompany me was named Alis'te, which is also the name of the wisp of cloud which trails away from a larger cloud mass on the back of a vagrant, independent breeze. I had saved his life three years ago, when he was just a day-old, coal black, wingless hatchling the size of my thumb.

His mother had foolishly laid her egg in a crack in the canyon wall overlooking the Panicblood River. With the spring thaw, the frozen trickle became a turbulent torrent, murky with minerals and silt, muscling violently through the narrow channel. The rising water level soon threatened the onfrit's once secure nest, even as the pouring rain made it impossible for her to fly her hatchling to safety.

I, fretful and rebellious after the long confinement of winter, had taken a forbidden solitary walk along pathways made treacherous by the rain. When the onfrit found me, I was daydreaming about the day still two years and more in the future, when I would at last grow my wings and be free to wander wherever I chose. She led me up a steep precipice along a pathway littered with tiny shards of crystal and split through with razor-edged, gaping cracks, to the edge of the canyon overlooking the river.

The depth of the canyon and the knife-edged foot-holds did not frighten me, but, as with all Aeyries, I am terrified of water. I climbed down that sheer cliff to a point so close to the river that its spray numbed my already cold feet and hung there, shaking like the luffing sail of a becalmed windmill. Blood from my cut hands dribbled down both my arms, and smears of it from my gashed feet decorated the crystal wall before being washed fussily away by the housekeeper rain.

The onfrit pushed her hatchling out of the crack into my hands . . . and I never saw her again. Whether she had been hurt, or was too wet and tired to make the climb, or was taken by surprise as the first wave of water washed into her nest, I will never know. By the time I had sprawled into safety, gasping for breath and shivering with pain, the rising water had obscured the crack in which she sheltered.

There are no orphans in the onfrit house. When I was allowed to walk again on my injured feet, several days later, Alis'te's foster mother had gotten so protective of her feeble infant that she would not allow me near him. After a few months, I returned to the onfrit house, hoping vaguely to bond with the rescued onfrit, now that he was weaned and winged. Perhaps I thought to substitute him for the younger l'frer I longed for and would never have. But his talents had developed early, and he was already in training to become a messenger.

So from the day I carried him home to t'Cwa sheltered in my bleeding hands, to the day of my banishment, we never met again. That Alis'te remembered me seemed impossible. Yet after I asked for a companion, he had buffeted two other onfrits out of the air so that he would be the first to reach my shoulder.

And I, though I had never seen him as an adult, knew him at once.

Alis'te flew the fey wind almost casually. I followed him through the turbulence immediately surrounding the Ula, into the more predictable currents of the updraft. Below me, the brightly painted rooftops of t'Cwa wrapped the mountain peak like a gigantic, eccentric necklace. As we continued to circle in a climbing spiral, the last water tower, surrounded by spinning, clanking windmills, dropped below me.

"Do you know a h'loa t'Fon?" I bellowed up at the onfrit. His black wings had been rowing him steadily upward, two arm's lengths over my head, with the distance between us increasing. But he dove down promptly at the sound of my voice, to repeat blankly, "H'loa t'Fon?"

"H'lana," I corrected myself. Onfrits are literal, linear thinkers, and I had confused him by using the word h'loa, which describes a soft wind, a gentle, widespread motion sometimes compared to a rising tide in the sea, when I meant to say h'lana, a river wind, which could carry me long distance in its powerful current.

"Follow me," Alis'te said, to my great relief. Though I knew in theory how to locate and ride a h'lana, I had never actually done it.

He broke out of the updraft to guide me toward the northeast. I dug my wings deeply into the unsteady air, tasting it with my membranes like a new food on my tongue. We climbed through a troubled layer of air full of hesitations and unpredictable eddies, into a relatively calm layer where a few small clouds were resting. Far below, a brook trickled like a blood vein in its bright red channel, weaving its way amid the uneven terrain toward the river.

We slipped around the peak of a great mountain, the one we call Sh'man because of its mane of white clouds. I twisted my head to catch a glimpse of t'Cwa as it was eclipsed by the dark orange of the mountain's tremendous ridges. Then my home was gone from sight. I found I could not breathe steadily, and struggled dizzily in the wake of my guide.

My wings prickled suddenly. Alis'te and I began to climb again, through a layer of air where my skin itched and my hair crackled with electricity, into a sudden turbulence which violently demanded my attention, buffeting my wings almost closed and nearly turning me onto my back. Alis'te, tossed about lightly like a toy, fluttered onward, but I had to fight with each stroke to retain my equilibrium.

At last I broke through, and was sucked irresistibly into the current of the h'lana. My first panicky wing-flap gave way to awed acceptance, as my effortless speed doubled and tripled. I was caught up in a pattern beyond my understanding; the h'lana, even as it moved me, being moved by some other global force.

I spread my wings to their fullest, and then tucked my chilled hands into my armpits and tried to relax. Passivity did not come easily to me: time and again I caught myself trying to exert my will, an effort which would only put my resources of energy to waste.

The landscape hurried below me as if I were scanning a map. This had to be the Gorge A'shana-re, the north-south route used in the springtime to the exclusion of all others because of its rare obstacles and dependable h'lanas. If luck were with us, we would see the first of its shelter flags before sunset, and we could avoid spending the night on a barren, wind-scoured ridge.

Ahead of me, I spotted Alis'te, black as a misplaced shadow, struggling against the current to slow his speed. When I had caught up with him, I anchored him to my greater weight with a tether of astil. I offered him a bit of c'duni, and we ate companionably as we floated across the surface of the earth.

"How long will it take us to reach t'Fon?" I asked.

"Two days," said Alis'te, then, looking sideways at the sun and downward to measure my speed in relationship to the passing landscape, recalculated. "Three days."

"Onfrits fly the wind much faster than Aeyries," I said.

"Yes," he replied smugly.

"Do you remember before you were winged, when I climbed down the cliff to save you from the river?"

Alis'te looked at me, bright-eyed as if with humor. "Onfrit people remember, tell the story many times."

"Of course, you were just a hatchling then."

"Why does Laril leave t'Cwa?" asked Alis'te rhetorically. "There is no gladness in your heart."

I shook my head, setting strands of my mane to tangling before my eyes.

Alis'te offered me a sliver of his c'duni, and I ate it, even though it was sticky with his saliva. I was in no position to be able to refuse anyone's friendship, even that of an onfrit.

All l'shans, when they are very young, are told this story, so they can understand more clearly the cooperation and affection between the Aeyries and the onfrits:

At the beginning of time; the two winged people, the first onfrit and the first Aeyrie, were equal to each other. But the onfrit, like all the other creatures of the earth, split itself in half; one half male, the other half female, so that they could mate. The Aeyrie alone remained intact in idreself. Instead of mating, id chose to focus all ids attention on the pursuit of knowledge and the creation of new things in the world: art, science, magic, music, literature, history, dance, and drama. Soon the onfrit population had grown to many hundreds, but the first Aeyrie lived alone, in a nest filled with tools and telescopes, books and paintings, charts and scrying glass, and all manner of wonderful inventions.

The Aeyrie had no one with whom to share ids creations, except for ids friends, the onfrits. But as the years passed, the Aeyrie's work increased in complexity and subtlety, until the onfrits, being preoccupied with the work of seeking food, mating, nesting, and raising young, could no longer understand idre.

Therefore, one day the oldest onfrits, who had been the first Aeyrie's friends from the beginning of time, came to visit. They said to idre, "Even before we were split into male and female, we have been your friend. Therefore, hear what we have to say. You have grown beyond our understanding, and you have become a great mage. Use your magic to create a friend for yourself, to be your companion and share your discoveries."

The first Aeyrie heeded the wisdom of the onfrits, and went to stand before a mirror to work a great magic. Day and night id considered ids own image, focusing all ids loneliness and all ids longing upon the Aeyrie in the mirror, until at last the image Aeyrie turned ids head independently of the first Aeyrie, and greeted idre in a voice like the whispering of wind over crystal.

Then the first Aeyrie was glad, for at last id had someone with whom to share all of ids life, ids thoughts and dreams, ids works and creations, ids arts and magics. Hour after hour, day after day, the mirror Aeyrie listened, watched, and understood as the first

Aeyrie spoke, danced, worked spells, wove on ids loom, or studied in silence.

But the day came that the first Aeyrie was once more filled with longing, and visited ids friends, the onfrits, to reveal ids heartstruth to them. "I rue the day I created the mirror Aeyrie," id said. "Now, day and night, I am tortured with longing. The mirror Aeyrie listens and understands, but does not imagine. The mirror Aeyrie watches me dance, but cannot dance with me. When the night is cold and stormy, I cannot lie down with the mirror Aeyrie, and share ids warmth, for id is cold, and hard, and has no heart."

Then the onfrits said, "You made a choice at the beginning of time, to remain both male and female, and therefore to be alone."

"I have never regretted the choice I made," said the first Aeyrie. "I have lived long and joyfully in my search for knowledge and beauty. But now it is time for me to die."

Then id lay down on the floor before the mirror Aeyrie, and refused to either eat or drink.

"I am nothing without you," said the mirror Aeyrie, pleading with ids friend to reconsider. "If you die, I die also." But the first Aeyrie only shook ids head and would not answer. Soon, the mirror Aeyrie also lay down and began to pine away.

Then the onfrits held a great convocation, and came as one to the Ula of the first Aeyrie. They said, "Many long years you have been our friend. You have cared for our young when they were injured or ill. You have showed us how to store food for the long winter, and how to read the sky so we can take shelter before the storms. You have delighted us with your music and poetry, and you have woven soft cloth on your loom to line our nests. Now, it is time for us to give in return."

So the onfrits took a great bowl, and as each one passed the bowl, they pricked themselves and let fall one drop of blood, and pulled out one tuft of fur from their body, and cried one tear. Then, each onfrit gave up into the bowl the ability to speak, to think about the future, to speculate and scheme, and to reason.

"This is too much," said the first Aeyrie when they were finished, and id took out of the bowl some of the ability to speak, and scattered it out among the onfrits. But id did not scatter it evenly, so that some of them could speak many languages fluently, and some of them could scarcely speak at all. Then the first Aeyrie took out of the bowl some of the ability to reason, and scattered it among the onfrits. Again, some of them received more reason, so that they remained equal to the Aeyries, and others received only a little reason.

Then the first Aeyrie took up the bowl, and threw its contents into the mirror. The mirror shattered into a hundred pieces, some of the pieces falling into the light, some into the darkness, some into the fire, some onto the wooden floor, and some outside into the snow. From the pieces that fell into the light rose up the Golden Aeyries, from those that fell into the dark the Black Aeyries, from those that fell into the fire the Red Aeyries, from those that fell onto the floor the Brown Aeyries, and from those that fell onto the snow the Silver Aeyries.

From that time forward the onfrits and the Aeyries have lived together. The onfrits, having given up so much, depend on the wit and reason of the Aeyries. And the Aeyries, who know they are forever indebted to the onfrits, live with them in respect, and care for them gladly.

As a l'shan, I loved this tale. But now, tears come to my eyes when I hear it. I must grieve, that a creature of earth was willing to give up so much, even if it was out of loyalty and friendship. Sometimes I understand that it is not the onfrits I grieve for, but for myself.

As the sun sank toward the horizon, the chilling air washed over my wings like snow water. The color of the glass had changed gradually from red to purple, and now shone a clear, deep blue. Some of the peaks were so translucent that I saw shadow things in their depths, as if the mountains cherished moving pictures of memory in their secret hearts. Something in the wind began to itch at my senses. I tugged gently at the tether which linked me to Alis'te. "How far is it to the shelter? Will we be there before dark?"

"After sun, before stars," said the onfrit.

"Will you be able to find it in the twilight?"

"I fly this way many times."

The sun slid down and speared itself on the upheld knife blade of a mountain, and the wasteland of blue glass was filled with blinding contrasts of white light and black shadow. On the horizon to my right, a fingernail sliver of a moon appeared, ghostlike, in the still bright sky. Then, as the sky darkened, a few huge stars appeared, bright as crystals in sunshine.

Alis'te tugged softly on the tether. After a last blaze across the cool blue crystal, the sun had slid below the horizon, and dusk lay its shroud over the bright ridges and dark canyons. I followed Alis'te down, fighting my way out of the h'lana into the turbulence below. For the first time, as I fought the playful, unpredictable wind, I realized how tired I was. My flight muscles felt rubbery and unreliable, and responded only reluctantly to the stimulus of the wind.

A mammoth, razor-edged summit grazed past us, trailing shreds of cloud in the twilight. The wind jumped me from behind like a playful l'shan, trying to bend my wings over backward, and running cold fingers over the soles of my feet. We passed the shelter flag, whipping and snapping in the gale. The wind tossed me upward, as if to impale me on one of those spiked crests. I peered anxiously forward in the half light, knowing that Alis'te could not see any better than I.

At last I spotted the shelter, a sturdy, ground-hugging building hidden in the windbreak of a cluster of prism-shaped spikes. I had to land in this gale without the assistance of overgrabs or railings, a tricky business of timing my stall between gusts of wind. I crashed onto one knee, crushing a wing painfully against the smooth, cold side of a chunk of glass, but other than some bruises I was not hurt.

Alis'te had already ducked out of the wind into the shelter's onfrit entrance. He abruptly reappeared, wings tightly closed across his back, squinting in the wind as he climbed toward me.

I sheltered in the leeward side of a crystal formation. As Alis'te drew near, I could hear him chittering anxiously under his breath. "What is it?" I asked.

"Walker smell," he said.

"Are you certain?"

Alis'te turned his back on me irritably, to let me know that I had questioned him one too many times this day. But I found it impossible to believe that Walkers had been here, in a place purposely chosen for its inaccessibility from the ground. "Maybe something is in the shelter that happens to smell like a Walker," I suggested.

Alis'te puffed out his fur and huddled down against the cold. He apparently had no intention of going back into the shelter, and was choosing to endure the night right where he was.

Out of all the onfrits in the onfrit house, I had been

picked out by one with a temper, as obstinate and opinionated as any Aeyrie. Shrugging my wings at him, I went to the shelter and let myself in.

The interior smelled of mildew and disuse. I lit the air lamp by the door with my tinderstick. The flare of light revealed a small, low-ceilinged room, its wooden floor covered by rugs, sleeping pallets rolled up neatly in one corner. On the far side of the shelter, the presence of a cookstove reminded me that it and the building materials would have been hoisted from a wagon below, using a block and tackle. For an Aeyrie work crew, the business of hauling materials would have been exhausting, frustrating labor, compounded by every handspan higher they chose to build the shelter. If an iron cookstove could be hauled up to the shelter site, then why couldn't a Walker climb up here?

Because, I reminded myself, Walkers were as terrified of heights as Aeyries were of water. Yet I examined the shelter nervously, checking in every cupboard and shining a light into every shadowed corner. I found nothing inexplicable or disarranged. Having discovered packets of dried foods in a rodent-proof cabinet, I engaged the windmill, which to my surprise was still functioning after a winter of storms, and soon a steady stream of water was pouring through the tap to fill the pot. I went out once to shout at Alis'te, but he didn't move from his huddle in the shelter of the rocks.

I cooked a stew of dried fruit and nuts, and brought a bowl of it out to Alis'te. The moons and stars overhead had been consumed by a heavy cloud cover. The cold, damp wind shivered with electricity. My wings shuddered involuntarily at the message they scried from that wind.

"It's going to be a bad storm," I said to Alis'te.

"There are no Walkers here now; come in out of the cold."

"No," said the onfrit stubbornly. He dipped a soggy piece of reconstituted fruit out of the bowl, and ate hungrily. I kept him company for a while, but the fierce wind drove me back into the shelter, where the last warmth from the cookstove was rapidly being sucked out the stovepipe. I made up a pallet with an extravagance of blankets and lay down to sleep, my muscles throbbing with weariness.

At t'Cwa, after a day's hard flying, I would rest my sore muscles in the steam room, perhaps with a friend or lover to massage my muscles and oil my wings. How suddenly my life had changed! How could I survive in a world so arbitrary, where disasters came upon one uncontrollably, where dreams became reality and parents became enemies? Mystified, I considered once more what had happened to me. I wanted to make sense of the events and arrange them into an acceptable order, but I could not do it.

There was Wand, who had used me in his sickness, but had no reason to hate or despise me. That id had encouraged me into folly I now saw clearly. But there was something more to the duel in the Well than just Wand's love for violence. Surely I could not have fought that cruel battle did I not also love violence. Surely a fantasy of revenge could not have become reality without my eager compliance.

I lay awake, staring into the darkness, torturing myself with memories of Jachim's wing ripping open before my knife, despising myself.

I awoke from a confused dream to the insistent tugging of a small paw on my hair. I murmured sleepily, "Changed your mind? Here, get under the blankets where it's warmer."

But Alis'te chirped in a hushed, fearful voice, "Walkers coming."

"What?" The wind howled outside, hushing through the stovepipe like waves in a hollow, screaming down the razor edges of the mountains, spattering a tattoo of rain across the roof.

"I see them. I smell them."

"How can you hear or smell anything in that storm? No one is abroad on a night like this. Come under the blankets, it was just a dream."

Alis'te gnashed his sharp teeth at me. "Laril thinks this onfrit is a fool," he said angrily. "Laril thinks I do not know dream from danger. I want to bite you!"

"Don't!" I sat up stiffly, untangling myself from the knot of blankets. The entire upper half of my body burned with pain, and my head throbbed with sleepiness. "I just don't understand why this would be happening."

"Fly now. Understand later."

I had no intention of trying to fly in this storm, in the middle of the night, but, having been drilled since childhood on what to do in case of a Walker attack, I pulled on my clothing and strapped on the various pouches containing my emergency supplies. When I unlatched the shelter door, the wind crashed it open and knocked me back against the doorsill. Cruel needles of rain dove through my clothing and fur to burn with cold against my skin. I picked up Alis'te from the floor and set him on my shoulder. He clutched my mane tightly enough to tug tears into my eyes. It was his terror which convinced me out into the gale to investigate, for onfrits are realists, not prone to wild imaginings.

I could not see anything, not even the ground underfoot or the sky overhead. I could only guess where the crystal shards and the edge of the escarpment were

located. Wings folded tightly so the wind wouldn't jerk
them awry, I felt my way one step at a time, the onfrit
whispering in my ear, "Right hand ways, coming up
the mountain. Smell them?"

I could smell only the rain. I crept cautiously toward
my right, ears straining for some sound other than the
screaming wind and the spattering rain. I heard nothing. But suddenly, as if a single star had broken free
of the cloud cover, I saw a light. Beyond that single
flame, wildly flickering in its protecting globe, a
shadow moved jerkily in a motion as familiar to me as
the motion of a hand turning the pages of a book. It
was an Aeyrie, refolding a wing knocked awry by the
storm.

Laughing with relief, I shouted a welcome which
the screaming wind snatched out of my mouth and
carried away. I shouted again, hurrying forward eagerly, realizing only now how lonely I had been this
long night. At last the Aeyrie seemed to hear me, turning sharply and standing rigidly against the overwhelming darkness.

"What are you doing out here in the storm?" I
shouted. "Come in out of the cold! There's a fruit
stew I could—"

The stranger leapt over the small light, and in two
more leaps was upon me. I was still pondering to myself the reason for this odd behavior, when by sheer
chance the faintest glimmer of light ran down the edge
of the blade which the Aeyrie held in ids hands. It was
a fighting weapon, held in the hand of a master. This
much my s'olel told me, in the fractured moment as
the glimmer still clung to the drawn weapon, just before the Aeyrie made ids strike.

Chapter 3

Crystal chiming on crystal awoke my haunted memories of the duel in the Well. As my singing blade once more blocked my unknown attacker's blow, I cried, "I am Laril of t'Cwa! Why are you fighting me?" But the other Aeyrie said nothing.

I scried the sum truth from the dance itself: that this deranged attack was no accident; that my opponent intended to disarm and take me prisoner without harming me. But I could not guess why.

My pale fur and white clothing glowed with reflected light. My opponent was only a silent shadow, dark against the darkness. I guessed my way through steps of the dance, my eyes blinded by night, my wings confounded by the wind. Three times the powerful stroke of my opponent clashed like a bell against my knife, rattling pain into my bones, forcing me helplessly backward a step at a time. I sought in myself the cruel, bitter rage that had empowered me in the battle with Jachim, but found only terror. Why was this happening to me? If I was so certain my life was not in danger, what did I fear?

The Aeyrie of shadows spread ids wings to propel another attack, the one that I knew would knock my knife out of my numbed hand. A gust of wind, catch-

ing in ids widespread wings, threw idre momentarily
off balance. I ducked into the darkness like a criya into
its hole, and fled, heedless of the unseen menace of
glass and chasm. The cold glass burned under the soles
of my feet. Alis'te clung to me in grim silence, claws
pricking my shoulder. I ran toward the shelter, with
the stranger clinging to my heels like a shadow. Almost too late, I realized that the shelter's safety would
be illusory: the security of its latched door and shuttered windows was that of a prison rather than a haven.

I veered wildly sideways, my wings knocking
sharply against the stranger's as I leapt past. A hand
clamped briefly onto my wrist, but I used the weakness inherent in such a grip to twist free, as a flood-
gate opened overhead, drenching me in a freezing
waterfall.

Slithering on the suddenly slick glass, I fought for
balance, nearly fell, dug my toes into firmer footing,
took a great stride forward, and collided into a knee-
high chunk of crystal. I fell over it, screaming with
fear and pain, into a helpless heap of wings and limbs.
In a moment the stranger was upon me, throwing ids
weight onto my sprawled limbs like shackles, breathing heavily with anger in my ear. I choked on a mouthful of rain, knowing that I had lost the battle.

Alis'te exploded out of the darkness into the face of the
stranger, chittering a shrill battle challenge. With a shout
of surprise, the stranger shifted backward, dark arms flail-
ing at the formidable claws and teeth of the enraged onfrit.
My groping fingers found my blade almost out of reach.
I hauled one leg under myself and aimed a feeble blow at
the stranger's shoulder. That weak nip at ids flesh was
enough to lift the last of ids weight momentarily from my
other leg, and I jerked free.

I spread my wings and took a desperate leap into
the storm. The fierce gale lifted me casually into the

air, shooting sharp needles of rain into my eyes. Then the wind cast me aside, and I fell. My wings sensed the empty gulf gaping below me. The cruel wind had tossed me over the edge of the cliff, then abandoned me to the merciless force of gravity.

As I plummeted into the screaming void, struggling my wings open to break my fall, the shouting voices of the Walkers halfway up the side of the cliff swept past me. *Alis'te, I should have believed you,* I thought regretfully. The wind slipped past me and pushed me upward, then twisted me cruelly toward the invisible crystal that I sensed slashing past me, first on my left, then on my right. Another sudden upward gust sustained me long enough for me to spread my wings properly, transform my fall into a hover, and begin to struggle in earnest for my life.

The fickle wind toyed with me mercilessly. I spread my wide wings, shut my eyes, and sought by s'olel to read the crazy mysteries of the impenetrable darkness.

The wind careened off the mountainsides and rebounded against the ground below. Piece by piece, I sketched the pattern of the shifting energies onto my mind. I saw the wind struggling in the gorge like liquid in a shaken bottle. I saw myself stalled five or six winglengths from the ground, having by sheer luck found my way to a relatively calm eddy between opposing whirlwinds. Using the rebounding winds as signposts, I located myself in relation to the walls of the gorges: a lone, tiring flyer struggling to hold ids own amid swirls of violent wind.

As if it were just a schoolroom exercise, I studied the picture. The solution to the problem was as clear as a pathway up a rugged hillside. Wingstroke by wingstroke, I began to climb.

Despite the groaning gasp of my lungs, as I pumped freezing air in and out of my burning throat, I wasted

some of my previous breath to call, "Alis'te!" My
voice wavered threadily away. A fluke of the wind
brought to my ears once again the alien sound of
Walker voices, speaking angrily over my head.

The Aeyrie who had attacked me would be as night
blind as I, but the Walkers might be able to spot me
even in the lightless storm. I hoped they would not
shoot me with their deadly crossbows. I hoped the
Aeyrie would not be so stupid as to go over the cliff's
edge after me.

The wind, which had calmed for a few moments, as
if to catch its breath, smacked into me suddenly,
knocking me sideways toward the invisible menace of
the mountainside. A razor edge, so palpable it almost
seemed I could see it, slashed a finger's width away
from my wing.

The wind jerked and twisted, screaming in my ears
until I screamed back at it, cursing its fey power. My
s'olel saw chunks of glass, spires and spikes and monstrous mountainsides, jump out at me tauntingly, only
to disappear again, in a malevolent game of Blind Bluff.
My vague intention of seeking out a spot to endure the
storm evaporated into panic at the dangers of the cruel
glass. I continued to climb my invisible path upward,
out of the gorge, vaguely astonished at the continuing
clarity of the wind map I had drawn in my mind.

Sudden downpours soaked me to the skin and chilled
me to the bone. Through wind and storm and cloud I
flew heavily upward, the mountainsides drawing slowly
back until I could sense them no longer. My breath
groaned and gasped in my ears. Suddenly, lightning
danced across the surface of the earth, and for the
fraction of a moment I saw the mountains and valleys
outlined with stark blue light below me. Shivering violently with cold and terror, I tried to shift my direction away from the lightning, but it erupted all around

me, flickering and dancing eerily among the heavy clouds.

I entered the damp, roiling center of a stormcloud, and struggled there like an insect caught in a puddle of treacle. After a time the length of a nightmare, I saw the mists fray away above me, to reveal glimpses of three ghostly moons, and a thousand brilliant stars. In an ecstasy of hope, I used the last of my strength to drive myself up out of the clouds.

At last I hovered above the storm, gasping and choking for breath. Lightning flickered faintly among the clouds below. Above my head, three moons consorted together, examining me coldly as I intruded on their dance. Stars hung like crystals burning with secret white flames, scarcely more than an arm's length out of my reach. The stormclouds were a wind-tossed, ethereal lake, illuminated within by flickering blue light, with stark, snow-crusted mountain peaks breaking through like islands. From the madness below I had ascended into a stark, empty, frozen world.

My lungs ached in the thin, cold air. I began to fly, using a ghostly mountain peak as a landmark, but even this small effort left me dizzy and coughing for air. I had no choice but to spread my wings like sails, and let the weak, unpredictable winds carry me as they willed. I ate a c'duni bar, which flushed its energy through my blood like a random passion, only to fade swiftly away. I sank into an exhausted, indifferent stupor.

The winds flowed like water, from weak stream to strong current, and then to a rushing river. I awoke a little from my daze when the h'lana sucked me into its crackling, roaring flood, but I was only an abandoned boat on its irresistible tides, and I could do no other than let it carry me.

The water in my mane and fur had frozen into ice. My feet trailed after me, unfeeling as blocks of stone.

But my warm hands reassured me that I was safe from hypothermia. The inevitable frostbite would only be an annoyance. If I could continue to muster the energy to keep my wings spread, I would not die.

I fell into a shallow sleep, and then awoke with a start, vaguely surprised to find that my s'olel had continued to maintain my stability in the air even as I slept. My people sometimes tell stories about desperate journeys, when a heroic flyer rode day and night on the back of a h'lana; sleeping, eating, and defecating in the air. As a l'shil, I had wondered how such a thing could be possible, but the knowledge of how to do it seemed to be woven into the very fabric of my mind. I could resist my exhaustion no more than I could resist the h'lana. Once again, I slept.

Cold water dripping from the tip of my nose awoke me to a pale dawn. The ice that covered me like hard candy had begun to melt in the wan warmth of the nearing sunrise. Stiff-necked, I raised my dangling head, and peeled the wet hair out of my face. One handful at a time, I wrung the water out of my mane and then knotted the whole mess at the nape of my neck. I glanced with a sinking heart at the alien landscape below. I certainly had outflown the storm, I thought dully.

Throughout the uneasy night, pain had wrenched through my flight muscles with every shift of the wind. Yet I cried aloud with surprise at the assault of agony that resulted from my first sleepy wingstroke. The heavy, warm object resting on my back between my wings stirred itself, startling me so that I jerked my wings, crying out again, my voice ragged with near hysteria.

The chirping voice of an onfrit said in my ear, ''Laril?''

"Great hellwinds!" I yelled angrily, and then relief washed over me and I gentled my voice. "How did you find me?"

"H'lana takes us both on long journey," said Alis-'te mildly.

I wanted to hug him, but had to settle for stroking the forehead peering over my shoulder. His fur was warm and dry. "Well you've had a cozy night of it," I said grumpily, wondering how he had managed to settle onto my back without me even being aware of it.

The sun rose at my feet, which in a moment's time shifted from numbness to pain. Light painted the wilderness below in pastel shades of rose and green. Jagged mountains rippled in the soft light of sunrise, cupping green hollows protectively between ragged fingers.

"Do you know where we are?"

"No," said Alis'te after a moment.

"I have never heard of glass this color."

The onfrit sighed in my ear, and then yawned. When the onfrits donated to the first Aeyrie their ability to anticipate the future, they had also lost their ability to worry about the unknown. Anxiety roiling like nausea in my belly, I saw the other side of the onfrits' great sacrifice, and fiercely envied Alis'te.

The wind weakened with the sunrise. I brushed a damp arm across my eyes, but my vision, blurry with tiredness, would not clear. Sobbing with pain as I forced my weakened muscles into motion, I began to fight my way earthward, gulping the thin air painfully into my raw lungs. I battered through the invisible layer upon which the h'lana skated. Then I could rest as the earth pulled me downward, into thick, warm, breathable air.

The mountains unfolded from around a pocket in which they sheltered a beautiful lake, bright as a sapphire in the early morning sunshine. I turned toward it, and landed at last, in a tumble of numbed and exhausted limbs, in a bed of ast on its banks.

It was so soft and warm there that I fell asleep where I lay, and slept away the entire morning without stirring, until hunger finally awakened me. In my dreams, I had been puzzling away at a problem. The circumstances that had brought me here seemed almost too random and senseless. Surely, if I only studied them long enough, I would uncover a pattern. Now that I was awake, I laughed at myself. One thing all sentient beings seem to have in common is the preference for sensible order, however illusory, over the reality of chaos. No doubt if I puzzled over my problem long enough, I would come up with some ridiculous conspiracy, easy to believe only because of the alternative.

I stood up stiffly, and reached first with one wingtip and then with the other toward a remote mountain peak that glowed softly in the afternoon sunlight. Filaments of pain shot through my muscles. It would be many days before I could fly again, no more than I could expect after such a night.

To my right, the lake lay like a gigantic fallen mirror. A puffy cloud floated in its impossibly blue sky, rimmed by the pink, uneven teeth of the mountains. The perfect image shivered suddenly. I rubbed my eyes before I realized that the blurring had been caused by the wind ruffling the water. The water licked the shore with wet, sucking sounds, and the ast rubbed its fibrous leaves together with a dry whisper. Then the image in the lake cleared, and the uninhabited wilderness filled with aching silence.

I looked around myself in a panic, until the sight of Alis'te dozing on a sunny perch nearby eased the terror of my loneliness. I stripped off my clothes to examine my various throbbing injuries. I could scarcely

bend the fingers of my knife hand, it was so badly
bruised. Various scrapes and other injuries covered my
body, but the worst of them were on my shins, where
I had battered them as I careened over the block of
glass in the dark. I had gashed open my feet without
knowing it, during last night's desperate battle. My
toes ached with frostbite. My flight muscles were so
exhausted I cold scarcely keep my wings folded.

The raw energy contained in my supply of flight
food would keep me on my feet for a day or two, but
c'duni and sh'duni could not nourish me into healing.
I needed to find some solid food quickly. I had noticed
from the air that the green collar surrounding the lake
had been wider at the western end where three streams
fed into it. Perhaps deposits of silt and minerals had
laid down a deep enough layer of soil so that something other than sucker plants could grow.

It was too early in the season for seeds or fruits to
be ripe, but I could subsist on alinsa, a starchy white
root that grew in swampy areas. I had studied the bo-
tanical drawings until I could prove to my instructors
that I would recognize alinsa, along with various other
edible plants, on sight. I felt embarrassed now, re-
calling my impatient resentment at having to pass so
many tests before I would be permitted to fly.

I limped so slowly along the lake's edge that Alis'te
winged impatiently ahead, returning from time to time
to check on me. I passed several budding ast patches.
Once they bloomed, Alis'te would eat well, but ast
blossoms were nothing more to me than a fragrant
herb for flavoring sweet breads. No sucker plant can
adequately fuel an Aeyrie's life fire. Our food must be
harvested from water, or earth.

This is the fundamental issue of survival for my
people: we are at home in the mountains, but the
mountains offer us nothing to eat. Now that the Walk-

ers claimed to own the lowlands where we had foraged since the beginning of time, our choices were either to trade, or to starve. Until the Walkers, our technology had been just one of many expressions of my people's intellectual curiosity. After the Walkers, it became our entire lives.

No one is alive anymore, who remembers what we call the Age of Balance, before the population explosion of the Walkers. But I think we all continue to grieve its passing, each of us in our own way. I understand my passion for Quai-du as a manifestation of that grief. Quai-du is part of the ancient lore, a tradition born of and exemplifying the Age of Balance. But the study of Quai-du, like many other arts, is no longer encouraged. It does not feed the people.

Soon I had to wade across a wide, fast-moving stream. It was not deep enough to drown me, but I panted with anxiety as the current tugged at my fur. As I limped slowly around the lake, past a criya catacomb echoing with shrill alarm cries, my hunger wrapped a pain through my belly and up into my chest.

At last I reached my goal at the end of the lake, a sodden marsh, redolent with the sweet smell of rot. I waded nervously into the silty mud, sometimes sinking into it as deep as my knees, in search of the fanshaped leaves of the alinsa plant.

It was nearly evening before I had wrestled a twisted root as thick as my arm out of the sucking silt. Without fuel for a fire, I had to eat the root raw, a watery, bitter meal. My stomach grumbled in complaint as I lay awake afterward in a crevice, wrapped in blankets, Alis'te a comforting warmth in my arms, looking at the stars.

I had never studied the star charts like I should have done. I knew that I had been carried far from settled lands, but how far, or where, I could not be certain.

I had been traveling westward when I awoke at sunrise, but the stars suggested that the h'lana had not carried me due west all night long. Perhaps this wilderness had been sketchily charted by some eccentric Aeyrie wanderer, but a map would have been of no use to me anyway.

If I flew westward, I eventually would find my way home, but I might never find a h'lana to take me the right direction. It was this possibility that brought my heart into my throat. To attempt the journey on foot would be a kind of suicide, for I would starve in a matter of days. To attempt to fly such a great distance without a h'lana would kill me even more quickly. Without a lucky wind, I was effectively stranded.

The chirping and croaking of swamp dwellers jeered into my dreams, and I awakened in the middle of the night, sobbing with loneliness under the remote examination of a single moon.

Daybreak found me thigh-deep in mud again, trying to pull an alinsa up by the roots, but succeeding only in sinking myself deeper in the mud with each jerk. Paddle-footed water creatures came up to examine me curiously. Feeling angry and foolish, I shouted at them in frustration, chasing them away for a brief respite before they came creeping back again.

Alis'te had flown off in search of ast or panja blossoms for breakfast. When I first heard a few faint musical notes, I paid no attention, assuming the song to be his. The strange, wailing half-notes attracted my full attention almost too late. I ducked into hiding amid a tangle of twisting vines, as a Walker waded through the knee-deep sucker plants that covered the slope to the lake, singing absorbedly and walking as if in a dream. A change in the footing cut off the song, and the Walker looked about in surprise.

I had seen and, to please my parent, even spoken with a few Walker traders, but they had never seemed anything but alien to me, with their strange, furless bodies, four limbs, and dramatic variations in height, hands, and coloring. Something about the shape of this Walker particularly bothered me, until the wind molded her loose tunic around breasts twice the size of mine, and I realized that I had before met only males, and this one had to be female. I wondered idly if she were lactating. If she was, she had left her hatchling at home. She was taller than I, and more heavily built. A short, unkempt brown mane covered her head. Golden pollen dusted her brown, hairless legs.

She waded fearlessly into the water of the lake, to work something free of the thick tangle of plants growing at the lake's edge. It was a small boat, which I had not noticed because the overgrowth hid it. With a dull thud she threw her basket into it, and then climbed into it herself, nearly tipping it over in the process. As she bailed it out, she began to sing a cheerful and lively song, as if to force herself out of her distracted, somber mood. I caught glimpses of her face as she worked. She seemed grim and preoccupied. Her short mane stuck in strings to her sweat-shiny skin.

At last she nocked the oars and rowed off briskly, the boat chucking softly as the strength of her stroke lifted its bow out of the water and slapped it down again. In the middle of the lake she shipped her oars, and picked up something from the bottom of the boat. It was a caricha net: I recognized it from an illustration in a book. I had tasted caricha buds once in my life; but as I watched her screw together the sections of the handle, my mouth began to water.

With diminished enthusiasm I turned back to my alinsa, and managed to finally pull it out, with a minimum of splashing and other noise. I crept through the swamp to more solid ground, where I made myself comfortable in the concealment of the lush plants, and watched her, for lack of anything else to do. The Walker worked steadily in the hot mid-morning sun. Sweat soaked her tunic, and she finally took it off and wore only a kind of skirt wrapped around her hips.

She seemed thin and terribly naked without fur, but the laboring muscles in her back and arms, so different from my own flight muscles, fascinated me. She had the body of an earthbound worker, which she used efficiently and joylessly to repeatedly bring in her net laden with shining spheres. I silenced my growling belly with bitter mouthfuls of root as I studied her technique.

What was she doing here? Walkers travel in the mountains only when they must, and that along established trade routes. That she had come so far inland on foot, without even a path to follow, seemed inconceivable. There had to be an overland route. If so, then I would be able to locate it from the air, once I could fly again.

Throughout the morning, the Walker swept her net through the lake. Sometimes I heard the lonely sound of her voice wailing across the water. Her song throbbed with sadness and loneliness, resonating so intensely in my own aching heart that I wondered if she were as isolated as I, stranded on this shore by some power as great and implacable as the winds which had deposited me here. But I knew I was only hearing myself in her song because I could not understand the words or the music. Perhaps her song did not seem sad to her. Perhaps her dour expression meant only that she was bored.

At midday, her basket full, she rowed herself back to shore, stowed her equipment inside the boat, heaved her heavy basket onto solid ground, and then, with a great splash, fell into the water. I was on my feet before I realized that she was not drowning, but taking a bath and washing her clothes.

Eventually she crawled out of the water to lie naked in the sun, her wet clothing spread on the plants to dry. I spotted Alis'te hiding in a crevice, watching both her and myself with bright, anxious eyes. I waved my hand to reassure him. At last, the Walker rose to go. She did not move so briskly now, but got dressed with what I perceived to be reluctance, but was probably just weariness, and walked heavily away, bowed over by the weight of the heavy basket.

She was scarcely out of sight before I had stolen her caricha net out of the boat and, with the handle extended as far as possible, was gathering what carichas I could reach from shore. She had made it look easy, but the heavy net dragged through the water, and it was all I could do to get my catch to shore. I gathered enough fuel for a small, smoky fire, in the coals of which I steamed the caricha on a bed of wet leaves. Alis'te and I had a feast that day, and many days afterward.

Toward the east, a single stream in a deep, clean channel carried some of the lake's water on the long journey to the ocean. After two days in which I did little more than sleep, weave a basket, and eat caricha, my feet had healed enough so I could do some exploring, and I followed this channel as far as I could to the east, half a day's precarious journey to a point where the water plunged in a steep waterfall to join with another stream below. Ast blossoms covered the glass like scattered blobs of scarlet paint. Alis'te unintentionally performed a service to nature, as he stuffed himself on the bright, sweet male flowers, spreading their pollen to the dull, bitter tasting female flowers. I found nothing fit for an Aeyrie's consumption, except for the water itself, which lost its musty lake flavor to become crisp and clean on my tongue, with a mineral aftertaste, like the water we pump up from underground lakes to supply the Ulas.

I returned in the evening to find that the Walker woman had been there, for the net was damp and the boat had been moved.

The next day, trusting that her return to the lake every third day was a pattern, possibly based on the growth cycle of the caricha, I followed her tenuous path up a plant-filled canyon. The path climbed a gradual slope, winding in and out of the jagged crystal cliffsides, spilling me out at last onto a fissured table that stretched, eerily barren and flat, to the base of a distant, monstrous mountain. Here her path was little more than a scuffed trail in the dust.

Feeling nervous and exposed, I sent Alis'te to scout ahead, but immediately regretted it. So long as he was with me, I seemed able to keep my anxious fears at bay. But as soon as he was gone, I sensed an enemy in every fissure, watching me with hostile, hungry eyes. I had not recovered yet from the shock of being violently and pointlessly assaulted by a fellow Aeyrie: If I could not trust a l'frer, then I could trust nothing, not the ground underfoot or the sky overhead.

Alis'te returned, his fur standing out along his backbone. "I saw a farm, a house, and a tower."

"Did you see any people?"

"I saw a furred person."

"An onfrit?"

"A draf."

I followed the vague path onward, wending around the fissures, which were two or three times my height deep, and full of the powdery dust which is all that remains of sucker plants after they decompose in the autumn. The path ended at a broad, shallow water channel which poured into a nearby fissure, narrow as a tunnel, until it suddenly opened up into a series of connected fissures. They, in turn, widened out into an odd valley, filled with sucker dust, and sectioned off by narrow, jagged ridges. In the spaces between the ridges, field crops, irrigated by the stream, startled the stark landscape with their lush greenery. The crops were growing in the sucker dust, I realized with astonishment.

Walking along the cliff's edge, I had traversed half the length of the valley before I spotted the squat, thatch-roofed cottage, with the draf in a fenced field nearby. A tower pointed like a black finger at the yellow sky. The house clearly was a Walker dwelling; no Aeyrie would willingly live on the ground, much less in a valley. But the tower could only be an Aeyrie dwelling. I did not dare draw any closer, for I knew that my shape pressed against the sky would be hard to miss, even at such a distance.

I squatted on the glass, which as the day advanced had begun to feel warm underfoot, and studied the landscape thoroughly on the chance I had missed something. "Aeyries and Walkers together," I commented to Alis'te, who looked as bewildered as I felt. "Do you suppose they could be from Triad?" I had already wondered this in relation to my midnight attackers. The Triad-re were rumored to be obstinately nonviolent, but many suspected this to be less than true, and even impossible, considering the storm of controversy in which Aeyrie, Walker, and Mer supposedly coexisted so peacefully.

"Are there any onfrits?"

"No onfrits," said Alis'te, a trifle sadly. He spread the claws of one paw and licked between his toes. "I will talk to the draf. Find out who lives here and what they do."

"Can you be careful so no one sees you from the tower or the house?"

Alis'te puffed out his fur haughtily, and I hastily apologized. His ability to reason might have been limited in some ways, but his intelligence was not; neither was his pride.

"Go on, then. I will wait for you here."

Alis'te chose an indirect route so that his small, fluttering shape would be camouflaged against a backdrop of greenery, rather than pressed against the blank sky. Once he had drawn close to the settlement, he used such caution that even I could not see him. The draf lumbered to its feet and wandered over to the edge of its pen, where it stood for a long while, flicking its thin tail and shifting its weight sleepily from one of its six feet to another. I knew Alis'te must be nearby, talking to him.

"They never talk to the draf," was the first thing Alis'te said when he returned to my shoulder. "He is lonely."

As the onfrit told me what he had learned from the draf, I started to retrace my steps back to the point where the stream entered the valley. Only two people besides the draf inhabited the valley: the Walker woman we had already seen, and a Red Aeyrie. The draf rarely saw the Aeyrie. The Walker did all the work. I looked at the valley below with renewed respect for her energy.

Sometimes, other Walkers and Aeyries were present, but they did not remain. How they arrived, or how they left, the draf could not say. The draf also could not explain his own presence. He was, Alis'te said smugly, stupid even for a draf.

From what I had seen of the valley, there was no

route by which a creature as large and clumsy as a draf could enter or exit. I had seen neither road, wagon-track, or wagon. Where had the materials to build the house and the tower come from?

I walked as far as I dared around the valley from the other direction, and once again I found no road, not even a path other than the one by which I had come. Even more mystified than I had been to begin with, I returned to the lake.

The next day, I decided to risk a short flight. I had been fretting about my limited diet, but apparently caricha, despite being a delicacy, was highly nutritious. Climbing to soaring height had never been so easy. My short flight stretched to the length of half a morning, as I scouted out the prevailing winds, and even circled in a wide loop around the inhabited valley, looking for a travel route I might have missed on foot. Either on land or by air, I located nothing encouraging.

Alis'te had already told me that there were no h'lanas nearby, blowing in any direction. Using what winds there were, I could work my way north or south, hoping to eventually encounter an eastward route, but I knew too well how much likelier I was to starve to death first. This caricha rich lake had been my only luck. Now that I had recovered from my preposterous night in the storm, my luck began to feel like a kind of imprisonment.

The next day, the Walker woman returned to the lake. I was expecting her, and had been listening for her singing, but she walked in silence. A whistle from Alis'te warned me of her approach, and I hid near her boat as the onfrit hurried to a rough landing on my shoulder.

She had been fussing with the boat for a while, almost as if she knew I was screwing up my courage to approach her, when I finally stepped out of hiding and walked down to the store.

"I've been using your net," I said in H'ldat, since I knew only a few words of the Walker tongue.

Before Alis'te could translate, the Walker looked up from her struggle with the rope, as calmly as if I were a neighbor she discussed the weather with every day and said, "I know," in my own language. "It was wet. Do you think I hadn't noticed?"

"I hope you didn't mind," I said stupidly, falling back on rote courtesy since I was too astonished to think of anything else to say.

"You took good care of it," she said, shrugging a muscular shoulder. "Help me with this rope, will you?"

I helped her untangle it, and found myself standing on the cushion of shore plants, holding the end of the rope in my hand while she nocked her oars and settled in the boat. "I was blown off course by a storm," I told her. "I am trying to find a way home again."

"Why don't you fly?" she said crisply, waiting impatiently for me to drop the rope so she could go to work.

"I—wish it was so simple. How did you get here?"

She looked up at me from under shaggy, unkempt bangs. Her eyes seemed black until the sun caught them from the right angle, and they blazed a dark, startling blue. "Magic," she said.

She was serious. It was too much strangeness for me. I dropped the rope into the water, and let her go.

Chapter 4

Long after her basket was full of caricha, the Walker woman dawdled out in the middle of the lake, sweeping her net idly through the water. She seemed to be hoping that I would tire of waiting, and leave her alone. But I had nowhere to go, and nothing to do, so I lay in the prickly ast, grooming the dust out of my fur with my fingers.

It had been unnerving to hear her speak so casually of magic. The mages of my people walk their secret ways unnoticed and unremarked. We are not like the Walkers, who with adulation tempt their sorcerers into the aristocracy of power, at the same time they belittle them by seeking nothing more of them than cheap tricks of occult chemistry: aphrodisiacs, love potions, and poisons. The Aeyrie mages mix no magic ingredients, chant no spells, accept no payment, and are granted no special privileges.

Apparently, an Aeyrie mage had rebelled against this tradition, to follow an even more lonely wind.

When the Walker woman finally rowed to shore, I politely helped with mooring and unloading the boat, concealing as well as I could my desperate fear of the water. "The Aeyrie you live with is a mage?" I asked.

She splashed me accidentally as she waded to shore.

Despite the heat, she had not taken off her tunic, and
now it clung to her back, soaked with sweat, dripping
lake water from the hem. I wrinkled my nose at her
alien scent as she brushed past me. She said sarcastically, "So you followed me home? Why didn't you
come in for dinner?"

I shrugged my wings. I did not choose to remind
this rude woman that an Aeyrie had no reason to trust
a Walker. "How long have you lived here?" I coun-
tered.

Her mouth narrowed to a thin line. "How long have
you been trespassing?"

Since Aeyries do not own property in the same way
Walkers do, she was forced to use the H'ldat word for
a violation of private space. I understood her unstated
alteration of the meaning and the threatening conno-
tation, and I stepped backward cautiously. To spar with
her seemed to only increase her hostility. "Maybe it
would be better if I talk to the Aeyrie."

"I am surprised you even bother to talk to a
Walker!"

"I knew you."

She made a dry, snorting noise, but said grudgingly,
"You will know the sh'man soon enough." She slung
the heavy basket to her shoulder and waded noisily
through the bracken. I hung back, but she never looked
to see if I were following her.

I could fly to the cultivated valley, leaving her to the
solitude she seemed to prefer. But her studied unpleas-
antness had done me no real harm, while this unknown rebel mage might well be very dangerous
indeed.

I picked up my amateurish basket with its skimpy
contents, and trotted after her, Alis'te skimming along
beside me. "My name is Laril," I said to the woman's

sweaty back, as I slowed to a walk behind her. "Can
I help you carry the basket?"

My attempt to carry such a heavy burden would only
make me look as foolish as a Walker attempting to fly.
To my relief, she did not accept my offer. After a moment, as if muttering an angry curse, she said, "Bet."

After her refusal to answer all the questions I had
put to her, this offer of her name seemed a kind of
victory, however short lived. Throughout the entire
long hike to the fertile valley, she did not utter another
word. Equally speechless, I followed after her, but
oddly, rather than enjoying the peace, I found myself
missing the haunting sound of her singing.

We climbed down the water-slippery path into the
narrow rift, and followed the brisk stream through the
maze of inter-connected ravines, into the cultivated
portion of the valley. The rising walls surrounding me
made me itchy with anxiety. Alis'te, as nervous as I,
abandoned my shoulder for the air, and flitted from
the top of one jagged ridge to the next, chirruping to
himself.

"What *is* that?"

In my already anxious state, the startling sound of
Bet's voice made my fur stand on end. "What?" I
asked casually, smoothing it down with my hands.

"That creature."

"Alis'te? He is my companion, an onfrit. Let me
introduce you." At my call, he landed reluctantly on
my shoulder, his fur standing on end as well, perhaps
in response to mine. "Bet, this is Alis'te." She looked
over her shoulder at him, and then at me, with unmit-
igated exasperation.

"Pleased to meet you," said the onfrit without enthusiasm.

She stopped in her tracks, the color draining from

her face. "It talks," she said blandly. She rubbed a hand over her arm. Perhaps she had no fur, but her skin seemed to be prickling.

"She talks," commented Alis'te, equally blandly.

Bet said not a word during the rest of the journey, covering the ground with a swift, angry stride that left me behind. She slammed herself into the shelter of the stone cottage, slamming a window shutter closed as well, in case I had missed the message.

"Maybe she is sick," said Alis'te.

"You are an ill-mannered brat," I said, as severely as I could, crossing my arms over the ache of laughter in my chest.

I waited uncertainly, but the cottage door did not open. Pans clattered angrily within, and a trail of smoke wisped out of the chimney. To knock on the door and apologize did not seem worth the effort, considering how unsuccessful my other overtures had been. I reluctantly decided to seek out the Aeyrie on my own.

Sighing, I followed the stone path around the cottage, through the fragrant disarray of a flower garden. A vine which had conquered an entire wall of the cottage hung in drooping, flower-covered fronds from the eaves. Though Bet had not told me how long she had lived here, I knew that the results of many long years of labor surrounded me.

A zigzagging stairway, constructed of the same grainy stone as the cottage, had been set into the rosy crystal of the cliffside. I climbed the stairway toward the blank, black walls of the square tower looming overhead. In its polished stone, sparks of light glittered like shattered stars. The stone had been fitted together with such skill that even when I stood at the heavy wooden door, I could not see the seams. Was the Walker woman a stonemason as well? That one person could be skilled in so many crafts scarcely seemed possible.

Alis'te hunkered down on my shoulder, examining the tower warily. "What's the matter?" I asked.

"H'mila taloica," he said.

"A meeting of crosswinds? What are you talking about?"

Alis'te shook himself all over, but would not or could not explain himself. I heard the faint sound of something shattering on the floor in the cottage below me, but not even the wind seemed to dare to whisper at the corners of the mute tower. No bells tinkled; even the ever-coiling, waterwyth shape of a wind banner was missing from the flight deck over my head. My ears throbbed in the unnatural stillness.

When I tapped my knuckles on the door, it swung soundlessly inward, to reveal the sunlight smoldering on a dusty wooden floor, in a windowless room cluttered with chairs, some of them built for Aeyrie bodies, and some for Walkers. At my touch the door glided shut again, blotting out the sunlight and leaving me blinded, wondering by what weird logic the tower had been built without windows.

I felt my way to the narrow, wall hugging stairway, and climbed it cautiously to a landing just above the ceiling level of the first room. There I walked into another closed door, which glided open before me, like the first had. The second dark room did not feel as empty to me, and Aeyrie musk heavily scented the still air. No one replied to my greeting, so I continued up the stairway, Alis'te's claws digging into my shoulder.

I had spread my wings to keep from bruising my nose again, but even as my s'olel insisted there was no door before me, I walked into one. I stopped short, my heart pounding irregularly in my ears. Suddenly,

I wanted nothing more than to be outside, under the open sky, breathing fresh air into my lungs. But I had to face this mage.

Alis'te shook his wings with a dry sound like wind ruffling through leaves. I knocked on the door which was not there, but could not hear the sound of my own knocking. I knocked again, hard enough to bruise my knuckles. Light abruptly blazed into my face, as if a curtain had been opened to the full brilliance of afternoon sun. My belly hollowed and my muscles trembled, but I stood my ground. Shading my tearing eyes against the painful light, I peered between the cracks of my fingers as if through the slats of a fence.

Rolling hills stretched before me, furred in green and decorated with clumped trees. A bizarre creature, that seemed simultaneously to walk upright like an Aeyrie and supine like a draf, paced steadily up a hillside. Heavy teats hung between its hind pair of legs, and three cubs frisked and tumbled in its wake. Suddenly, the landscape disappeared, and I was looking at the rooftops of a busy Walker city. The streets were crowded with brightly dressed, basket-toting people, pushing their way from one rickety booth to the next, where other Walkers held up embroidered wallets, lengths of astil like floating clouds, orange and red and green vegetables and fruits. They shouted at each other, straining to be heard over the din, but I heard no sound.

The view shifted again. To my left lay the fertile valley and the Walker woman's cottage. To my right lay the familiar rose and green of the beautiful wilderness which held me captive. I seemed to be standing on a floating platform of wood. Even though I could see to the horizon in all directions, and the sun shone overhead in a cloud scattered sky, my wings, reading the faint motion of the nearly stagnant air, insisted that I was in fact standing in a room with four walls and a ceiling.

My head ached with disorientation. Alis'te had long ago taken frantic refuge in my mane. I reached up absently to untangle him, for he was pulling my hair painfully.

In the center of the floor, on a carved and upholstered stool, an Aeyrie as red as blood examined me with eyes like glowing coals. "Taiseoch-dre Ishta Laril," idre greeted me formally. The voice was quiet, yet it seemed to fill every corner of the invisible room.

"Sh'man," I greeted the mage, witholding so much emotion from my voice that it sounded dull and flat in my ears. Aeyrie mages did not normally display their powers so lavishly. I was determined to not give idre the satisfaction of knowing I had been startled and frightened. I walked to the edge of the wooded platform. Clouds flowed toward me, carried on a wind that I could not feel. The air smelled musty and stale. I put out my hand, and touched cool, smooth stone. Below me, a criya scampered along the thatched roof of the Walker woman's cabin.

"I see why your tower needs no windows," I said.

Laughing softly, the mage got to ids feet. Tiny jewels glittered like star chips along the leading edges of ids bright wings. A beautifully worked knife sheath was strapped to ids right thigh, the product of some skilled crafter's workshop. Despite the age lines of fifty or more years drawn in ids face, id walked toward me as lightly as a l'shil, putting out a hand in greeting. My skin tingled as we touched palms. Seven days had passed since I last was with one of my own kind. In spite of the cruel lesson I had learned when I trusted the stranger at the shelter, every bone in my body wanted to believe that this eccentric stranger would do me no harm. In all that time, it seemed I had scarcely taken a deep breath.

"My name is Raulyn," the mage said.

"I have never heard of you," I said apologetically.

"I left my Ula twenty-five years ago. No doubt they think I am dead."

This skeletal history, and ids lack of parent names, suggested that idre was an exile like myself. I said, "I was blown off course by a storm."

"It was more than a storm that blew you off course."

I admitted it with a shrug. This mage could have been watching me for years through the walls of this room. Had idre seen me hatched and winged, watched me in my love bed or on the Quai-du floor?

As if sensing my discomfort, Raulyn stepped gracefully away, toward the center of the room. Where there had been only one stool, now two stood, with a game table between them. "I have been keeping watch on the Triad," idre said. "Why do you suppose they wanted to kidnap you?"

"I have no idea. I did not even know it was them."

"It was an impressive escape."

Flattered despite myself, my next question came out much less harshly than I meant it to. "I suppose it is just an accident that I ended up at your back door?"

"No," the mage admitted, as casually as if id were admitting to having sent me an astil scarf as a New Year gift. Id sat on one stool, and picked up the pack of triangular playing cards that lay on a corner of the table. "Do you play m'chiste?"

I perched on the stool, and watched ids deft hands shuffle the cards. Without surprise, I spotted the brand of a Quai-du master on the inside of ids right wrist. "Why?" I asked belatedly, as the mage dealt the cards.

"Maybe I wanted someone to play cards with," Raulyn said lightly.

I picked up my hand of cards, and examined them distractedly. I had never seen cards so beautiful. The characters were hand-painted in vibrant colors, and the soft, worn edges still retained traces of gilding. "These are old," I said softly, holding them up for Alis'te to admire, but he would not come out of hiding. "Why don't you just answer me?" I asked the mage. "I think I have a right to know."

"In truth? I watched a l'shil fly into a hellwind. Wasn't it my duty to help you to safety?"

I had been dealt a mediocre hand: a l'shil, a taiseoch, two different crafters, a weathermaster, and a librarian. I laid the l'shil face-up in front of me, and drew a card from the deck. A Quai-du-dre, that was better. Now I could lay down a solid triad consisting of the taiseoch, the weathermaster, and the Quai-du-dre, with power as the common trait. I looked up at Raulyn. Id was studying ids cards with an unblinking gaze. I decided to hold my hand, in the hope that I could make a more impressive move later in the game. "Your play," I said.

Oddly, the mage took my l'shil. I had never seen anyone choose a discarded l'shil before, for it was an inflexible card, rarely played.

"Would you be able to help me home again?" I asked.

"Easily," said the mage. "But what are you going home to?"

"I have friends in t'Fon."

"If the Triad-re find you again, they will be forewarned that you are not so easily captured."

I did not answer. I suppose I did not want to admit that anyone seriously was trying to harm me. I found it far easier to assume that the whole disaster had been a case of mistaken identity.

We had each drawn three times before the mage laid down six of ids seven cards in an impossibly complicated pattern in which each card enacted at least three different functions. The l'shil card held one of the three corners, sharing joy with the dancer and the scholar, and, in addition to joy, sharing the future with a l'per giving suck, and a mage with a scrying glass. Was Raulyn trying to tell me something?

"Do *you* know why they want to kidnap me?" I asked.

"Leverage with your parent, perhaps. Ishta's love for you is no secret."

"It's a secret to me," I said pathetically, but continued hastily before Raulyn could say the obligatory words of sympathy. "That makes no sense. Ishta has always wholeheartedly supported the Triad."

Raulyn wrote down ids score, and drew six cards. "Naturally. Ishta is no fool."

"What do you mean?"

"Now that all trade agreements are negotiated by Malal Tefan Eia, the life of every Aeyrie of every Ula is in idre's hands. One word from idre, and the people of t'Cwa would starve to death. Of course, Ishta supports the Triad; how can any taiseoch do otherwise? But your parent has been negotiating in secret with the Walkers, to agree upon a treaty which would make Ula t'Cwa entirely independent of the Walkers, as in the Age of Balance. No doubt the Triad's spies found out about it, and Eia was seeking a method to block Ishta's initiative. Eia will not tolerate any interference with ids power, whether it is to the good of the people or not."

"Ishta never mentioned such a treaty to me."

"Of course, idre confides all things in you."

"No," I admitted. "But how do you know about it?" Remembering the game, I played a single card, in recognition that I could not impress anybody in a game I had already lost.

Raulyn marked the score and nodded at me as if I had done something clever. "You are not quick to believe whatever someone tells you, an admirable quality in one so young. I have my windows—" With a gesture, the landscape over which we seemed to hover shifted, and I found myself in the middle of a rainstorm. "—And I have many eyes," the mage concluded. "I have seen—too much. I know a great deal about the world. More, perhaps, than anyone." Id casually laid down three more cards. With a sigh I reconciled myself to a drubbing.

"But how did the Triad know I would be at the shelter that night? I didn't even know I was leaving t'Cwa until—until I left."

"Now there is a mystery," admitted Raulyn. "I am certain only of this: it stinks of magic, or, more likely, sorcery."

These words finally silenced my questions. Truly, I had flown into a hellwind, if I had unwittingly become an object of contention between mages! In a fair fight, I could stand on my own feet, or concede my loss gracefully. But in a storm such as this, what could I do without help? I looked up with sudden gratitude into the mage's kindly gaze. How fortunate I had been, to be aided by such benevolence.

We had played two games and were just starting a third, when the Walker woman materialized out of the rainstorm, carrying a covered tray. Lightning flickered eerily behind her head. "Why are you sitting in the dark?" she asked, addressing her comment to some remote point in the room.

Raulyn changed the scenery, to once more overlook

the valley. The sun sat on a mountain, and the valley below had already filled with twilight. Whether I wanted to or not, I would be a guest for the night. I rubbed my aching eyes, wondering why this possibility made wings flutter in my belly.

Bet slapped the tray onto the game table, scarcely giving us time to snatch up our cards. Without another word she marched over the edge of the platform and disappeared.

"I'm afraid my onfrit was rude to her," I said.

"Bet will always find some reason to be in a temper," said Raulyn indulgently. Id stood up stiffly, vivid fur shimmering in the burning sunlight. The thin, wavy scar of a knife wound was drawn across one wing membrane. I noticed with astonishment that the tiny jewels in ids wings were mounted on posts which pierced through the membrane to fasten on the other side. Why would anyone endure such pain, just for the sake of decoration? But their winking, delicate chips of light perfectly complemented ids dramatic coloring, rich fur, and powerful build. Ids erect nipples poked through the fur of ids chest, colored a soft black, like the velvet darkness which follows twilight. Something had aroused idre.

"She is a very good cook," id continued, still talking about Bet.

I distracted myself from Raulyn's appalling beauty by lifting the tray cover. The intense, mouth-watering scent of caricha washed over me. Despite the violence with which Bet had set the tray down, not one drop had spilled from the soup bowls, and the plates of fluffy cous with caricha, vegetables, and sauce were works of art. Even the cutlery had not shifted from its careful arrangement. Created in the midst of a tantrum, was this rich, beautiful meal no gift, but a mockery?

"Are you hungry?"

"Yes," I said fervently. My body seemed oddly at war with itself, so hungry that it felt like nausea, so lusty that it felt like terror.

Raulyn poured me a cup of wine, and then smiled at me, the setting sun burning in ids eyes. "So am I," id said.

Later, we stood on the flight platform at the top of the tower, looking out at the stars. Alis'te, as soon as he found himself truly in the open air, dove into the darkness and did not return when I called him. I gave Raulyn a more or less honest account of the duel in the Well. Id listened in sympathetic silence, prodding me with a gentle question when I faltered.

"What was your parent thinking of!" id finally exploded. "To blame you for rejecting a Companion so badly chosen, only to abandon you to Wand's influence; and finally to send you out into the storm without even a decent hearing, while the one who is truly at fault remains to destroy the life of some other suggestible l'shil! I always thought Ishta to be a person of more sense."

I leaned against the railing, glaring fiercely at the blurring stars. The Cleata's tail was pointing at the Red Star; spring already turning its way toward summer.

Raulyn put a warm arm around my waist. I wiped away a tear under the guise of scratching my cheek. "Well, it has given me a chance to see the world."

"Not joyfully, as a l'shil should see it. It angers me, to see you robbed of your youth like this."

The wind had made me unsteady on my feet, but I could lean into Raulyn's embrace, and tip back my head to watch streaks of light, brief as lightning, flash across the sky. "A star shower," I said. "My luck is turning. So is yours."

Raulyn laughed softly, ids mouth close to my ear. "I do believe it is." Ids finger stroked tentatively down my wing. My muscles shuddered in the wake of ids touch. "I made my choices as I had to do," id murmured. "But I have paid. Every moment of my life, I have paid. Loneliness and more loneliness, until sometimes I almost forget—"

I was no fool, to turn down the thing I most wanted, when it was offered to me so willingly. I pressed myself into Raulyn's arms, running my fingers through ids hot, soft fur, until my hands found ids hard nipples. I pressed them softly between my finger, Raulyn taking in idre's breath sharply as if with surprise, and then bringing my mouth roughly to meet idre's. Blood surged in my veins; and I knew the sweetness of power.

Chapter 5

Late one morning, I awoke to find myself alone in Raulyn's musty bed. From the scrying room above I heard no sound: not the scraping of a stool on the stone floor, or the sighing of a bare foot brushing through the dust. With a sinking heart, I knew that Raulyn had left again.

Usually id returned by nightfall; but recently, three long days had crawled past, each one as empty as an unfurnished room. There would be no Quai-du lesson punctuated with breathless, groping kisses; no endless games of m'chiste as land and people I had never even dreamed of filled the scrying wall; no lovemaking to make the Universe swirl around me.

The tower echoed with emptiness. Soon I too would be little more than a despondent ghost, heavy and stale as the air. I hastily tossed aside the dusty blankets and stumbled through the windowless gloom toward the stairs, but the sunlight, when at last it spilled over my fur, was as dull as a copper pan in need of polishing.

Already, the glass glowed like coals under the burning summer sun. The sky was a well-used pottery bowl, its glaze chipped and faded and beginning to yellow. The air smelled old and dusty as a doormat.

Only the rhythmic, hollow scraping of Bet's hoe punctuated the silence.

What was I doing here in this timeless, motionless place? Had I flown into a circling eddy, in which I now hung suspended, deluded by the illusion of motion, the wind's fool? All the days that had passed before, lush with playfulness and passion, seemed suddenly only transparent illusions.

So it always was, with Raulyn gone. Moping aimlessly about, I would waste the day away, and despise myself by sunset. *But not today,* I vowed. I went back into the tower for my knife, and disciplined myself to a long series of Quai-du drills that Raulyn had assigned me. To train with such a master had fed my passion for the art, but today I danced in determination rather than inspiration, sweltering in the hot sun. When at last I was finished, I felt relief, but no satisfaction.

I had lived here nearly thirty days. My home, parent, and friends had moved into a shadow world of memory, the passions of the past totally eclipsed by the bright, vivid, joyful present. I was in love; nothing else mattered.

No one had ever loved like this. No one had ever loved anyone so deserving of service, so noble and beautiful, so kind and sensitive, so self-sacrificing and undemanding, so intelligent and gifted. I breathed my every breath, and thought my every idea only for Raulyn.

Bet roamed through that love like a ghost, inexhaustibly serving us and the land, her secret rage drawing her mouth into a thin, tight line. Following the sound of the hoe, I found her this morning waist-deep in the grain field, chopping rhythmically at the weeds. Sweat burnished her bronze skin to a rich shine. Behind her, a trickle of water crept through the furrow, reducing the dry clods to shapeless blobs of mud, smoothing like a potter the marks of the hoe. The thirsty plants lifted up their leaves and brightened their color, like subjects blessed by their god.

At my greeting, Bet brushed her forehead against her shoulder, her damp hair sticking in wet strings to her sweat. "I suppose you want to eat," she said.

"I can help myself."

"Generous of you." A puff of dirt rose from the blade of her hoe, powdering her dirty bare feet with more dust.

"Raulyn is gone again," I said. "I don't know when id will be back."

Bet grunted, whether at me or at the weeds I was not certain. Alis'te appeared suddenly in the shade of the grain plants, chirruping peacefully to himself as he patted the soil with his hands in a vague imitation of Bet's efforts. I had seen less and less of the onfrit, until I finally realized that he had adopted Bet. My brief jealousy had flared and then sputtered, like a candle in a downpour. Let them have each other, I thought generously, I have Raulyn. Now they were inseparable friends, and Alis'te scarcely seemed to notice me anymore.

Bet also acted as if I were not there, not even bothering to reach for her tunic to cover herself as she had used to do. The trickle of irrigation water seemed to be gaining on her, only to be stalled by a dirt clod. She gained two steps before the water overcame the obstacle.

"Well," I said, suddenly angry. "It has been a nice chat."

She focused me in her sharp, sardonic gaze. "What do you want of me?"

"Why do you dislike me so?"

"Because you are so stupid," she replied curtly.

Obviously, she was in one of her moods. I wandered away, to help myself to bread and fruit out of her larder, and drink water from her bucket, giving her something else to complain about: that I was too lazy and contemptuous to even walk the few feet to the stream.

In the afternoon, I leapt off the flight deck and winged my way tediously upward through the baking, shimmering air. The sun blazed like a fire in a kiln. I climbed the stairs of the wind, until at last I had outflown the reflected heat of the glass. Cooler air ruffled through my sweat-damp fur, chilling my temper from irritability to a more endurable vague unease. I soared over the valley, which lay still as a painting in the paralyzing heat, its verdant swath vividly green amid the dusty rose of the cracked plateau surrounding it. Bet had finally taken refuge from the sun, but her abandoned fields shimmered with thin strands of water where the captive stream continued to irrigate the land.

I followed the course of the stream northward, across the plateau, which rose gradually toward a new outbreak of jagged mountains. Each peak, a perpendicular, many-sided crystal, shimmered with hot sunlight. One of the mountains had been riven through from top to bottom. Half of it lay at an angle against the other half, resting like a fainting flyer in the arms of a friend. Between the two halves of the mountain, a pile of glass shards, more precious than jewels, glittered manically, as the water of my stream washed over them, welling like blood through the rent it had torn in the glass.

The sun was expiring its last hot breaths when I landed on the flight deck of the tower. For a while I had outflown my moodiness, but, as the sun sank, I began to dread the lonely night. At the sight of the light spilling across the deck from under the door of the scrying room, all my dread evaporated. I ran my fingers quickly through my tangled hair, and joyfully pushed the door open.

Raulyn straddled the floor before one of the walls, where three Aeyries grasped each other's hands in welcome. Though the images I had seen in the walls had always been silent before, this time I could hear the murmur of voices exchanging warm greetings. The air lamps lighting their meeting place also lit the tower room. Half hidden in the evening shadows, a dark, ghostly painting hung. On its muted surface, Aeyries and Walkers fought or danced, frozen in perpetual ambiguity.

Two of the Aeyries in the scrying were strangers, but one of them was my parent.

"Raulyn?" I said in disbelief.

As if the scene were a mirror image rather than a vision, Raulyn and one of the Aeyries in the vision simultaneously jerked with surprise and turned sharply to face me. Raulyn put a hand to ids mouth, an impatient, angry gesture. The strange Silver also put a hand to ids mouth briefly, as if warning the others to be silent. Then id unsheathed a glass blade and lifted it to ids eyes.

Raulyn turned back to the scene, and with an angry exclamation gestured it into darkness.

I wrapped my arms around myself in the sudden gloom. Raulyn said nothing, but I could hear ids heavy breathing, as if id had just fought a battle or averted a disaster. "What's the matter?" I asked.

Raulyn's voice was tight with anger. "Leave me."

"But—"

"Leave me!"

I fled down the stairs, to huddle on the bed in misery. Whatever I had interrupted had been terribly important, this I did not doubt. Would Raulyn forgive me? When Raulyn did not want to be disturbed, no one could enter the scrying room from below. I had assumed this to be true for the flight deck door as well, so I had not knocked. Never before had I been prohibited to speak; how was I to know that if we could hear the people who were being scried, they could also hear us?

Why had Raulyn been scrying Ishta, and who were those people with idre? The elegant, self-assured Black, with suppressed energy concealed behind id's smooth, liquid motions, had been arresting; but the Silver, with id's open, thoughtful face and piercing glance, had been riveting.

When Bet brought supper up the stairs, pausing for a moment to peer at me in the gloom, I did not stir. She continued upward, and was admitted through the magic door. Soon I heard her footsteps returning. ''Laril, the sh'man would like your company at supper,'' she said.

''Is id angry with me?''

''Perhaps,'' she said nonchalantly. But when I trudged reluctantly up to the scrying room, the air lamps had been lit, and Raulyn was uncovering the dishes on the supper tray, with ids usual proprietary air. Id turned with a smile as I entered, holding out ids arm to embrace me.

''There you are, sweet child. I'm sorry I was angry with you. You could not have known what you were doing.''

So all was well, and in my gratitude I never asked Raulyn for an explanation of what had happened. Like ids unpredictable comings and goings, what happened in the scrying room was mage's business. My duty was to love, not to questions.

"It must be lonely for you when I am gone." Raulyn said one day. "Bet is not much of a companion."

"I have Quai-du," I said with a shrug.

"Surely, to occupy the body is not enough for you. Let me give you a puzzle to solve."

Raulyn's belongings were piled hodgepodge on the floor, crammed into ornately carved wooden chests, and packed into rough crates, shrouded with hunter-worm webs and dust. I had offered to organize the clutter, but Raulyn was afraid that id would never find anything if it was all put away. Id opened one of the crates piled in the bedroom, and, in a cloud of ancient straw crumbling to dust, dug out of it a small pottery jar, plugged with wood and sealed with was. "What is it?" I asked.

"In this jar is a powder. I found it—well, it is too long a story. It is an alchemical compound, but that is all I know."

"Where did you find it?"

"What does it matter, if we share the same elements worldwide? I have always wondered what it is. Perhaps you can find out."

"I know practically nothing of alchemy! I don't even have any equipment."

"Weren't you educated in t'Cwa?" id said, patting my shoulder in a way I found secretly irritating. "As for equipment, I will bring you everything you need."

I had studied the art of alchemy, but in the same halphazard manner in which I studied everything. I had been more concerned with inventing ways to puncture my teacher's pomposity than with learning. But soon, Raulyn having once more disappeared, I found myself dredging up my memories, to discover that I had absorbed a surprising amount of knowledge despite myself.

Alchemy, perhaps the most obscure of the arts, is a study which tends to attract only a few serious practitioners, people noted as a group to be eccentric, socially isolated, and markedly short-lived. The alchemists seek to understand what the Universe is made of, how to reduce matter to its most basic elements, and how to recombine these elements to create a new Universe.

Many of them are mystical people, who speak of power without magic and of the remaking of the Universe. Others, like Mairli the inventor, are more practical. It was id who had first claimed that air is a combination of gases, one of which will burn if separated from the others. To prove this claim, id invented the air lamp, which has since become as commonplace as pots and pans.

Keeping in mind the alchemists' propensity for poisoning themselves as I unenthusiastically took up Raulyn's little puzzle, I was painstakingly careful to avoid breathing the fumes or tasting the concoctions produced by my crude experiments. Raulyn's powder was a light, airy gray stuff, as fine as dust, with a sharp, acrid scent. By mixing it with water I discovered, to my dismay, that various ingredients had been combined together to make the powder.

"This is an impossible task," I complained when Raulyn reappeared, accompanied by a crate of alchemists' equipment and books. "I have to figure out what each of these ingredients is, and how it interacts with the other ingredients, and how much of it is in the compound. It could take my entire life."

But Raulyn smiled, devastating me with the softness and pride in id's eyes, and soon I found myself agreeing with idre that maybe it was not an impossible task for an untrained l'shil, even though it would baffle a sh'man. So I labored through many long, hot days in the workshop we had set up for me on the bottom floor of the tower, mixing and distilling and evaporating until I was able to divide the powder into three unidentified ingredients. Wading through the obscure writings of the alchemists, I plodded through the complicated steps of various experiments, designed to identify the ingredient. After many long days, I still could not identify the powder, though I could be reasonably certain that it did not contain some ten known elements. It was increasingly clear to me that my supply of the powder would run out long before I had solved the mystery.

One afternoon I looked up from my work, to find that Bet had slipped soundlessly in the door, and was sitting quietly in a chair, watching me. "Is something wrong?" I asked sharply. Except for the first time I saw her, I had never known her to cease her toil. Surely she slept and ate, but not when anyone was watching. To see her sitting so still almost frightened me.

"What are you doing?" she asked.

I immediately felt absurdly foolish, for wasting so much time and energy on Raulyn's pointless puzzle, while she, without apparent payment or benefit, labored ceaselessly to feed us. "It's nothing. Just an—an exercise."

"Not magic," she said vaguely.

"Magic? Oh, no. Raulyn asked me to identify this powder."

"What does it do?"

"I don't know."

"Wouldn't it be easier, if you knew what it did?"

I said, "Yes, but I have to be careful. It might be poison, you know."

"Is it a sorcerer's powder?"

"How am I supposed to know?"

"I can tell you." Bet came over to my ornate set-up, and pinched a bit of the powder between her fingers. I turned to look with surprise into her spare, sun-brown face. She shuddered suddenly, rubbed the powder hastily from her fingers, and then brushed them clean, leaving a faint gray blur across her dirt stained tunic. She looked up at me. The sunlight spilling through the open doorway crossed her face, outlining harshly its drawn lines, its shadow of anguish, its weary despair. Then blue spears of light flashed in her deep, secretive eyes, like sunlight in deep, swift-flowing water.

She said quietly, "You are a child playing with death."

Her words shot like a glass-tipped arrow into my breast. I turned and fled up the stairs. But as I leapt off the flight deck onto the back of the wind, I saw her in the doorway below. She stood with her hands hanging empty at her sides, as still as a becalmed boat on a windless sea.

Chapter 6

If Bet were a seer, imprisoned here in the service of a more powerful mage, who could blame her for her sardonic, sarcastic, bitter anger? But I could not endure this sinister notion for long. I brought the afternoon's strange encounter to Raulyn, like a funny joke that fell oddly flat.

"But of course you realize that Bet is a little mad," said Raulyn.

The glass arrow embedded in my breast dissolved away, a nightmare in daylight. "Of course," I said, with a casual laugh.

"She was brought to me so I could cure her. I could not, of course, but I did come to understand that what she most needed was stability and predictability, a clearly-defined role, with boundaries within which she could have complete power and control. So this farm has become her life purpose, her saveline to sanity. So long as she respects her own boundaries, she does not get too unbalanced. Sometimes, though . . . " Raulyn's stroking hand paused on my shoulder. "Were you afraid, sweeting? She is not dangerous, I assure you."

"Afraid?" I said, hiding the irritation which rose in me at the condescension in Raulyn's voice. Was this how id perceived me, easily frightened and helpless, a dependent child?

"I would not leave you alone with her if I thought she was dangerous. But no, she is merely pitiable."

"I can take care of myself," I said.

"Of course, of course," said Raulyn soothingly.

The next day, id's irritating overconcern still rankled. I sweated away the morning over a particularly demanding experiment, but my attention perpetually failed me, distracted by other, wilder chimeras of thought. Raulyn did not respect me, was that it? And why should id respect a parasite who slept in another's bed, ate the fruits of another's labor, and when asked to do something in return, whined about the difficulty of the task and refused to take any risks for the sake of accomplishing it. There was nothing to respect here.

What had happened to Laril the hellion? My own parent would not have recognized me, so well-behaved had I become. Had falling in love stolen away my courage, or was it my self-blame over the duel with Jachim which immobilized me?

"So I made a mistake," I said out loud. "Is that any reason to stop living?"

I took up a tinderstick and the jar of gray powder and, with a rude gesture at my cluttered workspace, walked out of the tower.

The midday sun blazed across the glass, surrounding me in a blinding glare of light. I had not walked far from the tower before my fur began to plaster down with sweat. Even though I had molted the last of my winter undercoat, this blasting heat, unameliorated by plant life, was too much for me. Soon, I began to feel dizzy.

Near the edge of Bet's Valley, I paused to drop a

pinch of gray powder onto the glass. It scattered as it fell, dusting the rosy, irridescent surface with the gray of ashes. I squinted at it blurrily, and decided not to try to gather it back into a neat pile. As I reached down with the tinderstick, I thought, *Next, I'll taste it. We'll see who's a coward!*

The explosion left me momentarily deaf and blind. I know now that if I had taken the time to pile the powder neatly, the blast would have damaged my senses permanently.

When my vision came back, crawling with white spots and odd flashes of light, I was on my knees, staring at my arm, where tiny trails of smoke floated from a patch of black, shriveled fur.

"Laril!" Someone shouted from far, far away. I turned to see Raulyn, sprinting toward me.

"I know what the powder does," I shouted over the ringing in my ears.

Raulyn knelt to examine the glass, where a tiny webbing of cracks frayed out from a star-shaped smudge of smoke. "How much did you use?" I could scarcely hear ids remote, tinny voice.

"A pinch," I said. "Why do you sound so funny?" I began to pant irregularly, but Raulyn did not seem to notice. Id rubbed the cracked glass with ids fingertip, nodding in satisfaction. I could smell scorched flesh. "Raulyn," I said weakly, sick with fear. There was something wrong with me, but why didn't I feel any pain?

"And then what?" Id picked up the tinderstick I had dropped. "You sparked it?"

I spotted Bet down in the valley, standing rigidly in the grainfield, looking up at us, her hands hanging empty at her sides. Pain boiled up out of nowhere, like a winter storm, and I fainted.

* * *

"I'm sorry," Raulyn said "I didn't realize you were hurt." Id's hand stroked my mane without agitation, almost absentmindedly.

I burned in a pool of pain, scarcely able to see Raulyn through the strange smoke that filled ids dark bedroom. "You never asked," I said. Though my words seemed traitorously critical, Raulyn did not react to them. Perhaps I had not truly spoken.

Ghostlike, Bet floated through the fog. "This paste might ease the burn."

Raulyn gestured impatiently. "Whatever." Id stood up and abruptly left the room. Even as the door latched shut, I peered wildly about myself, looking for idre. I could not believe that id had left me in the care of a madwoman.

"Raulyn?" I said, cursing myself for having criticized idre. "Don't leave me."

When Bet touched me, I screamed. She smeared pale, sticky mud on my raw flesh, holding my arm in an unbreakable grip as I struggled wildly against the pain. "Raulyn!" I screamed.

"Raulyn! Raulyn!" But the door through which Raulyn had disappeared did not open.

Then my pain was abruptly extinguished, leaving me panting and sobbing among the sweaty, tangled blankets. Bet laid my arm down. She, too, was breathing unsteadily. "I think it would have burned to your bone," she said softly. She looked down at me uncertainly, as if she wanted to apologize for having hurt me.

"Some kind of acid?" I asked hoarsely. I poked a weak finger at the sticky stuff on my arm. "What is this? How did you know it would neutralize the acid?

Bet glanced around Raulyn's bedroom, her gaze resting briefly on the stool in the corner, but she finally knelt uncomfortably on the floor beside the rope bed. "Don't you ever air the blankets?"

I should have known, I thought in disgust. When did Bet respond to direct question, no matter how harmless? All I would ever get from her was questions and opinions. In fact—I looked at her, startled. She stared back into my eyes with an unnervingly steady gaze. Her failure to ever make a simple statement of fact was a startling consistency. It was almost as if she suffered from a kind of selective muteness.

"You aren't really out of your mind, are you?" I said.

Bet wrapped her arms around her knees. Before my wingling, I had used to be able to sit like that. Less than a year ago.

"You aren't mad." I said the words again, but my heart would not accept them. My heart screamed hysterically, Raulyn would not lie to me! But Raulyn had not cared or noticed that an acid was eating my flesh to the bone, and id had ignored my screams of pain. What was a lie, after such neglect? Was not everyone in Raulyn's life, especially ids lover, merely a means to an end?

"Is that what the sh'man told you, that I am mad?" Bet's words flaked into the silence like soft powder, but her eyes were like chips of black glass.

This had been Bet from the beginning: this contradiction of voice, words and body, which I had told myself over and over was only a difference of culture, a contradiction which to a Walker's eyes would not exist. But as I looked at her, through the cold clarity which remained once the fog of pain had lifted, I trusted myself for once, and saw a woman living under intolerable restrictions, unable even to communicate, except through those very contradictions.

"You are not mad," I said again, flatly. "But you are under some kind of spell that controls what you can and cannot say."

The corner of Bet's mouth quirked slightly with a smile, or with grief. "You are not so stupid after all," she said.

I shut my eyes with a sigh, too weary for this conundrum. *Tomorrow,* I told myself. *This has been enough for one day.*

But the next day, the cold clarity of my understanding was gone, and I laughed at myself in disbelief that such an unlikely explanation for Bet's peculiar ways had ever even occurred to me.

My foolish experiment with the explosive powder left me with a swath of raw, weeping flesh, that in the next two days made no progress toward healing. But it was not just the constant pain from my injury that made me moody. Raulyn had disappeared again. Though I had rejected yesterday's unlikely insights, coming up with a new explanation for ids neglect of me proved difficult.

Almost by accident, I finally identified one of the elements of the gray powder. I had relearned caution, however, and when a white froth suddenly boiled out of the vial in the course of another experiment, I fled the tower and paced the cliff for several nervous hours, half expecting another explosion. I eventually returned, to find that the froth had been transformed into a harmless, gluey gray syrup which dribbled in long strands to the floor.

Among all the likely or unlikely results of the experiment which had been in progress, this one seemed to be unheard of. Long after Bet had brought my supper, as quiet day fell into silent night, I searched through my alchemy library for an explanation. Once, as I paused to rest my burning eyes, I felt how the stillness of the night crept into my belly. I could have been the only person in the Universe, toiling mindlessly away at a pointless project, without which I would simply die for lack of purpose.

As I began to turn the thick pages of the last of my books, an ancient, mystical work, more a book of philosophy than of alchemy, I promised myself that soon I would go to bed. My supply of the gray powder was almost extinguished. One of its ingredients was probably unknown even to the alchemists. I would never solve Raulyn's problem; I had failed. I felt oddly relieved.

The door crashed open. I thought I heard an anguished screaming, as if the very wind were under the power of a malevolent torturer. I clutched the book of philosophy to my chest like a shield, staring in disbelief through the open door.

Nothing was there: neither moons nor stars, clouds nor wind, light nor darkness. In that emptiness, Raulyn's voice spoke sharply, and, like a lantern flashing, something appeared in the void.

Two Walkers came through the door, huffing hoarsely, carrying between them a heavy wooden crate. After them came two more, also carrying a crate, which they set with a creaking thud onto the floor. Raulyn spoke angrily. The Walkers turned to face the door, shoulders heaving with their ragged breathing, faces shining with sweat. Either they had not noticed me, or they did not care who I was.

Like light sparking from a tinderstick, Raulyn appeared in the nothingness, unruffled, wings slightly spread as if for balance. The door slammed shut behind idre. "What are you doing here Laril?"

I gestured wordlessly with the book, my tongue paralyzed.

"I will speak with you upstairs."

I fled.

In Raulyn's musty, airless bedroom I sat with the heavy book across my knees, the ancient paper creaking in protest as I angrily turned the pages. Voices spoke below, muffled and oddly far away. I rubbed my burning eyes angrily on my shoulder, breath choking in my lungs. Once again, Raulyn had treated me like a child—no, a servant, a convenience. But I wanted to be respected, not indulged!

Two pages of the book were stuck together. I peeled them apart with my fingernail, paying little attention to what I was doing, until the brittle paper tore. I looked more closely at the book. The pages were not stuck together by an accidental spill: they had been purposely pasted together.

My angry hurt abruptly gave way to a cold stillness. I took my knife and trimmed the edge of the pasted pages. From between them I extricated three thin sheets of paper, crackling with age. I knew, before I looked at them, what they would be.

The books, the arcane equipment of alchemy, these all must have been taken from the same place as the jar of gray powder: some alchemist's secret workshop, abandoned, perhaps, when the alchemist died suddenly. Somehow Raulyn had found the workshop, and for some reason had wondered what the alchemist was working on when id died. Had wondered enough to transport the entire workshop to me, on the chance that the solution was inherent in the books or equipment. And id had been right, more than id knew.

The first two pages of the notes contained not only the formula for the powder, but how to find and distill the ingredients. The third page was covered with small diagrams, detailing how to create a strange mechanism, with a sort of a tinderstick at the bottom of a cylinder. The purpose of it escaped me. On this last page also was written an epigram in faded, spidery handwriting: "What curse is this, to be able to imagine that which should be unimaginable?" And, underneath, a nearly unreadable signature, which I deciphered one letter at a time: Mairli.

When the door opened once more into the Void, and the winds of the Universe bent once more to serve the mage's will, I once again sensed the screaming protest of those winds, despite the walls which now separated me from the door. If Raulyn lost control, would the travelers embarking on their ghostly way wander forever? Could the entire earth be imploded into that Void, or even the entire Universe, if Raulyn could not shut the door again?

I was trembling with fear. How did I know the danger of that opening door? "Who are you?" I asked the shivering stranger inhabiting my body. I felt as if I had been ripped apart.

I carefully slid Mairli's notes back into their hiding place, and left the book lying carelessly on the floor. The trimmings from the edge of the pages I took with me up to the flight deck, where I tore them into bits and scattered them onto the soft breeze. Trying to still my trembling with great, gulping gasps of the fresh air, I stared hard at the stars. Only now that I recognized my strength did I recognize my weakness. Only now that I had lost my trust did I realize how little I was trusted.

"I am just a toy, aren't I?" I said, when I heard the flight deck door open.

Raulyn said placatingly out of the darkness, "I am never certain of the Walkers. I did not want them to know about you."

"If you had bothered to explain to me—"

"I am trying to protect you."

"Protect me!" I turned on idre in a fury. "I am your lover, I am your partner! But you would keep me in ignorance and make me a child!"

A dark, hooded shadow under the burning stars,

Raulyn said nothing for the space of two heartbeats, which shuddered through my body like shifting tides. Then id said, "I'm sorry, I have wronged you."

Id's voice was so coaxing and gentle, that I stepped toward idre without thinking. "Come here," id said, and I found myself in ids arms. But I flinched with pain as id touched my injured arm accidentally.

"What's wrong?"

"It's the burn—"

"It has not healed yet? I must have a look at it." Id's wing embraced me, wrapping me with warmth, enveloping me in the sweet scents of musk and sweat. With a deep breath, Raulyn began to speak, and, as if my ears had been opened, I heard for the first time how carefully id chose idre's words. Though I was already half seduced, I listened equally carefully, not for what id had to say, but for what id did not say.

"Laril, I am not just a solitary mage, who scries the world but does not live in it. You know that I have my—involvements.

"For many long years, it was not so. It seemed I had been an exile since the day of my hatching. I reconciled myself to living and dying in a world where I did not belong. But at last it occurred to me that it was not I who was wrong, but the world as we have arranged it. The Aeyrie people are flying willfully toward extinction. We refuse to use the power which is our birthright, but we bow down under the power which the Walkers hold over us like a knifeblade. We have allowed ourselves to be made into servants.

"But in all things except physical strength, we are superior to the Walkers. We are more intelligent, more gifted, and more thoughtful. Is it not so?"

I nodded automatically, my head against Raulyn's shoulder. I felt exhausted. Yet I fought my weariness, and listened.

"I have devoted my life to resolving this inequity. At every turn, my greatest crosswind has been the community of Triad, and the great persuader, Eia. Id unashamedly used even a tragedy like Teksan's War to build ids own personal power. Id's greatest creation, the myth of inter-species equality, is a pretty and intellectually appealing notion. So our people have given up to Eia what remaining power they had, in pursuit of this mythical 'h'loa p'rlea.' When the Walkers turn against us, as they inevitably will, how will we stand against them?"

I said sleepily, "I thought it was due to the Triad that Teksan's War did not massacre the population of t'Han."

"Very conveniently!" said Raulyn. Id sounded irritated—was id not expecting me to ask question? "Before Teksan's War, no one gave any credence to the Triad-re. But afterward, everyone read Eia's books, and to visit Triad actually became something of a fad. In fact Teksan's War was so successful in empowering the Triad, that I have to wonder . . . How could the power behind the war have originated in a lowly Walker sorcerer? Surely it was the Aeyries who actually engineered the war so that they could make themselves into heroes. I would not put it past either Eia, the brilliant politician, or that remarkable propaganda artist, Delan."

"Delan!" I said waking up a little. Something in my gut rebelled against hearing ill of the revered artist.

"A selfless artist, yes? Every bit as persuasive in id's way as Eia. Whose personal fortune exceeds that of an entire Ula. No, these heroes of the people are not heroes at all. They are not truly fighting for the liberty of the Aeyries, but for their own self-

aggrandizement. No one is, except myself and a handful of others.''

At last what Raulyn was saying dawned on me, and
I said with shocked horror, ''You are a separatist!''

Raulyn sighed. ''Do you see why I was reluctant to
tell you anything? 'A separatist,' you say, as if it were
an incurable disease! No, child, I am merely an advo-
cate for the Aeyrie people. I wish to make it possible
for us to claim our birthright. That is all.''

''And you have Walkers helping you?''

''The Walkers understand even better than the Aeyries the benefits of a properly ordered Universe.'' Id's
hand stroked my fur gently, soothing me into somno-
lence one again. ''Oh, Laril, you dropped into my
lonely life like spring into winter. I do love you, my
sweeting. I know that sometimes it seems as if I do
not. I must serve my destiny, even if our love sometimes must suffer. Please forgive me for hurting you.''

''Of course,'' I murmured, in the soft warmth of ids
embrace. Yet, deep inside me something remained un-
convinced. Raulyn had not told me about ids thievery
from Mairli's workshop, and had not even mentioned
the explosive powder. Id had not explained why id had
been scrying my parent's activities, many days ago. I
did not know if id was lying to me, but I did know
that id withheld part of the truth.

Yet I gave myself over to Raulyn's increasingly passionate caresses; ids fingers, awakening my wings'
sensors, pleasuring my fur; ids powerful, athletic body
rubbing against mine. I let myself become only a
mindless hunger. But I know now, as I could have
known then, that even as I lay sated and easy in Raulyn's musty bed, I remained empty and unsatisfied.
My appetite was gone, but my hunger remained.

Chapter 7

One hot night, crowded with bright moons and clamorous with star-shouting criyas, I stood like a lost wraith on Bet's cottage doorstep, watching my knuckles rap on the sill. "What?" she replied irritably. Her windows hung ajar, the faded curtains glowing with light.

I did not know what to say. I had lain awake beside Raulyn, my heart burdened by ids secrets and indifference, until I could bear no longer to hear the sound of id's deep-breathed sleep. I had wandered out into the raucous night, and the light from the windows of the cottage in the valley drew me like a signal lamp in a storm. But I did not know how to explain without seeming a fool. I said, "It's Laril."

Bet jerked open the door, and stood wiping sticky red juice from her hands onto the towel that draped her shoulder. Beyond her, baskets of brilliant ruby ocopods, like a miser's hoard of precious jewels, cluttered the floor.

"What do you want?" Bet asked.

"Could you use some help?"

Bet examined me suspiciously, her eyes strangely luminous in the white light of the air lamp. But she abruptly stepped back from the door, and I followed her into the cramped cottage. From the rafters hung with dried herbs, Alis'te flung himself to my shoulder. "We are very busy," he said pretentiously, patting my fur with sticky paws.

"So I see," I said dryly. He looked as if he had been rolling in ocopods. His belly swelled like an overstuffed pouch between his legs. He look ridiculous. It astonished me, how much I had missed him.

Bet handled me a small, sharp knife. "You'll have to stand, I'm afraid. I don't have any Aeyrie chairs." She showed me how to split the pods and scoop out the seeds with a crooked finger. It looked easy enough, but at my first attempt, seeds landed everywhere except in the bowl. Straddle-legged because of his full stomach, Alis'te chased seeds across the floor, and I shamefacedly gathered them from the tabletop. But Bet did not seem to notice.

She sat opposite me, and split and emptied the pods in efficient silence. My spilled seeds kept Alis'te busy, until I suddenly mastered the knack of getting them to pop neatly into the bowl without bouncing out again. After a while, the onfrit climbed to my shoulder, and sedately set about washing his sticky paws again.

I said to him, "Do you miss other onfrits?"

"Yes."

"I want to go home," I said. "Why do I feel like a prisoner here?"

Bet looked up from her busy hands to say vaguely, "Maybe you are."

"Raulyn would help me home if I asked idre," I said, wondering even as I spoke why I needed to continue to lie to myself.

"Then why don't you."

"Because—" I hesitated. Did I fear Raulyn would deny me? Did I hesitate to hurt ids feelings? Did I still love idre? "Because I can't," I said.

"There are prisoners," Bet said. "And there are prisoners."

Sighing, I slit open an ocopod. Bet could not answer my questions, or perhaps it was I who could not endure this conversation. We filled bowl after bowl of red ocopod seeds, which would dry in the sun tomorrow, protected from the marauding criyas by Alis'te's jealous guard. My fingers slowly learned the rhythm of the work, until I could keep pace with Bet, pod for pod. From time to time, our eyes met across the table, not in suspicion, but in companionship. *If I am a prisoner, then so is she*, I thought to myself, and was comforted.

Two of the moons had set and the criyas had fallen silent when I climbed the cliff path to the tower. I had left the bedroom in darkness, but now an air lamp burned, and Raulyn lay awake, leafing idly through the book of alchemical philosophy, in which I had discovered and rehidden Mairli's notes on the explosive powder. "Where have you been?" id asked.

"I couldn't sleep. I was helping Bet shell the ocopods."

Raulyn cast a surprised glance to where I hesitated in the doorway. "She asked you for help?"

"I offered," I said. "I feel so useless."

Raulyn waved the book of alchemy at me impatiently. "Ocopods! You could be making the greatest discovery of our age, and instead you are shelling ocopods!"

I sighed heavily. I was weary to death of Raulyn's explosive powder, but, like the crusted burn on my arm, the subject would neither be resolved nor go away. No matter how often I explained that I had done all I could, Raulyn did not seem to understand, or perhaps simply did not wish to hear. Jars and boxes, marked with faded alchemical symbols on peeling labels, filled the two crates that the Walkers had brought through the Void that awful night. Raulyn repeatedly tried to convince me that with guesswork I could put together the powder from these raw ingredients. Id treated my careful explanations of what was and was not possible like the excuses of a child. The longer I delayed unpacking the crates, the greater Raulyn's displeasure. It was almost as if id knew, somehow, that I truly could have done as id asked, but chose not to.

Without speaking, I lay down beside Raulyn, my stomach knotted with anxiety. To my relief, id put the book down. Tomorrow I would find another hiding place for Mairli's notes, I promised myself. Raulyn stroked a hand through my fur, then squeezed my nipples sharply between ids fingers.

"Leave me alone." I was still a l'shil, with indiscriminate and easily roused passions, but now that I had lost my trust, lovemaking felt like a chore. To love with only my body left my heart empty. I did not want to do it any longer.

"What's wrong with you tonight? Don't you love me anymore?"

"Yes," my mouth said stiffly, like the mouth of a puppet. "I love you very much." As if on strings, my body turned back to face Raulyn, even as my stomach churned with nausea. I felt dry and withered as a dead leaf in autumn. Id's fingers hurt me, but I could not pull away. I did as id wished, feeling nothing but the sickness in my belly, until id hurt me so sharply that I cried out.

"You have such passion," id whispered.

When at last it was over, Raulyn fell asleep in a sprawl. I cringed away from ids hot body, trembling. I stared into the dark wall, as if I could see through it, but I saw only myself, complaint as a well-trained animal, betrayed and shamed by a body that seemed no longer to be mine.

"I think Raulyn raped me last night."

Bet, who had been trimming vegetables for the canning kettle, looked up at me sharply.

"I must do as id wishes. I cannot refuse. But my stomach—" I looked at the mess I had made of the late breakfast Bet had fixed for me. I had not been able to eat more than a few bites. "My stomach knows the truth."

Bet covered her face with her hands. I had not meant to tell her so much, but now I heard myself saying urgently, "Do you understand?"

She nodded, pressing against her eyes with her fingertips, then abruptly got up to clear the dishes.

Raulyn had been gone when I awakened that morning. I had to search the tower three times before I could believe my good fortune. Standing on the flight deck, I yearned toward the remote horizon. The barren wilderness glittered mockingly in the sunshine. Never had a prisoner a larger prison, I thought bitterly. I could fly until I fell like an autumn leaf from the sky, but Bet and I both would still be prisoners.

I fled out of the tower, down the cliffside, to Bet's cottage, where she was just constructing my breakfast tray on her stained and scarred kitchen table. I had brought a pen and paper with me from the tower, and now I dipped the pen into the ink bottle and began to draw some crude pictures: a head of grain, a piece of fruit, an ocopod. Bet glanced over my shoulder as she lugged the bucket of water to the dishpan. I tapped my pen on the paper to draw her attention, not wanting to speak out loud. What if Raulyn came home suddenly, and wondered what I was doing in Bet's cottage? If id scried me here, let id think we were playing some kind of guessing game.

I drew a picture of the caricha boat, piled high with boxes and jars. With emphatic lines I tried to show Bet that the boat was supposed to be laden with the produce. She frowned at the paper, then looked up at me with a startled hiss of breath.

I showed the boat floating in water, among the cruel edges of the jagged mountains. I drew a bowed figure at the oars. Overhead, a spread-winged Aeyrie pointed at some obstacle farther down the channel.

Bet took the pen out of my hand, and drew a hand mirror with the little boat reflected in it. To escape a mage's scrying, her drawing reminded me, was no easy task. I took the pen back, heart pounding, and sketched Raulyn's tower, surrounded by fire, with blocks of stone flying away as if in an explosion.

It was the first time I ever saw Bet smile.

The tower weighed upon me like a mountain about to avalanche. My fingers itched to scrabble hurriedly through the tightly packed crates, but I forced myself to a methodical search of the boxes, bottles, and jars, glancing often at the book beside me as I deciphered the alchemical symbols. I handed a bottle to Bet, and she held it up to the light of the open doorway, peering curiously at its contents, before she settled it into her half full basket.

With each sigh of air or motion of dust, I feared anew Raulyn's return. I rubbed mold from a label, and set the box aside without opening it. Much of this collection consisted of dried herbs sweetening the air for one last time with their faint, musty fragrance before crumbling to dust. None of the containers remaining in the crate were of any interest to me.

I peered at Mairli's faded handwriting, the crisp paper trembling in my hand. "Ziodin," I said unsteadily. "I think that must be the new element. I can't find it here, but I have directions for distilling it from Conli's Ast. Do you know which ast that is?"

"I can find out," said Bet.

We cleaned up the mess carefully, repacking the containers in their musty straw, and even nailing the lids back on the crates. By the time I closed the tower door behind us and followed Bet down the cliff path, my fur stank of fear. If I didn't take a bath or exercise vigorously to mask the smell, Raulyn would know that I had been up to something.

I caught up with Bet in time to open the cottage door for her. Alis'te flew down from the rafters to poke curiously through the contents of the basket, but backed away, chittering irritably, when I warned that some of it might be poison. "I have something important for you to do," I told him.

On her knees before an open cupboard, Bet removed bottle after bottle of pickled caricha. I found a small, empty bottle in a drawer, and whittled a cork to fit it with one of Bet's kitchen knives. Alis'te hurried excitedly back and forth, alternately getting in Bet's way and in mine, until Bet said in exasperation, "Are all onfrits such pests?"

"He just needs other onfrits to play with." I rolled up Mairli's notes, put them in the bottle, and sealed it with the cork. "Take this, Alis'te. Hide it where only you can find it."

After much pacing and talking to himself, Alis'te clutched the bottle to his chest, and flew out the window.

He did not return until after Bet and I, having concealed our pilfered goods in the back of the cupboard behind the pickled caricha, were leafing through a book of botany that Bet had produced from under her bed. It was a beautiful, rare book, with hand-colored plates, which listed both the Walker and the Aeyrie names for the plants. How she came to have a copy of the valuable book moldering in the dust under her bed I could not guess.

Conli's Ast grew only in the spray of waterfalls. Its poisonous sporepods were an essential element in a healer's unguent against lice. It had distinctive, variegated leaves, but no blossoms. It was very rare.

I wanted to hide my face in my hands and weep, but I said sturdily, "I don't care how rare it is. I will find it."

Beside me, Bet was as silent and solid as a mountain.

So began the most wearisome and discouraging days of my stay in Raulyn's tower. To locate waterfalls and look for Conli's Ast growing in its spray, when I had no maps and a limited range, was no simple task at all. With a pouch of dried fruit from Bet, I found I could stay in the air for most of the day, if I flew carefully and made good use of the winds. But after two days of this I had to spend a day earthbound, nursing my unbelievably sore muscles. Because I could not bear to be in Raulyn's presence, I forced myself into the air again the next day, but I still had to come home and sleep in ids bed at night, and somehow find a way to act as if nothing had changed.

Soon, my discouragement hovered only a wing-stroke shy of despair. By the fifth day I searched in a confused daze, unable to remember which streams I had followed and which I had not, and uncertain why it mattered. I no longer searched because I expected to find what I sought, but because I did not know what else to do.

The last waterfall, little different from all the others,

spilled in a sheet over the beveled edge of the precipice, breaking apart on a cluster of jutting shards, to
shatter into a rainbowing spray. I landed near its base
and knelt, groaning with pain, to drink the sparkling
water. It was as I stood up again, fumbling in my
pouch for the last of my dried fruit, that my gaze rested
on the broad, variegated leaves of Conli's Ast.

In the scrying room, Raulyn's unoccupied chair
faced dark, blank stone walls. As I hurried from empty
room to empty room, my footsteps on the spiral staircase echoed in ghostly whispers, swirling dust in the
gloom. The ground floor door hung ajar, but no airless
winds screamed beyond. I stepped nervously outside
into the sunshine, listening until my ears ached for the
sound of Raulyn's footsteps. The door creaked faintly
in a breeze, and I wondered suddenly if Raulyn would
be able to return through the Void once this door no
longer existed.

I longed to lie down in solitude and sleep, free for
once of the intrusions of hideous dreams. I felt aged
by weariness, my heart gone dead inside me like a
burned out coal. But there would be no rest for me
tonight. Ignoring the angry protest of my aching muscles, I flew across the valley in search of Bet, and then
followed the vague smudged line which was her pathway to the lake. I found her halfway home, hurrying
to beat the sunset, carrying an empty basket on her
back. As I dropped down to land, my flight muscles
gave way like frayed thread before the pressure of the
air. I could not stall soon enough, and skidded into a
heap. I got up hastily, hot with embarrassment. Bet
had taken off her hat and fanned herself and Alis'te
with it, panting in the heat that lingered in the narrow
canyon. She made no comment about my landing.

"I found some Conli's Ast," I said.

"How far?"

"If we go now, we could be home by midnight."

Bet sighed heavily, rubbing her purple-shadowed eyes. She had sacrificed sleep to ferry foodstuff to the lake under cover of darkness. Perhaps she, too, had hoped to rest tonight.

"When will the sh'man return?"

"Not until morning is my guess."

She settled her hat again over her sweat-soaked kerchief. "Will you show me the way?"

"I'll walk with you. I can't fly anymore."

When we reached the stream which passed through Bet's Valley, we followed it northward to a stark pillar which I often used as an aerial landmark. The sun sinking behind the mountains at our backs, we cut across a plain of standing glass shards. The sunset shaded the deep rose of the glass with red. In the twilight I lost sight of my own bare feet. Soon Bet, too, had disappeared in the shadows, only to reappear suddenly, impatiently shuffling her callused feet in the rattling gravel as she waited for me to catch up.

"I can't see in the dark," I reminded her.

"You Aeyries have such restrictions! You can't see in the dark, you can't swim, you can't carry a burden, you can never be far from a flight tower—Is it worth it, just to fly?"

I felt rather taken aback. "Yes, of course it is."

"Well, I think it's no wonder that Walkers rule the world."

"At what cost? There's more to success than over-population."

With a snort, Bet stalked stiffly away, but I managed to keep up with her so I could say apologetically to her rigid back, "I'm not trying to offend you. You are the one who brought up the subject."

Bet said softly, "I hate Aeyries. I hate their arrogance. I hate their—'' She shivered in the warm twilight, and hurried away, leaving me to grope my way after her as well as I could. This conversation was over.

Moonrise found me wading up a slippery stream bottom, gritting my teeth as the strong current tugged at my ankles. Bet splashed steadily ahead of me, oblivious to my fear. At last we reached the waterfall, where Bet gathered plants and brought them to me, and I stripped the leaves into the basket in utter silence. For a time, I had forgotten that Bet and I were natural opponents, our people under an uneasy, angry truce. For a while, I had been treating her as if she were an Aeyrie, as if she were my friend. Now I did not know what to say to her.

The basket full, Bet squatted beside me at the water's edge. The pale light of three moons trickled across the dark glass, and shattered over the black water. "I'm sorry," Bet said suddenly. I could scarcely hear her voice over the waterfall's tumult. "I do like you."

"You have no reason to like me," I said wearily. "And you have no reason to love the Aeyries. I don't know what Raulyn has done to you . . .''

"I don't even remember anymore," Bet said sharply. The musty scent of wet kipswool washed over me as she got heavily to her feet. I helped her drag the basket's carry straps over her shoulders. Without speaking, Bet's hand found and grasped mine in the darkness. Swaying under the heavy burden in her basket, she led me homeward.

I held her hand tightly, until the alien smoothness of her hairless skin no longer troubled me, but it did not ease my guilt. I had discounted her, accepted her servitude, and never questioned Raulyn's absurd account of her madness. Even now, I found myself choosing words carefully, as I would with a child, assuming simpleness in her speechlessness. Raulyn had enslaved her, not I. But I, too, had wronged her.

Bet collapsed into sleep on her plain rope bed as soon as we were in the door of the cottage. Though I was tired into numb stupidity, I set up a makeshift workshop on the kitchen table. By daybreak, I had distilled more than enough ziodin. I had all the ingredients I needed to make up a batch of the explosive powder.

I lay down beside Bet and slept, until the silent screaming of the winds of the Universe entered my dreams. I woke up, my heart pounding, to find Bet sitting bolt upright beside me, her face pale in the light of late morning. "Raulyn is home?" I said.

She turned a piercing, startled glance on me. For a long moment we stared at each other. And then she nodded silently.

All was ready, yet I hesitated. To take the last step of compiling the powder required me to decide to use it, at a cost to Raulyn that I could not calculate. I fretted away at questions I could not answer, hoping stubbornly to find somewhere the clarity and certainty of mind that I had always thought everyone else possessed. What were the laws of magic? How does one distinguish lies from truth? How could some people live their lives so blithely while others died hopeless? My petty anger at Raulyn for failing to be the fantasy lover I had thought id to be gave way slowly to a deeper, slower rage. Step by step, Raulyn had taken me from independence toward slavery. How I knew this for certain I do not know, yet how could I not know? Raulyn had taken control of the winds themselves to make me a prisoner here. But had I not made myself a prisoner by choosing to love? Was I fleeing from Raulyn, or was I fleeing from myself?

One night Raulyn awoke me from my sleep, to once again force me into a cynical caricature of lovemaking. Id walked away afterward, into the Void. I followed after id like a sleepwalker, but the tower door led me only to the top of the cliff, and down the path to Bet's doorstep. Shuddering with horror in the warm air, I waited dully for her to open the door. When at last her tousled head appeared at the window, I said only, "Today is the day."

So in the end it was Raulyn who taught me that there is a time to doubt and question, and a time to decide. For me, that time had come.

Chapter 8

By afternoon, the hot air simmered like soup on a stove under the cover of gray clouds that had swept across the valley. Sticky sweat plastered down my fur as I lay lengths of oil-soaked string across the tower workroom's wooden floor, winding it around the clutter of stools, chairs, and crates, and under the debris of my abandoned alchemical workshop. I buried them in the mounds of gray powder that Bet had spooned along the bottoms of the walls. As I worked, I tried to pretend to myself that I did not know that the accumulation of Raulyn's entire life occupied this tower, not merely an accumulation of wealth or objects, but of labor, and energy, and power.

Since before daybreak, Bet and I had been laboring side by side, grinding and mixing and cooking our potions, until our eyes were grainy and our hearts numb with too much hope and fear and weariness. At last, every pot and bowl filled with the dust of destruction, we had cleaned up every trace of our labors. Mairli's notes, once again sealed in the bottle, were buttoned into Bet's tunic pocket.

Pale with tiredness and grim as a judge, Bet anchored the oily string with her foot as I backed across the floor and out the door. I paused to twist the four fuses together, then backed away from the tower, still twining together the four strands into a grimy rope. At last I stood at a loss, rubbing sticky grease from my hands onto my fur. What if I had made the fuses too long, or not long enough? What if the flames went out before they reached the powder?

I patted the tinderstick tucked into the sheathstrap beside my fighting blade, and said to Bet, who had followed me, step for step, "That's it, then. I'll catch up with you in the canyon."

The false calm of my voice convinced neither one of us. As each success brought Bet and me closer to this moment, my abhorrence for such willful, devastating destruction had threatened to immobilize me. Now Bet looked knowingly into my face, then turned away without speaking. She picked up a small bundle from the ground, called Alis'te to her shoulder, and strode away along the ridged edge of the valley.

Below her, the neglected grain had gone limp with thirst. The draf bawled plaintively in his pen, having not yet noticed the opened gate admitting him to the verdant riches of Bet's long labor. Bet did not turn her head once to look down at the cottage, the farm, or the flower garden. I have no regrets, her stiff back and unwavering stride said to me.

Someday, I swore to myself, as I watched her walk away, we would converse with each other, equal to equal. Someday we would sit down together and not rise up again until we could truly call each other friend.

When Bet had disappeared beyond the end of the valley, I began counting to a thousand. At any moment, Raulyn might come walking through the tower door, but it would endanger Bet as well as myself if I lit the fuses prematurely.

Shivering in the heat, I rocked back and forth on my

weary, aching feet, watching lightning flicker among the clouds. My heartbeat throbbed like a drum in the breathless, skin-crawling stillness of the approaching storm. At the sharp crash of thunder, I gave a startled jump. Rain and wind might put out my flames if I waited much longer to light them.

From my tinderstick's spray of sparks, a few settled onto the rope. The oil smoked fiercely, but I had to coax it into flame. It suddenly flared vigorously, and sprinted away from me, up the short distance to the tower.

The single flame broke into four and raced through the doorway of the tower as I leapt wildly off the edge of the cliff and fled skyward. I dug my wings frantically into the storm-sullen air. Never had I imagined that the flame would move so quickly! I climbed into the sky like a thief running up a staircase, as storm-clouds billowed suddenly toward me and thunder grumbled among the mountaintops. Almost too late, I remembered to clap my hands over my ears.

The explosion shredded the air and emptied my gut. It tossed me carelessly forward and then snatched the wind from under my wings. For a moment, I hung suspended, then the neat rows of Bet's farm rushed up at me from below. I watched this pell-mell charge with odd indifference, pondering idly how ineffectual we Aeyries are, being too heavy to fly easily, yet too light to do anything else. My wings worked of their own volition, the membranes puffing and stretching in the strain of the uprushing air. I slipped past the oddly beautiful random curves of a knife's edge of glass, grazed my belly on the sharp heads of the unharvested grain, then swooped skyward again.

My ears hurt. My head turned as if pulled on a string, and I saw a pillar of dust and smoke rising from the mound of rubble that had been Raulyn's tower.

Beyond it, the shouting storm fired burning bolts into the mountains.

Bet stood in the canyon with her hands in her pockets, scanning the sky. When I flew into her line of vision, she waved a brief, businesslike greeting, and resumed her journey down the path. I flew ahead to the lake, then circled back to meet her again, and landed to walk the rest of the way at her side.

"I doubt that a single stone is left standing," I said.

She wore her triumphant smile as if it were the clothing of a stranger. I reached out to take the bundle from her hand. "We're going home!"

Her mouth narrowed. "What to?" she asked heavily.

Chastised, I swung the bundle rhythmically back and forth, counterbalancing its small weight by spreading my opposite wing. What to, indeed? "This mystery," I said finally. "The questions I could not ask Raulyn. I have to find out the truth."

"Are you a fool, to toy with a mage? I doubt id will be very forgiving, Laril."

"I know I am not ids match. But the Council of Mages—" I shrugged. "Well, I will do what I can. But what about you? You have been imprisoned here for—five years? More?"

She stopped nodding her head when I reached the number seven. By the same awkward method I determined her age, only twenty-five, though her habitual cynical air made her seem far older. "Then you were not much more than a child, when—I wish you could tell me what happened."

Bet held up her hands in the air. "Like this," her hands seemed to say to me. She ripped open an imaginary piece of cloth, so violently that it seemed for a moment that I could even see the blood.

The storm spattered us briefly with warm rain, then passed us by. Thigh-deep in the lake, Bet loaded the boat with the bags and boxes that I carried down from their sheltered storage spot against the cliff. Given the choice between the burdens and the water, I had chosen the burdens.

"This is the last of it." I handed a heavy, rattling box across the water. As Bet secured it among the rest of our supplies, the boat sank perilously under its weight, until the water hovered just a finger's width below the edge.

"How are you going to ride in the boat?"

"I doubt I will," Bet said. "Even if the boat would not sink under me, where would I sit?"

"What shall we do, then?"

Bet produced a length of rope, with which she replaced the shorter, frayed mooring rope. She came out of the water, silt and mud streaking her legs.

"We tow it behind us," I said.

"I think we would have ended up walking most of the distance anyway."

I sighed, my dream of a relatively easy journey fraying away. We would not float homeward, borne on the currents of the water and the air. We would have to struggle every step of the way.

"Well, it's not as if we could change our minds," I said. "Shall we go?"

We walked the length of the lake together, Bet pulling the boat behind us, until we reached the single stream flowing away eastward, which I had once followed until it spilled over a cliff. The afternoon had given way to evening, but we pulled our load into the stream and walked on. We did not lie down to rest until the mountains had supped on the burning sun, and the stars burned like bright windows in the dark palace of the sky.

* * *

The next morning, we stood at the edge of a cliff, watching the stream plunge like a silver ribbon into a rippling pond below. We had grounded the boat in a bed of multicolored gravel, chips of glass that had been tumbling in this stream long enough for their sharp edges to wear smooth.

I pointed out a potential path, where the sheer cliff degenerated into a series of shattered crevices, but Bet covered her eyes at the thought of climbing that steep way with her arms full. "And what about the boat?" she added.

"Do we have a rope?"

I flew down, carrying the lighter burdens, and climbed the path back up for my next load, while Bet lowered the heavier boxes by rope. At last the two of us lowered the boat, Bet wincing as it scraped down the cliffside. She climbed down last, painfully slowly and deliberately, as I stood below calling instructions and encouragement. As Walkers go, she was a pretty good climber.

The sun hung directly overhead when at last we had reloaded the boat and could continue our journey. "Hellwinds," I said in exasperation. "So much effort for so little!"

"Like farming," Bet said dryly.

"I hope we don't have to do this again."

I suppose it is just as well that I did not know we would carry out this routine almost daily, and sometimes two or three times in the same day.

I could have crossed in one day's easy flying the distance that it took us three days to cover on foot. We slept at night on the bare glass, under the open sky, and got up in the morning groaning with pain, bruised by the hard bed, aching from the labor that had passed, and sighing at the labor yet to come.

Work-hardened Bet toiled sturdily, watching for the dangers of the sharp glass with one eye as she nursed the boat's precious cargo down the narrow, shallow stream. I flew for only a short time each day, to scout ahead and locate alternate routes, though I was often tempted to remain airborne, disdaining any interest or responsibility in the unending struggle to move our supplies across the ground. Yet, every day I landed, to share the duties of the tow line, cursing with each step the absurdity of the natural laws that required me to burn up my energy transporting the food that I needed to eat in order to have the energy to burn.

One afternoon, as the two of us dragged the listing boat through a shallows, the hull grating along the streambed, Bet suddenly stopped pulling, and gripped me by the elbow. I knew it was foolish to sacrifice our momentum like this, but I stopped gladly. The shoulder over which I slung the tow rope felt as if it had been battered with a stone hammer. ''What?''

Bet pointed wordlessly at my bloody footprint imprinting the ground, and waded into the stream to get some rags out of the boat with which to bind my feet.

Two days later, the callused soles of her own feet had also worn away. We sat together by firelight, using our eating knives to hack my flightsuit into ragged strips of astil. This, my first article of clothing, given to me at my winging, should have lasted ten years or more before finally being folded away in a chest to show to my children. But I destroyed it with only a passing regret: if we could not walk, we could not survive.

The mountains have no easy ways. Only the wandering medog, with its prehensile feet and tall, can easily traverse its jagged, hard-edged, often perpendicular routes. My people are flyers in the unforgiving land for good reason.

Our stream followed its own tortuous ways through the wilderness, circling back on itself, edging the base of the greater mountains, and more than once plummeting into deep chasms or slipping under mountains of debris. The days we could not follow the stream's route, we had to pick our way over the rugged, trailless terrain, carrying burdens and boat with us. We took turns walking in the lead, guiding the way across the treacherous landscape, supporting each other's fragile balance as we carried our awkward burdens. The boat was always the last, and the worst.

One day, we progressed so slowly that when we bedded down at twilight, the campsite where we had awakened that morning could still be seen. But we carried plenty of supplies, and were never far from water. Someday, whether in a ten-day or a season, the stream would have to reach the sea. Eventually, we would cross one or another of the major flight routes, which Alis'te would recognize even if I could not, and I would be able to find my way back to Aeyrie lands.

"Where are you going to go? What are you going to do?" I asked Bet. She speculated about relatives in Derksai who might take her in, and commented that most farms could always use another hand at the labor. But as she spoke, her eyes opened like hollow caverns, in which pain rose and fell like the tides of the sea. Raulyn was far from us, perhaps even had been crippled by the destruction of ids tower. But Bet still could not tell me the truths of her heart.

"Do you miss your valley and your farm?" I asked her once, but she could only laugh bitterly, and fling a shard of glass to ring shrilly against the stark side of a crystal mountain.

"What about you?" she said to me. "What do you need to do?"

"I will never fall in love again," I said passionately. But this vow was only a stone dropped into the impenetrable darkness of a well. In the center of my being, where I might have expected to find grief, or anger, or determination to pick up my life where I had left it off, was hidden a mystery.

"I need to study," I would say to Bet. "There is so little I know. I need to learn—I need to . . ." And then I would fall silent, shaking my head with bewilderment, only to find her gaze fixed on me, steady and knowing. "Do you understand?" I would say desperately. "Explain it to me."

But she would only hold her hand over her mouth, resignedly reminding me that she was, in her way, an amputee.

When the color of the mountains turned from pink to gold, I might have been able to chart our position, had I been in posession of an explorer's map. But I did know that golden mountains could be found several days' flight west of t'Cwa. That morning, when I awoke at dawn, I studied the sky as the sun's leading edge appeared on the horizon, hoping to spy an Aeyrie's great wings. Bet had huddled into my fur in the dead of night, seeking my warmth as blindly as a hatchling. Now she edged away, still asleep, as the first rays of the sun blasted away the chill.

I had hidden away a portion of the medog chips we had gathered several days ago, in anticipation of this day. I got up painfully, dislodging Alis'te from the cozy nest he had made for himself in the blankets. In the morning, before the sun's heat and the effort of travel numbed my senses and dulled my mind, the pain was always worst.

I limped down to the stream, where our tethered boat yearned toward the east. Now that several streams had joined ours, I could not cross from one side to the other without flying, though Bet still waded into it each evening to wash the sweat from her body and the dust out of her clothes. I could not bring myself to wash in running water, though my fur smelled like a rug long overdue for its spring cleaning. If Bet minded the smell, she kept it to herself.

Having claimed my bag of medog chips from the boat, I emptied it onto bare ground, and squatted over it with my tinderstick. I blew softly on the dry, fibrous lumps of partially digested sucker plants, and was rewarded by a brief flame, which quickly settled into smoky smoldering. As Bet sat up, suddenly awake in the new morning, I brought a pot of water from the stream, and rested it over fire.

"We get a hot meal today," I said. "To celebrate."

"What are we celebrating?" she asked groggily.

"No matter how much farther we still have to travel, the hardest part of our journey is over." I let her stare at me for several moments before I relented and told her a secret. "We reach a river today. At least I can fly, and you can row. It will be easy."

Bet knit her long fingers together over her bent knees. "I suppose so," she said, but shook her head wearily.

She always awoke depressed. Only the tedious demands of the day's work seemed able to cheer her. I wondered if the bitter hard labor of farming the wilderness, in which she had engaged so doggedly, had been only a drug to alleviate her perpetual pain.

"Come with me to the Aeyrie towns," I said, not for the first time. "Surely a mage can undo what another mage has done."

Bet shook her head patiently.

"At least to try. What is the harm of it?"

"Have you forgotten that I am a Walker? An Aeyrie has to have reason to help me."

"I have learned that it doesn't matter."

"And who are you, Laril? Are you going to change the world?"

"Why not?" I said, but she smiled at me indulgently, like an aging grandparent at a clumsy hatchling.

We reached the river at midday. Even after jettisoning some of the supplies to make room for Bet at the oars, the boat still threatened to sink under her weight, but Bet insisted that we did not need to lighten the cargo any further. She set the oarlocks and pushed off smartly into the strong current, Alis'te fluttering anxiously over her head. I climbed wearily up a mountainside to get myself airborne.

By the time I caught up with them, they were floating swiftly down the center of the river. Bet had shipped the oars, and lay luxuriously at ease, grinning up at me. How anyone could be so relaxed, with only a tipsy wooden shell between themselves and all that water, was beyond me. Alis'te had finally settled atop the cargo, but he held his wings nervously outspread.

With the prevailing winds working against me, I could not fly much faster than the river current carried the boat. I had explored this section of the river yesterday, and knew that it turned back on itself in a gradual eastward curve. With a wave to my water-riding companions, I cut cross wind toward the opposite shore, and flew overland to check ahead for waterfalls and other obstacles, and to scout out a mooring place for the night.

This old river had long ago smoothed the land to suit itself. It traveled with scarcely a ripple through its ancient channel, its water so clear that I could see the smooth, sunlight-streaked riverbottom. I spotted schools of waterwyths, like tangled wads of writhing black yarn, and lush green gardens in the occasional backwater, obscuring the water's surface with floating white blossoms.

Where the walls rose high on either side of the river, perhaps there had been a waterfall thousands of years in the past. But now only a few patches of whitewater remained. Somewhat beyond it, the river curved again, around a narrow beach, glittering with ground glass and scattered with debris.

I would not rest easy in the shadow of those looming walls, and I would have to climb at least halfway up those cliffs to get airborne again, but it was as good a place as any to spend the night. I turned around, and rode the wind upriver.

I encountered Bet sooner than I expected. I never would have expected the quiet river to increase its speed so much. Bet leaned into the oars, her skin shining with sweat. I hailed the boat, and in a moment Alis'te winged up to me. "Something is wrong," he said. "Bet wants the little boat to rest a while because of the fast water, but it will not go into the quiet places."

Far below, Bet's pinched face turned up to me.

"Tell her to tie the long tow rope to the bow, and I will try to pull the boat out of the current. Alis'te, you will have to fly the end of the rope up to my hand."

Another quiet backwater lay just beyond the next bend. There, surely my wings and Bet's powerful arms could break the boat free of the current. But the boat was far more stable in the water than I was in the air, and I knew that one misstroke of my wings could plunge me into the river.

The boat shipped dangerously to one side as Bet

abandoned her oars to tether a length of rope to the bow. I dropped my altitude until I hovered only a length over Bet's head, matching my flight speed to the speed of the boat. Alis'te flew up to me with the end of the tow rope in his mouth, and I wrapped it several times around my wrist.

"Ready?" I shouted at Bet. She leaned into her oars. I made a tight, swooping turn, and let the wind fill my wings like sails. I braced myself for the jerk of the boat, ready to dig my wings in sharply to counter its pull. But it did not happen. The wind had filled my wings, but I continued to move with the boat.

The same current that carried Bet had taken hold of me as well. Too late, I realized that we had fallen into a trap. A rent opened in the fabric of the air and the land, like a knife cutting through a painted canvas. "Bet!" I screamed at her. "Throw the bottle overboard! Throw the bottle!"

The mage's h'lana sucked us inexorably forward, and we fell into the Void.

Chapter 9

It was not the silence of a day at dawn, or even the silence of an empty room. This silence pressed against my ears, squeezed shut my throat, and sucked my heart as flat as an empty purse. I floated, a pinprick of dust in an empty, horizonless sky, on a lightless night, in the bone-freezing cold of an endless, timeless winter. No wind ruffled my fur, no gravity pulled at my flesh, no muscle tensed or throbbed anywhere in my body, no heart beat in my throat, no tear flooded my eye. I hung suspended in a thoughtless, emotionless, bodiless void.

Out of that emptiness, something came at me, something like a speck of light, which ballooned out to become a formless fire. It grew to a terrible brightness which filled the horizons of the Universe. Suddenly I was falling, my heart thundering with panic in my breast, my stomach churning with violent nausea, and wild, fragmented thoughts crowding my mind like frightened, clamorous, disorganized children.

I plummeted, like a carelessly tossed handful of rubbish, into a tumbled pile on a bare wooden floor.

For a moment I could not move. Had I come so far, only to have all my accomplishments negated by a lazy twitch of a mage's hand? With a grunt of effort, I used my wings to jerk myself to my feet, even as my fingers groped to pull the slipknot which had tied my knife in its sheath. I landed in a crouch, knife in hand, wings spread threateningly. But besides myself and Bet, who climbed heavily out of the listing boat to stand in the puddle of water spreading across the floor, the only other occupant of the barren, windowless, stone-walled room was Raulyn.

Id sat in an ornate, low-backed chair, examining us with heavy-lidded, blazing eyes set in a flat, expressionless face. Ids shining, sleek fur glittered in the light of the air lamps as if it were made of polished stone. Id twitched a fan of Walker-style rectangular playing cards through the cool, stale air, then abruptly set the cards down on the nearby tabletop. "Well," id said sardonically.

My rage exploded within me like a fire in paper, and I crossed the room in two leaps, shouting, "You had no right!" Raulyn watched my charge across the stone floor with disinterested unconcern. When I was within striking distance, I paused, my knife dangling foolishly from my hand. If id would not draw, then I could not attack.

"Honorless coward!" I screamed. But all the worst insults I could conjure out of my mouth only ricocheted off ids impenetrable fortress, and fell uselessly into silence.

Then at last id spoke. "You have wronged me."

"*I* have wronged *you!*" I screamed in outrage.

Raulyn stood up all in one motion, reminding me that this was a Quai-du master in whose face I had been screaming hysterically. I jerked my blade up into a guard position, but Raulyn plucked it out of my hands as if it were a weed in a garden, and tossed it casually toward the center of the room.

A blue bolt of lightning crackled through the still

air and shattered my blade into a hundred shining shards. They glittered in the air like raindrops as they fell. I felt a pain in my chest, and looked down at my fists clenching in my own fur. I whispered, knowing it would make no difference, "I gave up my l'per and my Ula for that blade's sake."

"Then share in this lesson that you have taught me, Ishta Laril. It is a true fool who invests ids heart in anything which can be destroyed."

Raulyn turned away from me, knowing as well as I that I would not be so foolish as to attack idre again, and strode toward Bet. She stood like a sullen draf, eyeing the mage listlessly from the shelter of her overgrown bangs. "Ysbet," Raulyn said.

"Sh'man," she responded tonelessly.

"You will look at me."

She raised a face as empty as a beggar's plate. "Did I do wrong, sh'man?"

Id struck her face with a sharp smack, whiplashing her head on her neck like a caricha on its stem. But her feet stayed planted firmly on the wet floor, and she uttered not a sound.

Having turned ids back disdainfully on both of us, Raulyn lifted a box out of the boat, and emptied its carefully organized contents into a pile on the floor. Id sifted briefly through the snarl of spoons and knives, candles, thread and needles then emptied the next box, full of ocopod seeds, on top of the pile.

Bet and I cringed into ourselves, avoiding each other's gazes like admonished children as Raulyn plowed through the contents of our boat. But I could not help but watch as Raulyn emptied a nearly empty box of saltbread onto the floor. It was in this container that we had secreted Mairli's notes. No corked bottle rattled into the debris.

My chest hurt. I had clenched my fists into my fur

again. I loosened my fingers and forced my hands to my sides. Between my screamed warning and our entry into the Void, only a few moments had passed. That Bet could have found and disposed of the bottle seemed impossible. I risked a glance at her, but even when our gazes met briefly, her sullen, stupid expression did not change. An angry red mark had appeared on her face, where Raulyn had hit her.

Where, I wondered suddenly, was Alis'te?

Raulyn picked up a bottle of pickled caricha and flung it against the stone wall. Jar after jar sprayed its contents over the wall and onto the floor, until my eyes watered with the sharp smell of vinegar, and my muscles hurt from being held rigid so I would not flinch at the sound of shattering pottery. At last, Raulyn stood back from the boat, and with a gesture shattered it into splinters.

The room fell into a strained silence. I stared in disbelief at the scattered debris and the pile of damp splinters, remembering how many times I had dragged that boat through shallows, carried it and its contents over rugged, nearly impassible terrain, slaved over it by day and slept beside it at night, cursing it when weary, and blessing it when hungry. I surreptitiously rubbed my burning eyes, but I felt too stunned even to weep.

"Clean up this mess," Raulyn abruptly said to Bet. She hung her head and exited the room through its one door, leaving it ajar, to reveal a portion of a gloomy, nondescript hallway. What lay beyond the hallway I could not begin to guess, since the building in which the Void had deposited us could have been anywhere on earth, or even beyond it.

Raulyn said conversationally. "You would not even reach the door, l'shil."

I tore my eyes from the lure of the open door.

"Tell me something: whatever in the four winds came over you, to induce you to make a mage into an enemy?"

I did not miss the threat in Raulyn's voice, and I did not need to hear my own voice's waver to know that I felt desperately afraid of idre. I held my tongue.

"You didn't want to share the credit for discovering the powder, is that it?"

Outraged, I could not help but reply angrily, "I just wanted to go home!"

"You just wanted to go home?" The disbelief in Raulyn's voice shrilled painfully in my ears. "You corrupted and misled the female whom I left in your charge, you lied to and deceived me about the alchemical powder, you stole my belongings, and what you could not steal, you destroyed. You did all this because you wanted to go home?"

I could not argue without betraying Bet's role in our escape. I held my tongue.

"Please," Raulyn continued sarcastically, "explain it to an old fool. When you set foot in my tower, I promised to help you home again whenever you wished. Why did you not simply tell me you wanted to go?"

My outrage threatened my control again, but I bit my teeth on my tongue to hold it still. If I told Raulyn that after id had deceived me, held me prisoner, and raped me, I had no cause to trust idre, id would only have laughed in disbelief. Other than in the uncertain convictions of my heart, where was my evidence?

I would not allow Raulyn to make me doubt my own intuition. How could I live the rest of my life if I could not trust myself? It would be like losing faith in my s'olel—without that faith, how could I have the courage to leap onto the back of the wind and fly?

Raulyn waited, but I refused to give idre the weapons to use against me.

At last id walked away. I breathed some of the fear out of my body as id paced the room in such a convincing state of agitation that I began to doubt myself once more. At last id paused near me, staring at a wall and breathing heavily. Id spoke, in a voice heavy with grief. "I loved you."

I knew that this, at least, was true in its fashion. I shuffled my feet uncomfortably, feeling twitchy with guilt.

"I delighted in you. I gave you everything you wanted—everything! And you—threw it away."

"You knew it was slavery," I said weakly. Where had my conviction gone?

Raulyn drew close to me, and touched a hand to my shoulder. I felt the heat of ids body burning through my fur, as ids hands stroked down my arms. "I remember something else."

I felt nauseated. In the confusion of my mind, my body's honesty anchored me. "Don't touch me!" I said fiercely.

Raulyn snatched ids hands away, the tender sensuousness of id's expression disappearing like a costume mask. "Go!" Id shouted at me. "You foul my house!"

I actually took a step toward the door.

"But I insist that you recompense me for the loss of my tower."

"What do you want?" I asked, as if I didn't already know.

Bet came back into the room, carrying two wooden buckets into which she began loading the debris. She did not even glance at us.

"I want the powder," Raulyn said.

"I don't remember how I made it."

"But you wrote it down. No, do not insult my intelligence by denying it! You are an Aeyrie. You wrote it down, and you brought it with you. Where is it?''

"You never told me how you plan to use it."

"Why should I trust you?" Raulyn said, with such bitterness that a new wave of guilt washed over me.

"It was written down," I admitted.

Then I added calmly, "But I destroyed it."

Raulyn looked at me. I could not tell if id believed me or not. "So," id finally said, in a voice thin and sharp as a shard of glass. "You have made your choice."

I heard no signal, but two large Walkers appeared abruptly at the open door, dressed in strange, stiff outer clothing decorated with insets of shining metal. They carried wicked, graceless metal weapons.

So much unnecessary force made me angry. I kicked the first one in the stomach, and left him doubled over and gasping for breath while the other one chased me round the room. Every time he made a grab at me, I broke his grip with a blow of my wings. Had I achieved my full adult strength, those blows could have broken his arms.

Only when a third Walker came into the room did they finally manage to corner me. Then I regretted having led them such a chase, for while Raulyn may have forbidden them to use weapons, they had not been forbidden to hurt me.

They hit me in the belly. While I was doubled over with pain, they punched me in the face until I managed to turn to the wall for protection. I had learned my lesson and stood passively while they lashed my wrists behind my back. I could not stop my terrified trembling. One eye began to swell shut. I spat a mouthful of blood onto the floor, another mess for Bet to clean up.

As they began to drag me away, Bet raised her face

to meet my terrified gaze, and held aside her expression of stolid submission as if it were a veil. For the fraction of a moment, her rage comforted me, but then I remembered, as the Walkers forced me out of the room and down the windowless, airless hallway, that Bet's seven long years of bitter anger had made her not one whit more effectual against Raulyn's power.

When they threw me roughly to the floor of a bare, windowless room, I felt too dispirited to even attempt to break the fall with my wings. As I lay sprawling, gasping with pain, the Walkers stood over me, toeing my ribs roughly with their heavy shoes, and discussing me in their harsh, alien language. At last they cut my bonds, nicking my flesh while they were at it, and walked away. The door cut off the gloomy light of the hallway, leaving me in unbroken darkness.

I heard the rasp of a bolt sliding home, and the rattle of the door as the Walkers checked to make certain it was secure. I wondered if that door would ever open again. No one, whether relative, friend, or stranger, knew what had become of me, but even if someone did, who would consider me worth the trouble of rescuing?

I lay as I had fallen. Vague, muffled sounds itched at my ear through the floorboards. At last, I crawled painfully to my feet, and explored the room by feel. I felt along three solid wooden walls, and a fourth of stone. The floorboards fit together so well that they did not even creak. I found the door, but it had not even a keyhole in the knob.

The room was completely empty, without even a chamber pot. My wings made sitting on the floor an impossibility. My choices were to lie down, or to stand. I stood in a corner, and fixed my gaze on the thin, faint thread of light along one edge of the door.

I stared at it until my vision blurred, and I wiped away a fistful of tears.

I could not distinguish between day and night, but it must have been sometime the next morning that the door was jerked open and a small, limp thing landed with a soft thud on the floor an arm's length away from me. I recoiled from the horrible smell of it: the scent of blood and pain and terror, and the familiar scent of a friend's fur. It was Alis'te, and he was dead. But before he died, his wing membranes had been shredded into bloody tatters and his feet had been cut off.

I lay in the darkness like a bag of rubbish, and made the acquaintance of hunger. The niggling emptiness in my belly grew slowly at first, and I could quiet it by swallowing saliva, or singing to myself. But soon my mouth had gone dry for lack of water, and the pain of my hunger ate through my body as if I were consuming myself, bite by bite. I could think of nothing else. My muscle and my very bones hurt with hunger. I could not sleep without dreaming of food: great, groaning tables of it, not one mouthful of which I ever tasted.

Unbearable cramps passed through my abdomen and legs. By the second day, I had become too weak to stand, and lay on the floor in a stunned daze. My awareness of hunger slowly faded, having been replaced by a ravening thirst.

I could measure time only by the appearing and disappearing of the gray thread of light at the door. But by the third day, time began to blur as the barriers between worlds frayed away. Ghosts made themselves at home in my stinking, gloomy prison. Invisible other than in the faint shifting of shadows, speaking in voices as thin and breathless as the sighing of the wind, they engaged me in long, arduous discussions. "Aeyries die of hunger in seven days," they reminded me, as if I could have thought about anything else. "How many days has it been? Four? Five?"

"Four," I said firmly, though I had no idea. My voice crackled like dry sand.

"You are young. Your life has scarcely begun. Why should you die like this?"

"Why do you act as if this is my fault?" I cried. "If I give in to Raulyn, I will lose—" But I could not remember what was at stake anymore.

"It is honorable to die for a good cause, yes, but what cause is this? A power struggle between yourself and a sh'man? What will you gain? You can live, or you can die. Those are your choices."

"I will die, then," I said. But I knew, even as I said it, that I was not willing to die.

I screamed Raulyn's name at the solid door, pounding on it weakly with my fists. I screamed until my hoarse and ragged voice had frayed to a whisper, and the blood from my skinned knuckles stiffened my fur like glue. But the door did not open.

The thread of gray light faded. I lay on my side, panting and dizzy with effort. My mouth felt dry as a slice of stale bread. My eyes burned and prickled as if from staring too long into the sun. Grains of salt grated under my fingers as I rubbed my face. I had no water left in me with which to weep.

"You. Awake."

Whimpering, I shielded my eyes from the blazing light. I had not even heard the key in the lock.

"On your feet."

When I did not move, the Walkers lifted me summarily to my feet. I tottered shakily, weak-kneed, staring at the two Walkers in a bewildered daze. I tried to ask them a question, but my words mired themselves in my sand-choked throat.

"Come," they said in Walker.

I took a step, and nearly fell. Wrinkling their faces up with disgust, they each took one of my arms, and half dragged, half carried me out of the room, and down the gray hallway.

In a room that still smelled faintly of pickled caricha, Raulyn sat at supper. The Walkers dropped me to the floor before idre. At the scent of food, my dry mouth suddenly poured with saliva.

"What is it?" said Raulyn impatiently. Ids fork clinked softly as id twirled it in the thin noodles. Some of the savory vegetable sauce dripped over the edge of the plate.

I tore my gaze away from the food, and stared instead at the floor, at my scruffy, sticky fur, fouled by my own urine. Disgusted, I shut my eyes. "I remember how to make the powder," I whispered.

"What? Speak up."

I tried, but my voice was gone. "I remember how to make the powder." I whispered again.

"So?" Water splashed softly in a cup. I thought I would die of desire for just one sip of it.

"I will write it down for you."

"What makes you think I need it any more?"

"You haven't let me go," I said in stupid surprise.

Raulyn snorted. "I had forgotten about you."

Id cut a crisp vegetable, and chewed noisily. I surreptitiously wiped a corner of my mouth on my shoulder. "Then let me go, if you don't need me," I said reasonably. I felt more confused than ever, but if Raulyn had suddenly ceased to care about the explosive powder, what did ids reasons matter?

Raulyn's stool scraped on the floor. I watched ids sleekly furred feet pad away from me, but I could not even lift my head to follow ids progress. I knelt at ids stool like a slave, my wings crushed painfully against the floor, my head hanging over my chest. No matter how heavily I breathed, my lungs hurt for air. I realized abruptly that I still felt desperately afraid. My life lay in the capricious control of an alien, one I understood less and less with each passing day.

Raulyn walked up to me, and sat once more on ids stool. "What do you think of this?" Id held a paper before my eyes. I recognized it at once, the age-yellow third page of Mairli's notes, with its careful diagrams and neat, regretful epigram. So this was why Raulyn no longer needed the formula! And I understood at last why Alis'te's body had been thrown into my cell. Bet must have taken the bottled instructions out of their box and hidden them somewhere else in the boat, within easy access of the onfrit, whom she instructed to fly away in an emergency, taking the bottle with him. Raulyn, with ids typical disregard for Bet's abilities, had assumed the author of this diversion to have been myself.

I looked at the diagrammed paper, and looked away. Of course I had not been able to leave an unsolved puzzle alone, and I had suspected for some time why the powder was so important to Raulyn. But I could not lie to idre again. I could not face that dark room, with its incriminating ghosts. I could not accept that my destiny was to die. "It is a weapon," I said.

"Can you make one for me?"

I could not even rally my spirits to ask who Raulyn wanted to kill. "Yes," I said.

And suddenly I was a prisoner no longer, but an honored guest. Raulyn shouted the Walkers back into the room, railing angrily at them as they lifted me to my feet, and set me firmly onto Raulyn's stool. I felt strangely disembodied, indifferent to the whirling vertigo that all but blinded me.

A cup touched my lips. "Drink, just a few sips at a time," said Raulyn. I swallowed painfully. "Now, a little sustenance." Raulyn fed me, one small mouthful at a time. I opened my mouth, chewed, and swallowed, and felt my stomach clench around the food as frantically as an angry fist.

All along, I had intuitively known that if Raulyn had been able to make me serve idre against my will, id would have done so long ago. To become ids servant, I needed to offer myself up willingly. For months, id had been bribing me, but I had not done as id wished, not for love, for intellectual satisfaction, for fear, or for guilt. But for food and water, relief from pain, and the illusion of dignity, I finally sold myself.

Chapter 10

To stand and fight, to face the razor edge of another's blade, to see and smell the spilled blood, and to experience the pain of injury, this at least requires courage, however misguided. But to point a weapon at a living target and obliterate it with a flick of the finger, this is a coward's violence. It requires no skill, no art, no involvement in the other's struggle for survival, no involvement with the enemy at all. I had created a coward's weapon, which made effortless that which should have been impossible.

The night after we first tested it successfully, using a straw target, I revisited the walled compound in my dreams. Behind me stood crafters, metalsmiths, farmers, and fighters. Some of them were Aeyries, and some of them were Walkers, united to destroy the unity of our peoples, working side by side even as the shades of hatred scoured our hearts. We seethed together like an alchemist's potion, with only Raulyn preventing us from exploding out of our cauldron and destroying each other.

Almost immediately behind me stood one Aeyrie Black, a beautiful, lithe, poisonous person named Pau. To my other side, Raulyn stood, ids glorious colors brilliant in the blinding sunlight, sparks flashing off the jewels pierced through ids wing membranes.

Two young Walker males had finally set up the straw target to their satisfaction. The weapon, already loaded, hung heavy in my arms. Raulyn had insisted that I test the weapons, for only then would id trust their safety.

I turned my head back and forth, searching for—an escape, perhaps, or a friendly face. But I found neither when I spotted Bet, standing with the only other female in that household, one whose fanatical hatred of Aeyries bordered on lunacy. Solemnly, almost grimly, Bet pondered the straw target. She did not turn her head to look at me.

"Don't despise me," I pleaded with her, or was it to myself that I spoke? "I did what I had to. This is not my evil, but Raulyn's." These words, often repeated on my long, tortured, sleepless nights, rang in my ears with unfamiliar hollowness. I added hastily, "Someone would have stumbled across Raulyn's powder, sooner or later. It isn't my fault that it was me."

I lifted the weapon, pointed it at the straw figure, and flicked the tinderlock. The kick of the shoulderpiece into my breastbone doubled me over with pain, the explosion's blast of noise shocking through my ears like a blow. The straw figure no longer existed. Except for a few scattered, smoldering pieces, it had been completely obliterated. All around me, Walker and Aeyrie voices joined together in a shout of triumph.

Was it only I who saw that a great section of the wall had been blasted away? Beyond it, a burned field lay like some artist's metaphor of death, a smoldering wasteland where before must have been a verdant farmland. Beyond the field, the Glass Mountains rose, majestic and forbidding, husbanding in their bellies their unforgotten secrets. But a monstrous furrow the width of three or four mountains had been gouged through their ranks, all the way to the edge of the earth.

Beyond the horizon, the moons hovered in one of their more common cluster patterns. But where Ahbi should have stood at the apex of the figure was only darkness. I had blasted the moon out of the sky.

I awoke from the dream, shivering with horror. But without a window, I could not even look out to make certain that it had only been a dream.

In the morning, the exultant crafters fired their forges and kilns and set to work with renewed cheer. From the beginning, they had doubted their project, they had doubted Raulyn, and above all they had doubted myself. I had sweated under their suspicion as if I had reason to care about their opinion of me, but today I stood back indifferently and watched them at work, setting up the molds and feeding fuel to the fires. Despite my long confinement indoors, I knew that summer had turned to autumn. My fellow workers brought in the scent of rain and wet earth on their clothing, and so I knew that the first rains of the season had fallen. My wingday had passed, unremarked and unnoticed. Without a calendar, I had not even been able to be certain what day it was.

By now, all the other Aeyries my age had made the initial choices of adulthood. After the year of traditional estrangement, they had recreated their relationships with their parents. Perhaps they had grown weary of casual sex, and had fallen in love. But my life had gone from malaise to disaster to despair. Caught in a web of another's weaving, I had overseen the realization of a nightmare. I had not done one thing in which I could take pride.

My back against the soot-black wall, I watched the

Walkers lean eagerly into their bellows, their naked, muscular flesh gleaming in the red light of the fires. The precious ingots slowly melting in their cauldron had been imported from the mysterious East, and brought at incalculable cost. Whose wealth purchased these expensive wares?

"Make yourself useful," one of the Walkers snarled at me. Several like him, each larger and more brutish than the last, had been assigned to be my guards. From breakfast bell to bed, they never left me alone. A spell sealed the door of my room which they locked each night, so that only the key which my guards passed among themselves could open it.

I wandered over to my work table, lit the lamp, and shuffled through the scattered notes and sketches, most of them marked with the crafters' sooty fingerprints. For sixty days I and my helpers had studied, designed, redesigned, cast, and recast. Yesterday's test in the walled compound had not been the first, but only the first to succeed. Nonetheless, the actual weapon looked much like the one Mairli the inventor had drawn on paper a generation ago.

I untacked Mairli's original design from the side of the wooden partition, and laid it on top of the stack of papers. "Why didn't you destroy it?" I asked out loud. No one would hear me, or pay attention to me if they did.

"You knew what you were creating. Why didn't you destroy your notes, dissolve the powder, and die without ever telling anyone what you knew?" But I understood Mairli the inventor too well. Hadn't I gone out of my way to preserve the weapon design, even though I suspected what it was? Hadn't a shout of delight come out of my mouth when it obliterated the straw figure yesterday? I had shouted with gladness, even though my heart already perceived a future of a blasted earth

and mountains and the moon shattered in the sky. I
had shouted because of my power. How was I so different from Mairli, or even Raulyn?

My hand brushed a layer of dust from the empty
work table, as if I were a housekeeper fretting over
the dirt of that stinking, sweltering basement. The
stack of papers I carried to the furnace, and threw
them in, one handful at a time. No one took notice of
me. As an explosion of flame consumed the page of
paper I had extracted like a hidden treasure from between the pages of Mairli's old book, I sighed wearily.
Yes, it had been destroyed at last. But much too late.

We all ate together in a large, crowded dining room,
the Walkers at one end of the table and the Aeyries at
the other. Only Raulyn ate apart in ids own rooms. As
always, Bet served the meal with her gaze lowered,
silent and efficient as a wind-powered machine. Even
though she lived with her own kind at last, her solitude
seemed only to have become more absolute.

Bet and I had not exchanged a word with each other
since the day our boat crashed out of the Void into the
middle of Raulyn's floor. The Walker males often
talked about her, and as my facility with the language
improved, I realized that many of them wanted to make
love with her. They discussed the subject among themselves, as if Bet were a draf to be trained or an enemy
to be coerced. But soon Bet's ungentle rejection of
their advances had transformed their lust into angry
dislike.

So I realized that the Walkers lead lives as passionate in their manner as we Aeyries are in ours. Their
passion seemed foolish, and even crude to me. Perhaps our Aeyrie ways seemed equally foolish to them.

Tonight, the other female had cooked the meal. I
choked down a few mouthfuls of the tasteless soup,

before laying down my spoon and reaching for more bread. The other Aeyries were doing the same, but the Walkers, though they grumbled about how awful the food tasted, continued to eat.

"I don't see you in here cooking," the woman finally burst out angrily. "Trying to make a few postas and a handful of yellowroot into a meal for twenty-five. I'd like to see you do it."

"Is that what this is?" One of the Walkers put down a spoon with a clatter.

"There's been no food delivery this week," she said stiffly.

"What?" Several of the males started out of their chairs.

"We'll see about that. Talk to Jory—he contracted to—"

"Give the lackwit a taste of my—"

"I already talked to Jory," the female said loftily. "He hasn't gotten paid, he says. No pay, no food. The master already knows about it, too. So don't you go blaming me for the empty pantry!"

Some of the Aeyries looked up sharply at the woman's implication that Raulyn was to be blamed for to-night's poor meal. I stood up hastily and said to my guard for this evening, "I'm going to bed." When the simmering tensions of the household turned into a full-scale brawl, I had no desire to be present.

But he waved me back into my chair. "The master wants to see you after supper."

I never wanted to see Raulyn, but especially not this night, when fear for my life weighed so heavily on my mind. Id loved my fear, and grew fat and self-satisfied when I sweated and trembled in ids presence. Sometimes id made me stay and play cards with idre for half the night, until I became so exhausted that I did not care any longer what id might do to me. Only then would id let me go.

I sat down again, and nervously picked at the remains of my bread as Walker and Aeyrie snarled insults at each other. The Walkers lately had seemed inclined to lose faith in Raulyn. I wondered if they had begun to suspect that my destruction of the tower had limited Raulyn's powers. Without scrying walls, Raulyn could not keep an eye on their enemies, or interfere, as id seemed to love to do, in everyone's business. Perhaps something else had been interfered with as well. Could their source of wealth have been dependent on the scrying walls?

The argument over dinner finally ended with the Aeyries walking out.

"They've gone to their precious sh'man, no doubt," one of the males sneered. They all looked at each other nervously. I was not the only one who feared Raulyn.

"Let's go, Laril."

I got up reluctantly and followed my guard the length of the room and out the doorway. Behind me, Bet and the other Walker woman began clearing the abandoned meal. I sensed Bet's gaze tracking me, but I felt too tired to even try to guess what she wanted to tell me.

Angry Aeyrie voices rasped in my ears as we drew near Raulyn's room. The door had been left ajar, and yellow light spilled through the scuffed dust of the hallway. My guard took me by the arm. I paused passively beside him, willing to accept my reprieves in whatever form they came.

Raulyn's voice rose over the clamor. "I will speak with the Walkers tomorrow," id said unconcernedly.

"But what is this business about the supplies? And Willa said that Jory hadn't been paid—"

"Don't worry yourselves over it."

"Have the Walkers stopped supporting us?"

"Money? Is that what all this is about? The Walker and the Aeyrie peoples are behind us!" Apparently realizing that ids reassurances were not enough, a new timbre and vigor filled ids voice. With passion and conviction id said, "We are only days away from our greatest victory. All we have struggled for during all these long years may finally be achieved. Soon the Aeyrie people will come to us in gratitude, begging us to return home and lead them to a new future."

My heart leapt in my breast. *So soon!* I rejoiced.

Then I shook my head to clear it. Where had these foreign emotions come from? I muttered sardonically, "Once a rapist, always a rapist." The Walker beside me looked at me strangely.

The Aeyries who had entered the room angry and anxious, left it contented, self-satisfied, their eyes glazed with adoration. I pushed past them, feeling like the only sober person in a crowd of carousing drunks. I felt so disgusted that I forgot myself, and crashed angrily into the mage's sanctum.

I had taken idre by surprise. For the fraction of a moment I saw idre unmasked: tired, old, and almost desperate. I could feel no pity for idre, but something else came over me, a kind of anger at the stupidity of the Universe, which makes us so hungry, and so cheaply satisfied, so eager to be free of the turmoil of uncertainty that we will settle for the easiest of answers, and then spend the rest of our lives defending them to the death.

I said, "What is it like, to have to force your followers to love you?"

Raulyn looked up at me, and for the time it takes a spark to disappear, I thought that I saw in the depth of ids face the remains of a real person, a person who had loved and desired, and then had slowly distorted beyond recognition. What had happened to make this wreck, so powerful and so empty?

Then I thought of myself, and my selfish, head-strong, thoughtless ways, and felt afraid.

Raulyn did not bother to respond to my comment. "I have called you here to give you an opportunity to convince me that you can be of any further use to me." Id waited, eyes glimmering, for me to respond to the veiled threat in ids words.

"If I were gone, who would you play cards with?" I asked flippantly. I took a deck of cards out of the cabinet, a Walker deck with which I had been learning some of the artlessly simple, but energetically competitive Walker card games. "How about a game of 'Eyes'?"

To this day I am not certain what had happened to me. Perhaps I realized at last that Raulyn could not dance this elegant waltz of ego and power without a dance partner. Perhaps all of these others would not leave the sinister ballroom until their feet had blistered and their hearts given out, but I would dance no more.

Without another word, Raulyn sent me away. A fearful exultation filled me as I strode briskly down the hallway to my room, far ahead of the guard, and shut my own door behind me. Maybe someone would come with the one key to let me out in the morning, and maybe not. At the moment I did not care.

I crossed the lightless gloom and threw myself onto the narrow bed. Sometimes as I lay there trying to sleep, my body would remember the soaring sensation of flight. In sixty days I had scarcely even seen the sky. I knew that the other Aeyries living here were able to fly as they willed. But Raulyn never did, nor had id ever flown when we lived in ids tower at the edge of Bet's Valley. How could id bear to live so long without the wind under ids wings? How much longer would I have to live so?

A foot brushed softly across the floorstones. I jerked myself sharply out of bed and to my feet, but then I smelled the scent of soap and wool and kitchen herbs. "Is that you, Bet?"

A tinderstick grated a shower of sparks into the darkness, and then a candleflame flared in her hand.

"At last," I said, as if I had been waiting for her for a long time. "They are going to use the moonbane weapon to attack the Community of Triad, aren't they? There must be a way we can stop them."

She examined me by candlelight, as blue and gold flared through her eyes. Then she knelt to secure the candle to the floor with a few drops of wax. The sheet of paper she held in her other hand crackled as she laid it down. On top of it, she set an inkwell and a ancient, grimy pen.

I sat down once more on the bed, and waited for her to tell me what she had to say.

Chapter 11

Her hair had grown long enough that it could be tied back with a ragged strip of cloth, but half of it had escaped to frame her thin face in sweat sticky strings. Like myself, she appeared to be pining away in the windowless gloom of this stone prison. But her eyes burned.

Her pen scratched on the paper. She shoved her drooping sleeves up to her elbows and dipped the pen once again into the ink bottle. Reclining on one elbow on the bed, I pretended to feel relaxed. But the habits of captivity had been too long ingrained in me.

"I'm glad to see you." I said. "But what will happen in the morning, when the guards open the door and you will have nowhere to hide? It's only luck that they didn't see you tonight."

Bet uttered an amused snort, and dipped the pen once more. I caught a glimpse of the paper as the broad shoulder blocking my vision moved aside. I saw, not the drawing I had been expecting, but letters. "You can write!"

"What did you think?" Bet said sarcastically. "The question is, can you read?"

"Of course I can."

Bet looked up into my face, her expression almost solemn. Without another word, she handed me the sheet of paper. She had written two sentences in small letters across the top. But she had not written in the graceful H'ldat script that I had perfected as a child. Instead, the angular, disjointed characters of the Walker script danced mockingly across the page. I frowned, aware of her anxious gaze on my face.

Then I haltingly read out loud, "It never occurred to me that you might speak my own language. I know you Aeyries believe in book-learning, so perhaps you can read in the Walker tongue as well."

Bet expelled her breath in a relieved sigh. I continued, speaking this time in H'ldat, "My parent insisted that I study your language. My reading and writing has always been better than my speaking, though that has improved since we arrived here."

"Oh? Your accent is beyond description."

"Why thank you," I said, smiling weakly to let her know that I had not lost my ability to absorb her insults. "You seem to be able to write what you are unable to say. I guess Raulyn doesn't know you can read or write?"

"Apparently," she said. Her tone of voice reminded me that Raulyn seemed prone to drastically underestimating her.

I pressed the coarse paper back into Bet's hand. "Then tell me what hellwind possessed you, to come to my room like this. The only thing protecting you from the mage's anger is ids conviction that you are incapable of thinking on your own."

In a moment Bet had scratched her answer and handed the paper back to me. "Raulyn will never know," I read.

I got up and paced the little room as she continued to write. Four strides long and four strides wide, my shivering shadow walked with me from corner to corner. Bet's pen scratched once again on the coarse paper. The candle had begun to dribble wax down its side when at last I recognized the emotion driving me up and down the length of the room. It was fear, yes. But it was also anger. Anger at Bet, for making decisions for me, for involving me in her enterprise when I had been managing so well to keep out of trouble.

"Bet," I said wearily, "I have had to learn that I am something of a coward."

She murmured over her work, "Is it cowardice to fear a person who has absolute power over you? I think not."

"But you aren't afraid, and id has just as much power over you."

Bet looked up at me then, and though she did not speak, I read the answer in her face. Though we had labored and travailed many long days in each other's company, she remained a mystery to me. How much more enigmatic was she to Raulyn, who had fallen into the trap of believing ids own deceits rather than the truth? Perhaps Bet had never been truly submissive, or perhaps Raulyn had made the mistake of believing that she could never grow beyond it. Perhaps Bet herself had cleverly altered herself to match Raulyn's expectations, making it easy for idre to believe that the mask was reality. Whatever the reason, the cage that confined her had not been built strongly enough to hold her. And Bet knew it.

I came back to sit on the bed. The ropes stretched across the frame to support the thin pallet creaked scratchily under my light weight. "You'll only get the one chance," I said.

She nodded.

"It might be best if I don't know whatever you're planning. Raulyn can easily make me tell everything I know."

She nodded again, and handed me the paper.

"You have to trust me," she had written. "I will not abandon you or betray you."

"You trusted me when we escaped the valley," I reminded her, and kept reading.

"I only need two things from you. The first is that you explain to me how the weapon works."

That was all she had written. She still sat on the floor, her shoulders resting against the bedframe for support. I nudged her shoulder gently. "And the second?"

She shook her head. "You'll tell me later?"

She handed me the pen. I could see that something troubled her, but we already agreed that she would keep her secrets, so I did not press her. "Well, this is the last time I ever draw this damnable thing," I declared. Though I spoke lightly, I meant my words.

I talked to her as I diagrammed the moonbane weapon one last time. I told her about my dream and how it had haunted me all day. "I keep telling myself that this crime is Raulyn's, not mine. But the longer I think about what this thing can do, the more frightened I become, and the more responsible I feel. I could have destroyed the alchemical formula. I could have told Raulyn I would die sooner than build ids weapon. I could have stopped this somehow, and I didn't. At first I could excuse myself, but now . . ." I stopped speaking, surprised to find tears in my eyes.

Bet said nothing. But she had wrapped her arm affectionately around my leg, and the difference her gesture made in my dreary mood astonished me.

I explained the moonbane weapon to her. I told her everything there was to tell, every detail of the metal alloy, the triggering device, the loading, the braces. I explained to her the problems we had overcome, and the weaknesses that remained. I talked until the candle had burned down to a mere stub, and finally I could not think of anything more to say.

"Is that enough?" I asked.

Bet did not speak. She stared into the shadows that filled the corner of the room, the paper drooping limply in her hand.

"Don't ask me any questions; that might give me some clue as to what you're up to. But just tell me; do you want me to keep talking? I've told you everything, but if you want me to go over it again—"

Bet shook her head slowly, then raised her head sharply as if she heard something. I sensed it also, the skin-itching, electrical tension that suddenly pressed against the building, as if a screaming storm were struggling to overcome its stone walls, "So, the thief is going out tonight," I said. "Do you know, I almost felt sorry for Raulyn this evening, id is stretched so thin—"

Bet blew air through her closed lips, making a loud spitting sound. I laughed, feeling the pall of Raulyn's controlling presence lift away. "Id is gone."

Bet held up the paper, tapping a finger on the fragmented Walker scipt: "You have to trust me."

"I do trust you. We are friends," I said simply.

She tore the paper into four pieces, and then painstakingly tore each piece into bits the size of a fingernail. She handed half of them to me, and we swallowed them, side by side, as solemnly as any dignitary at a formal meal. I felt glad that it had not been a bigger piece of paper; we didn't even have any water to wash it down with.

"But what about the second thing?" I asked suddenly.

Bet took in a deep breath and got stiffly to her feet. She picked up the pen and the ink bottle and secreted them in one of her many pockets, then she abruptly pulled her tunic over her head, and dropped it onto the floor.

Somehow she had managed to wash herself and her clothing. I had contrived to bathe in a pitcher of water once or twice, but if this dwelling had proper bathing facilities for Aeyries, I had not yet heard about it. I hoped that my fur would finally get so rank that one of the Aeyries would volunteer to guard me while I bathed. Bet dropped her trousers and took off her shoes, then turned briefly to look at me, her eyes questioning me.

I only looked back at her, puzzled. She shook her head to herself, and took off her underclothes.

"You've removed all your fur," I said lightly. "Won't you be cold without it?"

The candle flickered its faint light onto her face, which had oddly lost its pallor and flushed a deep red, as if she had been working too hard in the sun. Keeping her eyelids lowered, she scattered the last of the clothing onto the floor, and lay down beside me on the narrow bed. Her cool, smooth flesh pressed against my thick fur. With so much hard muscle in her, I had never thought that some parts of her body could be so soft.

"Bet!" I said in astonishment.

She stroked a hand tentatively through my fur. "Will you tell me what to do?"

That Walkers and Aeyries could make love with each other had never occurred to me, no more than I would have considered making love to an onfrit, or a draf. That she felt no desire for me as well was obvious. I wanted to refuse her, but I had promised to trust her.

If nothing else, I would make the expected motions. At least my lovemaking skills were something I could be proud of. If I had been able to do something so shameful as to design the moonbane, then surely I could force myself to do this.

Her bare skin felt strange, but not unpleasant. Tiny, nearly invisible hairs tickled the palm of my hand like down. Her bodyshape differed from mine, yes, but not so much that I could not trace our common ancestor in our similarities. I held her close to me, and told her some of the bedsecrets that I had learned from my first lover, as if she were a wingling coming to a love bed for the first time, and I were the Companion designated to teach her the ways of pleasure.

She reached out to gently stroke the sensitive membranes of my wing. "Like this?" she whispered.

Even the shock of my first awakening, when I truly understood what it meant to be an adult and a neuter no longer, could not compare to this. From the center of my bones to the tips of my fur, I thrilled into awareness and shuddered wildly awake. I did not have to close my eyes and pretend she was an Aeyrie. Of everything that happened that night, this one discovery surprised me the most.

I had never found more respect and kindness in a love bed. That it came at the hands of one so unlike me mattered far less than that it came at the hands of a friend.

We fumbled and giggled like children, and then passion abruptly lifted us like a summer updraft. We loved each other into speechless astonishment. At last she mounted me, the guttering candle sending her shadow in a frenzied dance across the ceiling. I remembered suddenly the guard in his room down the hall, and tried to warn her to be still, but then I, too, forgot caution. Our caroling voices rang defiantly through the stale air, making the cold stone walls sing. I did not even hear the guardman's door open, or the key turning in my prison's magic lock.

He dragged her off of me, and struck her a blow that knocked her up against the wall. But she matched him, curse for curse, her fists clenched and her body rigid with anger, until at last he backed away from her. "Well, it turns my stomach."

"Don't try to tell me you never imagined what it would be like!"

"Just you wait until the master hears about this."

"No, don't—" Bet frantically gathered up her clothing. "Don't tell the master, he'd be so angry with me . . . Listen, I'll make a bargain with you."

The door had closed before I could hear what bargain they struck. But a fool could have guessed. They left me alone once more behind my locked prison door, my heavy breathing and my rattling heartbeat only just beginning to slow in my chest. Was it her cleverness, or her ruthlessness that made me smile to myself as the candle finally guttered out? Or perhaps it was the way my body felt, unfolded and aired out, like a blanket at spring cleaning. A dozen lovers at one time or another had shared my bed. But none of them had left me feeling like this.

I slept better that night than I had ever slept in that bed.

In the morning I was released into a flurry of activity as the Walkers rushed about, preparing for a shopping trip into town, coins jingling in their pouches like little bells. More than all my other suspicions and certainties about Raulyn, confirmation of ids petty thievery left me puzzled. To possess such power, and then use it for something so contemptible! But was it not the same pettiness which led idre to compel loyalty, to prefer rape, and to rule so regally over ids tiny, strife-ridden, artificial kingdom?

I could not believe any longer that id was serving

the noble Aeyrie cause that id claimed to be serving. Such idealism could only be a smokescreen to cover ids true purpose, something so small-hearted and narrow-minded, I could not even imagine it.

I saw Bet at breakfast. Her body seemed curled in over itself, like a flower past its bloom. She looked at me once, and then looked swiftly away. Was it shame? Like a campfire in a rainstorm, the small joy burning in my heart was abruptly extinguished.

My guard took me down to the cellar, where the forges already had been fired. They set me to work at the tricky chore of setting the triggers, which only I had been able to master. The night's chill had seeped into the building, giving the air the smell of winter, but here it was sweltering, hot from the fires and humid from the steam as the forgers plunged the red-hot metal into the cooling tanks. I thought I had gotten used to the claustrophic sensation of the underground, but today my skin crawled with it, and my concentration jittered like a bug on a hot stone.

The Walkers chattered as they worked. I had never paid much attention to their talk before, but today I listened intently; seeking what, I do not know. To understand, perhaps, why they were doing this monstrous labor. But after listening half the morning to their stupid prejudices and blind hatreds, I yearned to stuff my ears with cloth so I could hear no more.

At midday, the smoke-stained door slammed open. Pau, the Black Aeyrie with the poisonous manner, stood in the doorway, a shadow in the darkness of the cellar stairs. Something about ids sudden appearance wrenched fear into wakefulness in my heart. Id came into the light, and stepped aside with a flourish, like an actor in a formal drama. Raulyn stepped out of the darkness behind idre.

Id was glorious. The light of the fires flamed the

edges of ids fur. Ids mane flowed back from ids face, catching the light so ids head seemed surrounded with an aura of red, smoldering fire. The jewels in ids wings sparkled like stars. I remembered suddenly why I had loved idre, and the memory burned like acid in my chest. I set down my tools and rubbed my eyes with my fingers, as if the dim light and the smoke were too much for me.

"The future of the land is in your hands."

The magnificent voice had such power that id might have been standing beside me, shouting into my ears.

'The perverted dogmas of the h'loa p'rlea threaten to steal the minds and freedom of ourselves and our children. Shall we go forward chained side-by-side, Walker to Aeyrie, forced to walk in a lockstep rhythm beaten out for us on the drums of stranger? Or shall we follow our natures as we were meant to do, living Walker for Walker and Aeyrie for Aeyrie, raising our children and living our lives in freedom?

"Who shall decide the future of the Walker people? Who shall decide the future of the Aeyries? It is you, my friends! Will you have your children go hungry so that strangers of another race can eat? Will you have your children be schooled in an alien University, and return home so changed that you do not know whether to call them Walkers or Aeyries? Will you live to see the day that Walkers and Aeyries lie down with each other?"

The first rumble of response had grown to a roar. "No!" shouted the Walkers, with such rage that I flinched in my fur.

"Or will we coexist in parallel peace, the Aeyries in their land and the Walkers in theirs? It is you who will decide the future for our children."

Raulyn paused, and I lifted my face from my hands, hoping that ids speech was over and I could go back

to the obscurity of my work. But Raulyn had paused
only to pick up one of the nearly finished moonbane
weapons from a work table. "We will decide, you and
I together, and this is what we will decide it with. We
will drive the perverts from the land, and allow them
to poison our people with their lies and deceits no
longer. We will drive them out!"

Once again, the Walkers roared their approval. But
I snuffed out my light, so I could better hide myself
in the shadows, and endured the appalling irony of
Raulyn's speech in a kind of stupified daze. The magic
of ids voice, which at first had glamoured my vision,
washed over me in waves until I grew sick of its mel-
lifluous power. Yet it nibbled away at my will, and by
the time Raulyn had finished, with a great shout of
"Thirty days!", a great, bleak shadow lay over my
spirits.

Raulyn left the room, and Pau stepped in behind
idre, slipping once more from the light into the shadows. And my heart froze in my throat, for I knew at
last what was bothering me about the Black. Id was
the one who had attacked me in the storm, nearly half
a year ago now. And so this whole thing had begun.

Or had it begun with Wand seeking me out on the
Quai-du floor? Or even earlier? How long had Raulyn
been twitching at the threads of my life, and why?

"You heard the master," the Walker Afim said.
"Let's get to work."

By the next day, many strangers, Walker and Aeyrie
both, began to appear in the household. They worked
the forges in two shifts now, keeping the fires burning
all day and half the night. Several had been set to work
in the alchemical workshop. I was not permitted there,
but once I caught a glimpse through an open door.
Aeyries sweated and argued over burners and distill-

ers. As I watched, one poured a vial of completed powder into a wooden barrel.

In only one day Bet and I had made enough powder to destroy a building. Surely it would not take much longer to create enough of the powder to destroy the entire country.

Somehow, this madness had to stop. But my guards watched me more closely than ever, and Bet never even looked at me any more. I lay in my bed at night with my knees curled to my chest, and each time I closed my eyes all I could see was fire.

Chapter 12

"It's nothing to worry about. The door is locked. But listen to the sounds beyond the door. They have locked me in because something is happening."

My muttered reassurances fell into the gloomy, stale air of my room, like sparks falling into a rainstorm, quickly extinguished by fear. I paced anxiously from wall to wall, the heavy stone closing me in and weighing me down until fear made me frantic.

I bashed my fists on the heavy door. It thudded dully, adding yet another splinter to my bruised, bleeding hand. "Let me out!" I yelled hoarsely.

A key turned in the lock. I backed away, breathing heavily, rubbing my sweating palms on my thighs. My fur felt sticky with grease. I had survived for thirty more days without a bath. Thirty more days, without spreading my wings or feeling the sun, or touching the hand of a friend.

The Walker pushed the door open with his foot, set a tray of food on the floor, and tossed a bundle of clothing onto the bed. "Put those on."

"I want to know what—" I began, but the door slammed shut in my face.

The unfamiliar, heavy wool clothing included a worn and grimy quilted vest such as the Walker farmers wear for warmth in the field. All the clothing had been hastily altered to allow for my wings, but did not fit me particularly well. I got dressed anyway, and forced myself to eat the food that had been brought for me.

Then I paced fretfully up and down my tiny room, knocking my wings painfully against the wall each time I turned. They were bringing me with them on their day of triumph, in case something went wrong with the weapons, perhaps, or just so Raulyn could keep an eye on me. Maybe I would be able to escape my Walker guard. Maybe I could somehow warn the Triad Community.

But when at last the door to my room opened again, three of my guards crowded into my room, and they had a rope. "Raulyn never did trust me," I said lightly, though my heart's hopes were evaporating in my chest. I turned my back to them and voluntarily held my wrists together behind my back. "Today is the day, then? I never thought I might be permitted to go along."

For a moment I feared that they would not respond to my chatter, but at last one replied gruffly, "It's the day."

"We must be going through the Void." I allowed myself a tremor of fear. "Have you ever passed through the Void? I'd rather walk, let me tell you."

"Shut up now," one of them said angrily. In my haphazard probing I had struck a nerve. If I had been frightened and disoriented in the Void, how much more so would a Walker feel, who lacked my experience with the wind?

"Well, I can't wait to see the moonbane at work. We'll burn the buildings right to the ground. And the people of Triad, burning like those straw targets. Won't that be a sight! Say, did you know that over half of the people at Triad are Walkers?"

"I said, shut up!"

I tested my bound wrists surreptitiously. I had hoped to distract them into inadequately tying the knots, but I had been far from successful. One of the Walkers dropped a loop of rope over my head, and slid it tight over my throat. I swallowed painfully, and could not think of anything clever to say.

"Let's go. They're waiting for us."

I walked behind them with my head hanging like a draf, too frightened and desperate to conceal my shame.

Most of the others had already gathered in Raulyn's room, the Walkers and Aeyries whose faces I knew if not their names, and others who were all but strangers to me. I tried to count them, but I could not turn my head without choking. As usual, the Aeyries had segregated themselves on one side of the room. In the middle of the floor stood the crate in which we had packed the tested and retested moonbane weapons, each one wrapped in cloth and laid into a cushion of straw. A sealed wooden barrel also waited among them. I knew at once what its contents must be.

Raulyn sat in ids usual place, apparently unaware of the silent, shuffling people that filled ids room. I looked around for Bet, and spotted her at last among the other Walkers. She stared straight ahead of herself, blankly indifferent, as if she neither knew nor cared that, as with myself, a rope dug tightly into the flesh of her neck.

I had been keeping a small light of hope alive inside of my heart, a hope that Bet, somehow, would manage to stop this monstrosity from happening. That last bit of hope died, and I turned my face away from the sight of her. Raulyn's very strength lay in ids pettiness: a small heart is an invulnerable one. What had made me even imagine that Bet could fell idre?

When Raulyn stood up and began to address id's followers, I scarcely listened. The others shifted nervously in the tide of ids rhetoric, seeming anxious to get the fell journey through the Void over with, but by the time Raulyn ceased to speak, every eye glowed with inspiration. They knew that they would be remembered in history as heroes, and perhaps, I thought dully, they would indeed. Had I not been midwife to the hatching of a new age, in which weapons needed no skill, and killing needed no contact? War, already so much easier than negotiation, had become even easier. Teksan's War, with its one battle and mere hundreds of fighters, might someday be regarded as quaint and old-fashioned. We would lose our ability to be horrified. How could we value life, when with a twitch of the finger we could snatch it away?

In this new age, anything might happen. But ultimately the Walkers, because of their sheer numbers and cultural ruthlessness, would be the only survivors. Under the leadership of an Aeyrie, an Aeyrie invention had been used to commence the destruction of the Aeyrie people. Not for the first time, I wondered what Raulyn truly hoped to accomplish.

Raulyn went to the doorway. I knew what was to happen next, and yet when the door to the Void slammed open, it surprised me. The sensation of great forces, screaming in protest, the crashing open of the wooden door to reveal the rushing emptiness beyond, these I had learned to expect. But the ease with which Raulyn opened the door surprised me.

Where did the power come from? I wondered. Surely, to do so much required far more than a mere effort of will. Since I had grown up among mages, I never gave them a second thought. Except for a certain solitariness in their demeanor, they seemed little different from everyone else. I knew that the laws of magic, like the other laws of the Universe, applied indiscriminately to everyone. If to enact them required only an effort of will, then why could I not do it?

Raulyn stepped aside from the door, and gestured the first Walkers through the door. My guard tugged at the rope, pulling its grip on my throat uncomfortably tight. I glared at him angrily, but he only grinned in reply. I pretended, as he started toward the terrible emptiness beyond the doorway, that he did not exist. As we stepped over the doorsill, I shut my eyes, and took hold of the hard thudding of my heartbeat like an anchor.

The empty, airless winter of the moons froze my breath in my throat and the blood in my veins. I carried my frozen heartbeat in my hand like a polished stone, a talisman to comfort me through the wilderness. The mage's will carried me, but there could be no others in that nonplace, and I cherished the sudden solitude. I thought: In all these long months, I have never been truly alone. I mentally took a deep breath and looked around myself.

I will never have the words to describe what sights passed my awareness. Images, actions, patterns, and even thoughts, much of which reminded me oddly of the things sometimes seen frozen in the crystal of the mountains, all these flashed through my closed eyelids as I floated through space and time, riding on Raulyn's current. To visit the mind of one alien to me, a mind complex beyond description, with patterns of thought so beyond my experience that I could not even recognize them as patterns, this was the Void.

I looked down curiously at my own etherial body. It was composed, not of flesh, but of fire: a bright, trailing comet of energy, with a blinding bright core. This was my life-fire, and this startling core had to be my soul. The energy of my being pulsed round me. No, I was not powerless! I could easily free myself from Raulyn's influence. All I needed to do was use a little of that energy to propel myself free of the current. Raulyn would never find me again, in that timeless infinity. But I could not condemn myself to be lost to wander, forever unmoored, wearing a body of fire rather than flesh, in this empty, endless, cold, and alien place.

The second doorway rushed up to me, and I fell, wrestling to free my hands, spreading my wings to break my fall. I landed gently on my face in a wet meadow. I took in a deep lungful of the sweet, wet air. *I will never be confined indoors again,* I swore. *Never again!* Someone caught hold of the back of my flight vest and dragged me to my feet.

All around me, people snapped into being in the thin air, and tumbled headlong to the ground. My guard dragged me out of the way so they would not land on me, but I could not tear my eyes from the marvelous sight. Several of the Walkers, their eyes staring blankly out of white faces, lay helplessly puking where they had landed. The Aeyries did not have such difficulty with vertigo, and bunched rather disdainfully together, a distance away from the chaos. But I watched Bet land on her feet, more self-possessed than the Walker who supposedly held her prisoner. Just once, our eyes met, and a shiver thrilled down my backbone. For a moment, it seemed I could see the energy burning like fire in her dark eyes.

The crate of moonbane weapons and the barrel of explosive powder landed heavily. Raulyn, who had been the first to step over the threshold, stepped onto the grass and neatly shook the kinks out of ids wing membranes.

As the Walkers recovered from their disorientation, and the small army organized itself, I looked around myself. Only in my dreams had I ever stood in such a place: flat as a spread blanket, with a vast, unbroken darkening sky filling with stars overhead, and the last vestiges of a red sunset edging an absolutely straight horizon. I could have been standing on a monstrous platter under an inverted bowl. Only in the air had I ever before been able to see so far.

We had landed on the gradual slope of a hillside. Gigantic plants puffed out from the ridge of the hill: trees, I realized suddenly. I had seen them in books and paintings. A patchwork of farms spread across the land to my left, but to my right I could see only a vast, uncultivated field. It stretched, broken by tussocks of summer grass and the twisting of a stream, to an edge nearly invisible now in the fading light. Beyond that edge, I could see nothing but hazy darkness.

I took in another breath of air. It had a rich, pungent taste, not unpleasant, but strange. When I licked my lips, they tasted like salt.

''Where is this?'' I asked the Walker, as he dragged me into position behind the crate.

He answered me, unable to resist any opportunity to demonstrate his superiority. ''Northern Derksai,'' he said. ''Near the coast. See over there? The lights of a boat at sea.''

I looked at the distant lights spreading their reflection in shivering lines across the endless water. How marvelous it would be, to throw myself over that nearby cliff and float along the surface of the great, mysterious ocean, and listen for the sweet singing of the Mers.

The last clouds of a rainstorm that had apparently passed through earlier hovered above, edged with the last light of the sun. Enough stars had come out so I could identify the four directions. Several days' journey to my left, which was west, lay Ula t'Han.

I had heard that the Triad Community and the people of t'Han maintained several wayshelters scattered across the flatland, built on top of towers so the Aeyries could travel easily. At first, the shelters had been frequently sabotaged, but in the last ten years the Walkers of Northern Derksai had learned to welcome the increased traffic of goods and ideas. If I could free myself and find one of the shelters, I would find my way home.

The breeze was honed with a winter chill, but I shivered with fear rather than with cold as Raulyn began to hand out the weapons, and Pau to distribute pouchfuls of powder from the barrel. Never in the history of the world had Aeyrie done battle with Aeyrie in anything other than personal combat, but this would not even be a battle. It would be a massacre.

The Aeyries playfully pointed their unloaded weapons at each other and pulled the trigger. I wanted to be sick.

Clearly, the others had been instructed in the layout of the land, and even had drilled in preparation for this night. After a few moments of shuffling to mix the night-blind Aeyries with the seminocturnal Walkers, they formed a line and began to walk toward the northeast. Bet and I both walked near the end of the line, separated only by our guards. Behind me, a Walker named Edra brought up the rear, gingerly carrying the remainder of the barrel of powder in his arms.

I felt strangely calm. If I truly had the ability to escape the h'lana of Raulyn's will while in the Void, then surely my helplessness before idre was not nearly so great as I had thought. I opened my senses, and watched, and waited for some small thing to which I could turn my will.

The trail followed the curve of the hill, then down

into the flat grassland that led to the edge of the sea. As the trail curved, I could see Bet's powerful shoulders, recognizable even in the half darkness. It was she whose plans had been obstructed by Raulyn's decision to bind her. If, somehow, I could undo her bindings—

I imagined the fire of my body as I had seen it in the Void. Then I created in my mind a picture of Bet's hands, bound behind her back. The rope was wound tightly around one wrist, crossed between them, wound in the opposite direction around the other wrist, then it was wrapped crosswise, and tied off. If I could only loosen the one knot, then she would be able to work her hands free. Surely I could do such a small thing.

I reached out with the fire—so—and touched the tight knot. I felt something warm and living, as if I had touched, not the rope, but someone's hand. Startled, I lost my concentration, and stumbled on stones underfoot. My guard jerked sharply on the rope, choking a cough out of me with the strangling noose. "Watch your step. And shut up."

"Aeyries can't see in the dark," I reminded him impatiently.

What person had I encountered, already struggling to loosen the tight knot? Had we an unknown ally, Bet and I? Whoever it was had been having a hard time of it—how I knew this I did not know—and needed my help.

I concentrated once again. This time, when I encountered the fleshlike solidity of the other person at work, I did not pull away. I squinted my eyes until they hurt with peering through the restless shadows, and suddenly I could see the other's fiery hand. I overlapped it with mine. The brightness of our joined fires hurt my eyes: how could anyone else fail to see it? With one sharp tug, the knot gave way.

I stumbled again on the pathway, my ears roaring. "What is wrong with you!" my guard hissed over his shoulder. I fought for control, but I weaved wildly, like a hatchling finding ids feet for the first time. I peered blurrily into the darkness, trying to spot Bet's broad shoulders once again, but I could not see her. No cry of warning or sounds of struggle let me know that my success had been anything other than a self-induced hallucination. I focused my gaze miserably on the darkness in which my feet trod.

Great, gently-moving shapes blocked out the sky, a squadron of tall trees. Their dry leaves whispered fiercely in the strong breeze, and their twigs rattled together as if in warning. They grew in a formation too orderly to be natural. Perhaps they formed a wind-break to protect a farm's precious produce. I heard the Walker behind me moving forward, past us, and away into the trees, and realized that all the members of Raulyn's army had scattered into the grove.

My guard led me forward. I tucked my wings tightly out of the way, but the hazards of brush and low-hanging branches assaulted me in my blindness. Footsteps crackled faintly on the dried leaves. Somewhere ahead of me, I heard a low whistle. I collided with my guard, who had stopped in his tracks.

"What is it?" I whispered. My heart had begun to thunder again.

"There's something wrong," he said. We started forward again, more cautiously, then stopped again. "What's the matter?" my guard said.

"She's gone," replied another Walker. His voice sounded blank with disbelief.

"Who? Bet?"

"I was walking ahead of her, like you are, and all

of a sudden the rope swung down and hit me on the legs. She'd disappeared like—a ghost. Vanished into thin air.''

My guard turned sharply, and dragged me forward into his line of vision. "You didn't even feel a tug on the rope?" he asked the other Walker.

"Nothing. And I didn't hear a sound."

After a moment, my guard said nervously, "We had better tell the master."

"I suppose we have to." Clearly fearful of Raulyn's wrath, the Walkers started forward reluctantly, and then stopped again, to cautiously sandwich me between them. Somehow I managed to walk obediently, even though my heart was expanding in my chest, bewildering me with joy and wonder. I had helped her to escape! And now I could hope, if only just a little.

The trees opened up like curtain before us, and we stood at the edge of a cultivated field. My feet sank in the soft, light, recently-turned soil, the rich scent of it filling my senses. Off to my right, I could sense the sea once again. The stars had brightened in the sky. By their faint light I could see the clustered shapes of buildings, overhung by more trees. Scattered windows glowed with warm light. The breathless, hollow tones of a nishi flute whispered across the field, as a solitary musician played to an audience of stars.

I could not see the Walkers and Aeyries, pausing like myself and my guards at the edge of the rich field, but I could hear them stamping restlessly in the soft earth. One of my guards uttered a low whistle, and the night fell suddenly silent. The first rising moon, a mere sliver, sailed on the ocean's horizon.

The earth sighed as Raulyn walked across it. Id cupped a delicate, faintly luminescent light in one hand, with which to light ids path. The unearthly light glowed in ids angry eyes, and I quailed, like my guards, in the face of the sh'man rage.

"What is wrong?" id asked, very quietly.

" The woman is gone."

"What!" Raulyn looked sharply into the small woods. "And where is Edra with the barrel?"

My two guards drew closer together "He passed us, and went into the trees to our right," one of them said. "I should think he would be here by now."

"Yes," hissed Raulyn. "I should think so. Stay where you are. Do not take your eyes off Laril for even a second. If id escapes as well—"

Raulyn did not need to finish that sentence. The two Walkers hemmed me between them like walls, as Raulyn strode swiftly away.

The silence made my ears ache. How long had the musician been silent? I smelled the faint, earthy scent of an animal I had never before encountered. Someone spoke urgently. A tinderstick sparked, and an Aeyrie, apparently fed up with the darkness, lit a lightwand.

I caught only the briefest glimpse of the creature before I heard the distinctive click of one of the moonbane weapons being cocked. I shut my eyes tightly, and turned my face away, but when I heard the blast, it was not to my left, but to my right. The explosion deafened me. Light flared through my closed eyelids. My two bodyguards flinched and cried out, slapping their hands to their light-sensitive eyes. All up and down the line of trees, I heard the same shouts of surprise and pain.

But I did not understand yet what had happened until Raulyn hurried past us, shouting, "Attack!" From the left came a protest. "The cursed things don't work!"

I opened my eyes. The Aeyrie's lightwand still burned. I glimpsed the alien creature, bounding beyond the reach of the bright light, gliding with eerie speed toward the bright lights of the building. But with that loud explosion, the warning already had been thoroughly delivered. Even as I watched, the lights of the community were disappearing behind protective wooden shutters. A voice echoed across the field, a passionate, sweet cry, so alien it made my skin crawl. Scarcely had it fallen silent before other voices chorused in reply.

All around me, the attacking company clamored in scarcely-hushed argument. "What was that?"

"The idiot didn't use enough powder."

"Mine doesn't work, either."

Through the chaos, Raulyn's light moved more swiftly than seemed possible. And at last, a single word cut through the hissed arguments like a glass knife. "Betrayed!" id cried. "Someone has sabotaged the weapons!"

My guards both gave an enraged roar, and as one they turned on me.

Chapter 13

"What are you doing?"

One final kick of someone's foot, and the blows stopped at last. The damp earth felt chilly against my face, but I could no longer smell its sweet, heady scent. A hot trickle of blood dribbled from my nose down my cheek. Shuddering with fear and pain, I pressed my body into the earth.

Over my head, Aeyrie and Walker shouted at each other. I scarcely heard their words for the ringing in my ears, but I could hear the desperation and panic, and, above all else, the poisonous hatred.

"The traitor! Who else could it be? Who else knows enough about these cursed weapons?"

Raulyn's voice said mildly, "Why, any one of you who worked the forges could have done it."

"Not one of *us!*" they said. But what they meant was, "Not a Walker! Only an Aeyrie would do such a thing."

"Don't be an utter fool. Laril could not have damaged the weapons. Unless one of you guarding idre stood by and watched idre do it."

The Walkers, unable to argue with Raulyn's logic, chose instead to mutter angrily among themselves about the contempt with which Raulyn had spoken to them. I thought to myself, with strange clarity, *Raulyn has lost them.*

But Raulyn did not seem to realize it. Id gave a string of sharp orders, most of which I could not understand through the ringing of my ears. I gathered that we were to retreat. While the Walkers vied with each other to kick and hit me, the people of the Triad Community, having secured their houses, had organized a party to investigate the explosion. Since the hairy beast patrolling the land had already seen us, we could not even rely on the darkness to delay their search.

Someone dragged me, sobbing with pain, to my feet. My head throbbed. A knife-sharp pain dug into my side. "Walk !" one of the Aeyries ordered, but my knees buckled under my weight, and I slid to the ground. I tried to explain that I could not stand, but blood choked my words. The inside of my mouth had been cut open.

"Brainless, honorless idiots," one of the Aeyries muttered. "Did they think we were just going to stand by while they beat one of our own?" Apparently, even though the Aeyries were willing to turn these unbelievably destructive weapons against their own kind, there were some things they still would not tolerate. I wondered suddenly if their intention had been to kill only Walkers, not Aeyries. When the first Walker killed an Aeyrie, how would they have reacted?

"They're coming!" someone said frantically, sounding oddly surprised. Had it not occurred to them that the people of Triad might fight back?

Two of the Aeyries lifted me up between them, and we fled into the grove of trees. We did not get far before the two of them had to set me down, so one could feel out a route through the bracken. The other remained with me, supporting me with an arm around my waist so I could remain on my feet and peering nervously behind us.

I said thickly, "Why don't you just leave me?"

"What do you think?" the Aeyrie said. "You know too much."

"Raulyn promised me—"

"Take it up with Raulyn," the Aeyrie said impatiently. "Besides, what makes you think that they won't kill you if they capture you?"

I sagged against idre, hoping that by making the care of me as difficult as possible, I could convince them to abandon me. But as the second Aeyrie returned, I heard voices behind us, speaking a low, guttural, harsh language. Fear washed over me. What reason did our pursuers have to think that I was not an enemy? Wasn't I in fact the one who had engineered Raulyn's great plan? I had no friends in this place, only enemies.

When the Aeyries lifted me up once more, I did not struggle. Even though we traveled slowly, our pursuers did not seem eager to overtake us. I could hear them, making a heedless racket among the dry twigs and leaves that carpeted the earth, but the sounds of pursuit never drew any closer.

"They just seem to be making certain that we are leaving," one of the Aeyries muttered.

"What *are* those things, anyway?"

"Some kind of trained guard animal?"

We were not quite the last to come out of the woods. Two Walkers appeared a few moments later, carrying a third between them. "It's Edra."

"Is he dead?" asked Raulyn indifferently.

"Looks like someone hit him in the head. But he's alive."

Another Walker said anxiously, "Let's get moving; those creatures are right behind us!"

"They don't seem to be interested in attacking," said Raulyn mildly. "Did anyone see any sign of Bet?"

After a moment, one of the Walkers said reluctantly, "I was looking at those creatures, trying to figure out what they were. And I realized that one of them was carrying a body on its back. It could have been Bet."

My captors abruptly set me down on the ground like a sack of goods, and paced back and forth, shaking their weary arms. I lay on my side and stared bleakly into the darkness. All Bet had ever wanted was—What? Now I would never even know.

"Are you sure she was dead?" Raulyn's voice, remote and uncaring, asked.

"How could I be sure, at that distance? It looked like a dead body to me."

"I need to be certain," I heard Raulyn mutter.

As one, the Walkers drew together. "We're not going back," one of them said angrily. "Not without weapons."

"No, of course not," said Raulyn gently. But I heard an edge of anger in ids voice, and cringed my battered body closer to the earth. Someone would suffer for this night's work, and I knew too well how likely it was to be myself.

"Then what are we standing about for? Those creatures—"

The Walker fell silent, as all of them stared at something I could not see in the darkness. It was another who finished the sentence nervously. "They're at the edge of the trees, watching us. A good—fifteen of them."

Raulyn said, "You are under the protection of a mage, remember? Go ahead; I'll bring up the rear."

The Walkers were glad to oblige, but I heard, as Raulyn must have heard as well, one angry comment: "The protection of a mage didn't do Edra or Bet much good. I can't help but notice that only Walkers were hurt.''

The Aeyries hesitated in a disorganized huddle around Raulyn, as if seeking reassurance, but the mage only waved ids luminescent hand. ''Follow the Walkers. Their night vision will save you the trouble of finding the way. Take turns carrying Laril.''

''But—''

''Never mind them,'' Raulyn said blandly. ''I will see to them later.'' At first, I thought it was those mysterious creatures Raulyn threatened. But later, I realized that id had been talking about the Walkers.

I do not remember much of that journey. Never in my life had I been in so much pain, and every time the Aeyries paused to pass the burden of my body to another pair, I fainted. A pair of Walkers could have carried me the entire distance, no doubt, but my fellow Aeyries trusted them no more than I did.

Their voices murmured in the background of my pain.

''I always told the sh'man that it was a mistake to work with the Walkers. Did you hear them? Not one of *us!* It was enough to make me cut one of their hearts out.''

''If you could even find it.''

''Or maybe some portion of their precious male genitalia.''

They snickered among themselves.

''And it never even occurred to them that the only person who could have hit Edra in the head and exploded his barrel of powder was Bet.''

By the time we reached the crate on the hillside, the Walkers had already packed their weapons into it, and shuffled about impatiently, waiting for us. Edra lay on the ground beside the crate, moaning.

The Aeyries lay me on the ground, and left me unwatched. But with my hands still bound, I could not even crawl away. The Aeyries hurried to pack their weapons, and the Walkers rushed about frantically, picking up bits and pieces from the ground as if they were collecting tinder for a fire. They laid these sticks and stones onto the ground in the shape of a door. I watched them in some bemusement. There had been no doorway when we arrived, why did we need one to leave? Perhaps the experience of disappearing into thin air was too much for them.

The doorway slammed open, and two Walkers hastily shoved the crate of weapons through it. The rest of them rushed in, not even waiting for Raulyn, whose pale light had begun to dim in ids hand. I struggled against the ropes, but the knots had not yet slipped enough for me to work myself free easily. Two Aeyries picked me up by my armpits.

"Wait!" Raulyn said sharply. The Aeyries who had followed at the heels of the Walkers paused at the doorway. "It is unfortunate that the Walkers were in such a hurry," said Raulyn. "They did not let me go first to find the pathway home."

"Hellwinds," breathed one of the Aeyries carrying me. But no one dared ask Raulyn why id had not stopped the Walkers from rushing through the door. In stunned silence, we waited for the mage to go first, from darkness into emptiness. One by one, we followed, and came through on the other side, into Raulyn's room, where the air lamps still burned. But of the Walkers, or the weapons, there was no sign. Raulyn had very neatly taken care of the problem of the Walker rebellion.

I had never thought that I would be glad to see my prison room again, or the lumpy rope bed on which I had spent so many tortured nights. I slept like the dead for a day and a night, awakening at last when Pau came in to set a tray of food and a flagon of water on the floor near the door. My mouth felt dry as a summer wind, but when I begged idre to bring me a drink, id turned ids back, and shut the door once more behind idre.

My battered body had stiffened as I slept. Even moving in small increments, the intense pain made the drink of water seem scarcely worth the effort. Healing from my injuries would rapidly weaken me into true illness if I did not take nourishment. Weeping with pain and self-pity, I forced myself to get out of the bed and move the tray within reach.

The one Walker who had not traveled through the Void to Triad, the female with whom Bet had shared cooking duties, remained in the household. Though it scarcely seemed possible, her cooking had deteriorated. I could not bring myself to eat half of the food on the plate. She certainly would not have remained here willingly, with all the other Walkers mysteriously gone, and demonstrated her unwillingness through her cooking. Bet had rebelled against her captivity by cooking defiantly well, but that was Bet.

At the thought of Bet's rational absurdities, grief blew through my body, sometimes a gale and sometimes a breeze, but never still. I wept, and wept again, until at last, utterly wrung out, I fell asleep.

I tottered down the hall after Pau, toward Raulyn's rooms, too weary and weak for apprehension. When Pau told me that Raulyn wished to see me, I had shrugged indifferently, and followed.

As the days of our long effort to perfect the moonbane weapon crawled past, Raulyn had seemed increasingly weary and aged to me, as if every moment of our effort were blood drained out of ids body. After losing all the weapons and more than half of ids followers in the abortive attack, I expected idre to be weakened to the point of desperation.

But the sight of Raulyn shocked me awake. Id strode vigorously back and forth before what I would have taken for a particularly clever painting, had it not been moving. Once again, Raulyn had a scrying wall.

At the sound of our entry, Raulyn turned to me, moving with a Quai-du master's liquid grace, and said mildly, "Ah, Laril, there you are." But I recoiled from something in ids eyes, something very like madness. "I am glad to see that you are recovering from the unfortunate overenthusiasm of our Walker *l'frers.*"

I stood as steadily as I could, given my weakness, and held my tongue.

"I know," id continued, in the same light tone of voice, "that you believe my desire to destroy the Triad has been frustrated. It must come as a surprise to you to hear that our little excursion to Northern Derksai was a very productive one, very productive indeed."

It did come as a surprise, but I did not let it show on my face.

"I do have one or two questions on which I need enlightenment. I believe you know the answers. First, how did Bet find out how to sabotage the weapons?"

For the barest fraction of a second, I considered lying. But I feared that glint of madness in Raulyn's eye, and I replied, my voice shaking slightly with weakness, "She got into my room one night, and I told her everything about the moonbane weapon."

"Moonbane? Is that what you have been calling it? What a romantic you are." Raulyn quirked a corner of ids mouth with amusement. "And how did she get in?"

I told Raulyn everything. I had no skin to save but

my own, and all my instincts told me that my only chance of survival lay in telling the truth.

Raulyn perched on a stool as I talked, and sipped from a steaming cup that rested on a table nearby. "Well," id said when I was finished telling about how Bet had diverted suspicion by seducing me. "How very resourceful. I would never have expected it of her, a Walker no less, with so many inhibitions." Id pondered for some moments, as my stance grew increasingly unsteady, and a tide of queasy dizziness coursed through my blood.

"Now we know beyond doubt that the weapons functioned when we packed them into the crate. Pau here had the task of keeping guard on the crate at night, and id swears that nobody came or left the room where the crate was kept. How did Bet do it?"

I replied honestly, "I have no idea. I told her I wanted to know nothing of her plans, and she did not tell me. Whatever she did, we will never know."

"I see. And how she escaped from her bindings, you cannot explain that either, I suppose."

I could not risk hesitating, but this was the one thing I could not tell Raulyn. If some outside force had been helping us, perhaps it could help me again, if Raulyn were not given the opportunity to hinder it. If I myself had some small ability to work magic, I would not be allowed to use it if I alerted Raulyn to its existence. "Maybe her ropes were not properly tied," I suggested. "Or the Walker who was with her helped her somehow."

"It was not the Walker," Raulyn said. "And her ropes were tied as well as yours."

"Then I don't know." Raulyn was looking at me too intensely for comfort. I wracked my brain for some other explanation for what had happened. "I don't suppose it is possible Bet has some sorcerous pow-

ers?'' I said, and then could have cut my own throat
as I realized that it was the worst thing I could have
said.

Raulyn burst into laughter, laughter with that terri-
fying, raw hysterical edge to it. ''Bet? Our Bet?'' But
then, as I feared would happen, id sobered. ''But
maybe someone else,'' id said.

Pau took me back to my room, where I ravenously
ate the rest of the food that the day before had been
inedible. Then I collapsed onto my bed again, and
stared into the shadows in dull despair.

Chapter 14

In the dead of night, a faint crash startled me wide awake. I rubbed impatiently at my eyelashes, which were crusty and itchy with tears, and sat up reluctantly. Someone yelped in the distance, or was it crazed laughter? I peered into the impenetrable darkness, my heart thundering.

The nights had taken on a winter chill, and no amount of rearranging my blanket could make my bed warmer. For two nights now I had slept only fretfully, miserable with cold. Every day, Pau brought me a little less food, and so my body had a little less with which to keep warm. I thought that I didn't know why Pau despised me, until I remembered the night I evaded idre by jumping into the storm, and realized that my escape must have made idre a laughingstock among the Walkers.

The faint sounds seemed to be getting closer. I heard another dull thud, a cry of pain, and the crash of a nearby piece of furniture being knocked over. I got reluctantly out of bed into the chill, and felt my way along the coarse wooden wall to the locked door. After rattling the knob dispiritedly, I pressed my ear against the crack.

Glass blades clashed together, ringing sweetly in the

hallway. A body crashed up against the wooden wall, thundering a hollow echo into my ear. I heard heavy, hoarse breathing. "I submit!" an Aeyrie cried in H'ldat. To my surprise, the nearby sounds of combat fell silent, though the fainter sounds coming to my ear suggested that elsewhere, other fights continued. The last thing I would have expected of the Aeyries associated with Raulyn was for them to consider themselves bound by the Quaid-du rules of honor.

What dispute could have turned them against each other so fiercely? And why did Raulyn do nothing to stop them?

Whatever had happened, I did not want to call attention to my presence, lest the violence spill over onto me, as it had done before. I backed away from the door, barking my foot sharply on the corner of the bed. But a person in the hallway tried the door of my room, and called sharply, "Ishta Laril?"

I did not recognize the voice. None of Raulyn's people had ever called me by my full name; I doubted they even knew what it was. I said weakly, "What's going on?"

"This is Malal Tefan Eia. I'm going to get some help and break down the door."

"Eia Stormdancer?" I repeated stupidly. If a legendary hero from my people's past had spoken at my door, I would not have been more startled. Malal Tefan Eia, a taiseoch-dre of t'Fon, had retained possession of ids black blade longer than any Quai-du-dre in the recorded history of the Quai-du contests. Id might well have been the best Quai-du fighter that ever lived. But ids fame as a fighter was overshadowed by ids fame as an intellectual and political activist.

I collected my wits and called, "There is a spell on the door. Pau has the key. Id is a Black Quai-du master—"

''I know Pau,'' the voice beyond my door said grimly. ''I will return soon.''

As I made my way back to the bed, my fur prickled along my spine. I paused, a tremor of anxiety shivering through my wings. Without knowing why, I backed up against the wall, groping at the place on my thigh where my fighting blade had always hung. It, at least, had given me the illusion of power.

Something was happening in the center of the room, a dark shivering of the shadow, an eerie stretching and tearing of the air itself. My chilly prison suddenly seemed unbreathably hot, the air as thick as pudding. I could almost hear the tearing sound of the barriers of space and time rending open.

Raulyn stepped through the opening, and breathed into ids cupped hands to make a light. The pale light spilled between ids fingers to shine on me huddled in my corner like a thief.

''There you are.''

I felt sick and tired of being Raulyn's puppet, amusing idre with my ineffectual resistance and equally ineffectual misery. My hatred shivered through my bones like poison. ''Get out of here.''

Raulyn's mouth quirked with amusement. ''You should be flattered, little child. Out of all my followers, you are the only one I consider worth bringing with me. For your sweetness, my dear, and for your entertaining temper.''

''I am not your follower! And I am not coming with you. You will not do to me what you did to Bet!''

Raulyn's head jerked up with surprise. ''What lies has she told you?''

''I will not go into the Void with you. I would rather die.''

'That is exactly what will happen if you remain here, you fool! Do you think these people are your friends?''

In a rage of impatience, Raulyn started toward me. I pressed myself implacably into the corner, as if by sheer determination I could become one with the stones themselves. As soon as id was close enough, I aimed a weak kick at ids groin. But my many injuries and the slow starvation to which Pau had subjected me had bled away my strength. Raulyn caught my ankle in one hand, and with the other batted aside my frantically windmilling fists to grab hold of my mane. I slapped one punch firmly onto ids jaw, and heard my own fingerbone crack. But Raulyn did not even seem to feel my blows.

Id jerked my mane sharply, and, while I was still gasping with pain, let go of my ankle and slapped me in the face hard enough to make my ears ring. Id began dragging me by the hair, toward the center of the room. Though my eyes streamed with tears of pain, I forced myself to hang limp, a deadweight. Id had contemptuously not even bothered to draw ids weapon. Had I truly always been so easy to force into submission?

Or had Raulyn merely made ids assumptions, as id had with Bet, based not so much on fact as on ids own expectations?

I drew my feet under me, and abruptly threw myself against Raulyn, knocking idre off balance. With my left hand I snatched the knife out of Raulyn's sheath and struck at ids arm: an awkward, desperate blow that would never have made contact had Raulyn not been so sure of idreself.

The mage gave an angry shout and let go of my hair. I danced backward, guarding myself with the blade, but not attacking. All I wanted to win for myself was a little time.

Raulyn's light had gone out in the struggle. Now id lit another, and regarded me by its pale illumination.

Never had I seen ids hard eyes so frigid. Blood dripped from a shallow gash in ids arm.

"I will kill you if I have to," I said.

"No doubt," Raulyn replied, but ids voice contained only mockery. "Well, so the little taiseoch-dre has some fight in idre after all.

Then id laughed, and with a cry of pain I dropped the burning hot blade. Raulyn lunged forward to snatch it up, as I pushed past idre. I could think of only one thing to do. I ran headlong into the center of the room. I took one last breath of the stale air of my prison room, and then I leapt into the Void. Raulyn's surprised shout was extinguished behind me, swallowed up into the great, cold silence.

An image flashed across my vision. I could see into every room of the building simultaneously. Some of the rooms were cold and empty, with hunterworm webs shrouding the corners. In others, air lamps burned. Through the hallways, scattered Aeyries stalked, almost every one of them a stranger to me. I saw a few of Raulyn's Aeyries engaged in battle, but most of them had been imprisoned in a single room, sitting in glum silence as two of the strangers stood guard over the locked door.

But not all of the attacking Aeyries were strangers. The elegant Black Aeyrie, whom I had seen in Raulyn's scrying wall as id visited my parent, strode toward my own locked door, moving with the terrible beauty of a Quai-du master, dangling the key to the door from ids hand. And from the direction of Raulyn's rooms, the Silver I had seen in the same scrying ran full tilt in the direction of my room. As I looked, id raised ids head sharply to meet my gaze. "Trust," id said to me.

All this I saw in the flash of an instant. Then I sensed the mage on my trail, hunting me like a carnivore trailing its prey. When Raulyn implied that the Walkers who went into the Void without ids direction were lost forever, id must have been lying. Id could have tossed out a burning net to capture them, just as id had done to entrap me.

I saw it like a net of fire, spreading and stretching to entrap me within its web. The message of the Silver mage hung in my consciousness like a moon in the sky: Trust. Trust myself, trust the wind. I spread my burning wings, and leapt blindly onto a strong current of energy. Raulyn's net seemed to dissolve, but it could have been I who had dissolved, passing through ids net like dust.

It was not a wind which carried me, and it was not my wings with which I flew. A being of energy rather than flesh, I rode the mysterious currents which constitute the invisible Universe: the power which is the impossibly slow consciousness of the living mountains, and the dizzy whirling of the earth in space. The currents shifted and faltered under the wings of my will. When they moved, so did I. When they paused, I hung suspended in the timeless void.

I floated, thoughtless and timeless as an unhatched embryo, through a moment the length of an eternity. The secrets of the Universe surrounded me, but they were not secrets I had been born to understand. The ebbs and flows of energy carried me back and forth, like a driftwood on an ever-shifting tide. I floated, and trusted, and was at peace.

I realize I am no poet, to lay my words together like pieces of a mosaic. I cannot describe what it was like to be lost in the Void because the language itself is bound by the rules of time and space. Since one word must follow another, I must write as if there were a sequence of events, when in truth I had leapt into infinity, in which there is only the one moment. My escape happened simultaneously with the attempt to capture, even as the winds carried me on their secret currents, even as I hung motionless and at peace. Afterward, I wondered at myself, that I felt nothing, not even fear or impatience. But how could I have felt impatient, when all things happened simultaneously even as nothing happened at all; and how could I have felt fear when I had leapt beyond both past and future?

Time began again, when a force different from the energies on which I had been riding intruded into my awareness. It carried with it, like a h'loa p'rlea, the spores of the world I had left behind: a scent of air, a sound, and a fragment of emotion.

I remembered with a kind of a shock that I was a living being, that a heart beat in my chest, that I wanted to live, that a great deal of unfinished business awaited my attention. Like a baited waterwyth, I followed the direction offered to me, still trusting, until I found myself suddenly spilling out of thin air into a wailing rainstorm.

I landed flat on my face on an expanse of slippery glass. In moments the freezing rain soaked my fur. Each drop stung my skin with flecks of ice. Water ran into my eyes. A wicked wind snatched the last of my body heat away, and, abruptly, I began to shudder with cold. The wind howled in my ears, a hellwind, a flyer's nightmare.

My body felt strange and foreign to me, as if I no longer quite fit inside my own skin any longer. My brain, as well, felt much too small. I could not properly remember what had just happened to me, as if it had only been a dream.

My teeth chattered. I took a deep breath of the freezing air. My throat ached with the cold. In a sudden panic, I dragged myself to my knees. I had not survived so much only to die of hypothermia!

Rain spattered into my eyes. I could see nothing in the stormy darkness, but a second, deep sniff of the frigid, wet air told me that I had landed somewhere in the Glass Mountains. I stood up stiffly, my head throbbing with a fierce pain that threatened to split it in two. My sense of balance had gone awry, and I wobbled unsteadily as the wind shoved roughly at my wings.

I might be only a step away from a cliff's edge. I spread my wings, shuddering as the freezing rain hammered at the sensitive membranes. The winds recoiled from ridges, wrestled through narrow channels, and went screaming away into the night. Their forces spoke to my senses like the familiar voice of a friend. I would never forget these winds; the memory of them was graven into my brain like an etching in stone.

I had been deposited by the Void at the shelter near t'Cwa where my journey had first been blown so far off course.

Laughing with amazement, I glanced off to my right, half expecting to see a stubborn onfrit clinging to the bare glass, refusing to go into the shelter because it smelled like Walkers. Had the seasons run backward in time as I floated in the Void? But no, this freezing, driving rain tasted of winter, not of spring. Raulyn had tortured Alis'te to death. Bet had been killed when she exploded the half barrel of powder. For some reason, I had survived.

I made my way to the shelter, lit a fire in the stove and dried myself off, ate some food, and lay down on one of the pallets. I remember nothing else.

By autumn, even the homeless wanderers have settled in an Ula for the winter. I spotted only one traveler, winging north or south far over my head. I do not know what I would have said to idre, had id stopped to rest at the shelter.

I luxuriated in my freedom. I breathed the sweet, chilly air of autumn, and watched a nearby waterfall cascade into the canyon below. I got out of bed in the darkness, so I could stand on the frost-encrusted ledge and watch the sun rise. I slept whenever I chose, and ate as much as I wanted. I washed my filthy fur with water heated on the stove. Never before in my life had I felt so content.

On the third day I discovered a broadsheet published on the t'Fon press, which had been left in the woodbox by some previous traveler. I devoured the news almost as hungrily as I devoured the food supplies. In one of the articles, I read about myself. I had been kidnapped by Aeyrie separatists. They had demanded in exchange for my release that Ishta abandon ids plan to admit Walkers into the University. Ishta, the article continued, while very concerned for my safety, had no intention of complying with the kidnappers' demands.

Astounded, I got up from my reading to pace around the small shelter. I had opened the shutters to let in the rain-washed air. I paused at a window, looking over the red mountains of home.

The broadsheet had been published in the summer, when I still lived happily in Raulyn's tower, too love-besotted to realize that id held me prisoner. That Raulyn had been using me from the very beginning, long before id even mentioned to me Mairli's cursed alchemical powder, did not surprise me. But I wondered once again just exactly how long Raulyn had been manipulating my life.

In order for the ambush in this very shelter to have been arranged by Raulyn, ids followers would have had to know two or three days in advance that I would be sheltering there that night. How could they have known, had my exile itself not been orchestrated by Raulyn?

How long had id been twitching at the threads of my life? Was Wand's appearance at t'Cwa an accident? My friendship with idre had embarked simultaneously with the shameful binge of purposeless rebellion which had culminated in the duel in the Well. Had Wand been dancing on Raulyn's strings even longer than I had?

I looked northward. The winds had made their seasonal shift, and the same h'lana I had ridden south two seasons ago could take me north, to reach home in less than a day. Home, to set the Council of Mages on Raulyn's trail, to enter the University as I had always been expected to do, to oversee Wand's third exile, to glue back together the broken pieces of my life.

I felt a rush of relief. How easy it would be!

I shut the window abruptly, and walked back to the stool. The coals in the stove gave forth a muted warmth. I rested my feet on the warm hearthstones. Two days I had been resting here, as the sun crossed the sky by day, and moons crossed it by night. I had remembered again the passions of my body and the anguish of my heart, and I had begun to forget the ethereal, incomprehensible, beautiful world of the Void.

I could return home to t'Cwa, yes. But I could not turn back the passing seasons: I could not reclaim my lost Wing Year, or my innocent belief that good will ensured a good outcome. I could not become the person I once had been.

It was too easy to believe that something so simple as the truth could mend my shattered relationships and regain the lost trust of my friends, kin, and community. It was too simple to think that the Council of

Mages could stop the renegade Raulyn. And to think that I could just take up the thread of my life and start weaving again, forgetting all that had happened, was simply naive.

This business with Raulyn remained unfinished. And only I could finish it.

Chapter 15

Winter breathed through the autumn night, setting the dry leaves to shivering. Among crisp, sharp-edged stars, the moons roved like hunters. Below, the Walker farms flowed past me, each one silent in sleep, the doors closed and the windows shuttered against the cold.

I had become tireless as the wandering moons. There was much I had learned about the winds. I had slept on the barren, wind-swept ridges of the mountains, as the river below and the h'lana above flowed endlessly onward, like the currents of the Void or the pattern of my own life, purposeful only at the point where I could no longer comprehend purpose, powerful only as the dripping of a drop of water from a leaf or the opening of a flower is powerful.

I also flowed onward, sometimes on the back of a friendly wind, sometimes on the strength of my own flight muscles, flowing northward against the prevailing winds until I saw the towers of t'Han, and then eastward toward the sea. For three days now, I had slept in Walker lands, dozing in the shelter towers as the farmers worked in their fields below. They made their final preparations for winter, just as the Aeyries would be doing in their Ulas.

But I flowed in my own current, oblivious to the seasons, flying in the darkness, when the winds flowed toward the sea, and sleeping in the light. I had entered into a new kind of Void, in which I followed the current of my purpose and yet remained somehow motionless, as if my life, so rife with trouble and bewilderment, had finally come to a despairing halt.

So I came at last to the sea, as a full moon rose out of its depths, dripping a haze of faintly glowing clouds, and sprinkling the waves with silver dust. The wind carried me out across its sighing waters. They swelled and sank beneath me, wrinkling like the brow of an aged sh'man, as if in consideration of an ancient, unresolved puzzle.

I could have followed the wind out to meet the dawn, and then let it carry me shoreward again like the tide. But I had reached the end of my journey, so I turned my back to the rising moon and stroked back to shore.

I circled the fields of Triad, and landed at last, my flight to earth shielded from unfriendly eyes by the mysterious trees. My body heat vaporized the freezing air. My footsteps crunched through the frost-crisp grass, as I walked in a cloud of mist into the grove.

My wrists ached with memory of the rope that had bound them, and my skin crawled with the memory of Raulyn's people haunting the darkness. But tonight I was utterly alone in that tangled place.

I felt my way cautiously through the bracken, trying to keep my wings from getting tangled in the brush I could not see, and setting down my feet hesitantly onto the ground, lest I rustle a leaf or snap a twig. The tangled wood resisted my entry, and made me pay for my passage with many painful scratches and sharp, stinging pains where thorns had hooked my flesh.

At last I came out once more into the moonlight. The cut straw that blanketed the fields gleamed faintly, giving the farm the look of having been glazed with silver. Nothing moved across that frozen stillness, except I. I walked toward the house, beginning to shiver as the heat of flight dissipated. The moonlight and shadows were my only camouflage, but no one challenged me.

At the central, two-level building, a low wall surrounded a bedded down flower garden, but its gate hung ajar and unwatched. I slipped through, and then paused, irresolute for the first time since I left the shelter near t'Cwa. The first-floor windows were tightly shuttered against the cold. The doors also would be barred against intrusion. The second floor balconies were far out of reach. I should have approached from the air, I realized, and tried to enter from one of the balconies, or the flight tower rearing toward the stars at my right. Or I should have forgotten my guilt and waited for daylight, like any other visitor.

An *astil* wind streamer snapped overhead, and a whirligig gave a clattering whirr as the wind picked up. Even in the sheltered garden, the freezing wind burned against my sweat-damp skin. The cold had already numbed my feet. Shuddering, I turned around, to go out of the garden and scout around the house. Frost crunched underfoot.

A silent, bulky shadow blocked the garden gate. I saw the faint, green glow of eyes in the moonlight as the monstrous creature silently studied me. Perhaps it even had been shadowing me since I first came through the windbreak. I froze where I stood, remembering how swiftly these creatures could move if they chose to.

It flowed toward me. I smelled its furry, earthy scent. It paused again, rearing up its forequarters to examine me, face to face. In size it was worth a good three of me. I shivered in the cruel wind, and waited.

"I have smelled your scent before," it said in H'ldat. Its voice sounded strange, burred and distorted, as if it spoke a language for which its body were not designed, but I understood its words clearly enough. "You were here the night of the great light."

A tremor ran through my body which was not cold. I answered with difficulty. "Yes. I was here."

"Aarrrgh," it growled softly, almost sighing. "With one bite I can kill you."

I said nothing. I did not know how I could explain my convoluted h'lana to this alien, not even with the encouragement of its oddly gentle threat.

"You do not have weapons?" it said.

I held out my empty hands.

"Why have you returned?"

"I—" I shook my head helplessly. "I had to come here, to find out—to finish. I don't really know why."

The creature considered, and considered again, standing rock-steady as I trembled like a leaf before it. At last it said thoughtfully, "I remember the story I smelled in your trail. I smelled no danger in you." It padded to my side, snuffled thoughtfully at my fur, and then took my unresisting arm in the firm, clawed grip of its paw. "Come."

It led me up to the front door of the building, which swung open at a flick of the latch, and through into a dark, vaulted entry, through which a stairway swooped toward the second level like a rising cloud. "Are you cold?" asked the creature politely. "A fire burns in the kitchen."

Its bulk so filled the narrow hallway into which I was led that we could no longer walk side by side. I pulled ahead, but its gentle grip never let go of my arm. "Three steps down," it warned, but nonetheless I nearly fell down the steps and into the warm, dark kitchen.

Even in the dark, the room reminded me of an Ula kitchen, with its many stoves and the long, knife-scarred work table in the center of the floor. I saw the distinctive mess of an onfrit nest in the rafters. On the floor beside the one stove in which a fire burned, lay another creature like the one who had escorted me in. Our appearance did not surprise it, for it examined us silently from glowing eyes and did not rise from the floor.

My escort spoke to it softly in a language that growled and rumbled in the throat, yet had a sweet, almost musical echo. I looked closely at the creature in the faint light of the fire, and saw the glimmer of a flute hanging by a cord around its neck. "Sit down here," it said.

I found a stool, drew it near the fire, and sat. My escort scraped out of the kitchen door, but I remained sitting, for the other creature now regarded me out of unblinking eyes. Something stirred among my watcher's curled legs, giving a faint, yammering cry. She bent forward to lick it, without ever taking her eyes from me.

I remembered then where I had seen creatures like this before. It had been in Raulyn's scrying wall, on my first day in the tower.

"Is that your baby?" I asked.

After a moment the creature replied, "Yes."

"Could I see?"

"Baby ill."

"I'm sorry."

She said nothing, but the powerful muscles bulging under her shaggy fur seemed to relax. I huddled stiffly on my stool, reaching out my hands to the stove, but despite the warmth I could not stop shivering. The house felt heavy and silent around me. Once I thought I heard the faint cry of an Aeyrie infant, but it was quickly silenced. Then I heard a creak in the hall, and once again the six-legged creature scraped through the door, rumbling a greeting to the one on the floor.

"Someday we'll widen this doorway," said the Aeyrie following at its heels.

The creature gave a growl of laughter. "Someday. Someday you will widen the house, yes?"

The faint glow of the small air lamp in the Aeyrie's hand brightened the kitchen. Id caught sight of me, and paused in the doorway, utterly still, seeming for a moment not even to breathe. This was the third time I had seen this Silver mage, but the first time in person. Id's charcoal-tipped mane flared in an uncombed tangle about id's fine-boned face, in which perhaps forty-five years worth of laughter lines were drawn. A blade was strapped to id's thigh, but I saw no master-mark branded in id's wrist.

"Laril," id said.

I stood up from the stool, still shivering. "Sh'man. How do you know me?" My legs trembled violently under my weight, and I wondered suddenly how long it had been since my last decent meal. I could not remember.

"I visited t'Cwa often when you were just a hatchling, but of course you would not remember. We have met again rather recently, in the way of mages."

My knees gave way, and I saw down suddenly. "But—how could I be a mage? None of my kin are mages."

"That is not exactly true." The mage turned to the creature who had fetched idre, and spoke softly in its own growly, musical language. The monster padded out of the kitchen, as the Aeyrie slid a couple of pieces of wood into the stove, and fussed over the latch of the firebox. I gained the distinct impression that id was buying time. My appearance at ids doorstep had taken idre by surprise. And if this was whom I suspected it to be, then to be surprised was a rare occurrence in ids life.

At last id turned to me with a wry smile. "From my point of view, not a quarter of the night has passed since I gave you passage out of the Void. I know I placed you near t'Cwa, so you are the last person I expected to see in the Triad kitchen this same night."

"It has been eight days," I said uncertainly. My journey had flowed so seamlessly from one day to the next that I had not been able to keep track.

"Eight days?" The mage sighed. "Well, it could have been worse. My understanding of the Void has always been shaky. Are you hungry? I am not much of a cook, but we have bread and cheese—"

Without waiting for me to reply, the mage hurried to a cupboard. I put my hand to my face, startled by the trickle of a tear. What was wrong with me? "Why are you afraid of me?" I said to the mage's back. "I don't even know who you are."

Id paused, and set the plate down, and came over to me where I sat in such bewilderment. "Please forgive me. I am Delan."

I sighed, feeling a heaviness of dread in my belly like a great stone. "When I realized that the Black was Eia Stormdancer—of course you had to be Delan the artist. Raulyn hates both of you, you know."

"Many people do."

"What have you foreseen, to make someone like you be afraid of me?"

Delan began to smile, but then sadness overwhelmed ids face. "If only I could know the future with such certainty!" Id leaned wearily against the work table. "The great events of history seem to have such inconsequential beginnings. If I could know, and prevent the small events from happening . . . Well, I suppose it is just as well that I cannot. Who am I to be deciding such things?''

Id tugged ids fingers nervously through ids tangled mane, looking more like a harassed housekeeper than like a famous artist and seer. "I am not afraid of you, Laril, though I am curious what it is you fear I have foreseen. I am afraid of what I must tell you. I suppose I had hoped, by opening a Door for you so close to t'Cwa, that you would go home and hear it from the one who should have told you long ago.''

"I am an exile, how can I go home?'' I said vaguely. "I feared you had foreseen the end of the Aeyrie people.'' I spoke so confusedly because the color and form of this beautiful Aeyrie had suddenly riveted me, not out of lust or even aesthetic appreciation, but out of a secret knowledge that lay, long denied, in my heart. The fine-boned, triangular face, the stark white fur tipped with silver, the cloud-white wings marked with long-healed knife scars, the charcoal mane and the troubled charcoal eyes, all this seemed terribly familiar to me.

I remembered the odd moments of puzzlement that had punctuated my life: when I realized that my l'per should have been too old to have a child as young as I, when I wondered why my wings were white rather than gray like those of both my parents, and even more recently, when I worked magic even though I knew I had no relatives who were mages. All these small pieces fit together suddenly like a puzzle, and I gave a shocked cry. "No!''

The fire crackled busily in the stove. The creature on the floor, who had raised her head sharply at my outcry, laid it down again with a heavy sigh. I felt my pain, and then I felt the rush of relief course through my body. As if Delan also felt it, id finally spoke, saying softly, "Children always know when they are being lied to. You have just understood much that has puzzled you.''

"But a hearth adoption is not shameful.'' The steadiness of my own voice surprised me. "Why would Ishta—and the entire community of t'Cwa—break Aeyrie law by denying me knowledge of my blood parentage?'' I looked up then, directly into Delan's gaze. "And why didn't you do anything about it?''

Delan replied quietly, "I do not intend to try to justify either myself or Ishta, when I say that it is not always easy to know what is the right thing to do. I have been hoping, like everyone else, that id would voluntarily tell you the truth. I did not want to bring litigation against the taiseoch of t'Cwa. There are political reasons—''

With a gesture, Delan seemed to recall the fragile, tentative unity of our people, without which we could not stand against the overwhelming power of the Walkers, a unity which had somehow come to be invested not just in the community of Triad, but in the person of Delan's lover and partner, Eia.

"—And there are personal reasons,'' id continued. "When I had lived my entire life like a sideshow freak among the Walkers, Ishta claimed me, and gave me a home and a heritage. Ishta is my blood parent and my legal parent as well.'' Delan paused, and added as an afterthought, "My other parent, your grandparent by blood, was a wandering mage, Mairli the inventor. I never knew idre.''

The room spun dizzily around me. I said weakly, "I believe I will have that bread and cheese.''

The food steadied me. When I had emptied my plate, Delan brought me some fruit and a wedge of sweet spice cake. Id perched on a nearby stool and talked as I ate.

"Ishta could not seem to lay a fertile egg. And when at last it did happen, the egg was stolen from its hearth by the Walker sorcerer Teksan. I hatched into a remote, primitive Walker community, where Teksan had slipped my egg into their communal nest. Twenty years passed before Ishta's missing heir at last was found, but I wanted nothing to do with being a chieftain of an Ula. I had been raised as a Walker. I did not even know the language! So instead I gave Ishta back ids lost child.

"At first, id observed all the customs of a hearth adoption. But as my fame as an artist grew, Ishta began to be afraid, I think, that somehow id would lose you to me. Now that I am a parent myself, and one of my children has become a Merfriend, I understand a little better how easy it is to hold onto your children too tightly . . . Of course, no good can ever come of it."

I said grimly, "Well, I certainly have managed to make Ishta's life a misery." But for the first time in my life, I said these words without either glee or guilt.

"When id asked my help this summer in finding you, I think id had realized at last how the secrets between the two of you had damaged both of you. I think id intends to tell you, should you return."

I licked my fingers, and felt suddenly sleepy. More than half the night had passed. I heard faintly the haunting notes of a nishi flute singing sweetly to the moon. "These creatures, what are they?"

"Orchths, a fourth sentient race. They are singers and herdfolk, like the Mers, but not telepathic. Have you eaten enough, or are you still hungry? We have plenty of food here."

I patted my full stomach politely.

"You will guest with us, of course."

I uttered a harsh bark of laughter. "Where else

would I go?'' I took in my breath, and added wearily,
"This business with Raulyn . . .''

"Yes. We need to talk about Raulyn. But not in the
middle of the night, when we are both so tired. Tomorrow will be soon enough.''

I nodded passively. Tomorrow would be soon
enough to find out about Bet as well. I had endured
enough for one night; I would give myself one more
night in which to believe she might somehow have
survived.

Delan took the plate out of my hands. "Let's go find
you an empty bed, then. I think one of the upstairs
rooms is unoccupied.''

In a stumbling daze of exhaustion, I followed idre
across the kitchen. Delan mounted the stairs to the
hallway, but stopped short in the doorway, holding up
the air lamp. "Surely you should not be out of bed at
this hour,'' id said in the Walker tongue, speaking to
someone I could not see. "What is wrong? Can I
help?''

The person in the hallway replied in H'ldat, in a
voice stretched thin by fear and hope. "Is Laril here?''

Delan turned to me in puzzlement, saying to no one
in particular, "She does talk. And in H'ldat, no less.
How do you suppose she knew you . . .''

But I was pushing rudely past idre, saying wildly,
"Great Winds! Bet!''

"Careful,'' Delan said belatedly, and I drew myself
short. Bet leaned wearily against a wall, cradling her
bandaged arm against her chest. Her eyes burned fever-
bright in the air lamp's light. I reached out and eased
her gently from the support of the wall into the support
of my arms. She leaned heavily against me, puffing
hot breath into my fur. I wrapped my wings around
her, and held her. Her one good arm gripped me
tightly around the waist.

"Bet," I said. She took a shuddering breath, and snuffled like a child. "Stop it," I said unsteadily. "You never cry. It scares me."

She shuddered again, but this time with choked laughter.

"What happened to her?" I asked Delan.

The mage leaned in the kitchen doorway, regarding the two of us thoughtfully. "I gather you know her? One of the Orchths found her shortly after the explosion. As far as we could determine, Bet was running, and fell into a stream bed in the darkness. Broke her arm, took a nasty knock on the head, but not nasty enough to explain her silence since then."

"She is the one who set off the explosion to warn you of the attack. I don't know how she survived. Bet, I wish you could tell me."

"I wish it, too," she said fervently.

Delan leaned more firmly against the doorsill, mouth pursed thoughtfully, examining the two of us through narrowed eyes. I felt Bet become very still in my arms. Still, Delan studied us, with the unnerving intensity of an artist, until I too grew uncomfortable under that stare, and protectively tightened by arms around Bet.

"So," Delan finally said. "A convoluted puzzle indeed. Just to think of untangling it makes me yawn. Let's go to bed."

"You don't have to make another bed. I'll sleep with Bet."

"Of course," Delan said blandly. "Of course."

Chapter 16

"In hearth adoption, the blood parent lays the egg on the adopting parents' hearth. The egg incubates and is hatched and nursed by the adopting parents. But the blood parent continues to have some contact with the child. This is what should have happened with me."

"So your parent is your grandparent, and this Delan is your parent," Bet said. She sat by the open window, as the chilly late-morning air flowed in from the sea, filling the room with its salty sweetness. The window curtains puffed and twisted in the strong breeze, framing a brilliant blue sky filled with puffy white clouds.

I had awakened from my exhausted sleep to find her staring bleakly out to sea, wrapped in a blanket for warmth, her broken arm supported against the arm of the chair. Deprived by her injury of the drug of labor, she could relieve her sadness no longer. It lay across her features like a cloud of smoke over a bright summer day.

I said, "Ishta is legal parent to both myself and Delan, but id is my grandparent by blood. Delan is my parent by blood, but I have no right to call idre l'per because of the adoption. Any relationship we have with each other is a matter of choice, rather than duty. Do you understand?"

Bet murmured, "You Aeyries just love complications, don't you?"

"Like I love you."

She slowly turned her face from the window. Her eyes flashed with sunlight, but then became black as a starless night as she looked at me across the room. Her head tipped at a sardonic angle. "You Aeyries are frivolous lovers."

"What?"

"Did you know that Walkers mate for life?"

"So do we, sometimes, in couples or in triads."

"What I mean, is—" She struggled for words, but could not utter them. Her hand clenched, and came down with a silent thump onto the arm of the chair in which she reclined. She turned her face away from me, rigid with frustration.

"We don't have—" I used the Walker word, "—families. The community is our family."

"So how can you depend on each other?"

"Sometimes we can't," I said. "Look what happened to me."

She said nothing more. I wanted to continue, to try to explain why the frequent coupling and uncoupling of my people was an expression of our strong community rather than of frivolity, but I held my tongue, certain that to continue the discussion would only continue Bet's frustration. What was I doing, falling in love with a person of another sex and another species, with whom I could scarcely even communicate?

I got abruptly out of bed, and searched through the dresser drawers until I found an old fur brush. My winter fur had begun to grow in, but I never had the chance to brush out my shedding summer coat. My matted, tangled pelt looked and felt like a worn out doormat. Bet watched disinterestedly as I fought the bristles through the tangles. Fallen clots of fur covered my feet when she stood up abruptly from her lonely chair, and took the brush from my hand. "Let me do your back. You look like a bug-eaten rug."

"You say the nicest things."

"I'm sorry," she said after a moment, her voice muted. But the brush stroking firmly down my back felt so good that I would have forgiven her anything. "Why don't you lie down," she said.

Much later, we lay quiet again in each other's arms. The morning had warmed into afternoon as we made a tangled mess of the bedsheets and knocked most of the blankets to the floor. Bet had sobbed and wept as I investigated her uncharted secrets. Her joy seemed so tangled up with her sadness that she could scarcely seem to feel one without the other.

As for me, well, she had surprised me again. We Aeyries like to believe that no Walker can compare to us in any skill or art: it was Bet who taught me again and again how wrong we can be about each other.

I found the fur brush tangled with one of the blankets that had ended up on the floor, and began brushing her hair with it, laughing when she sighed with pleasure. Her head rested in the hollow of my shoulder. I said lightly, "You do know how good this feels. How clever of you, to make seducing me look like a mere accident."

"It's all my fault, is it?" she said, the bitterness that had been evicted for a while creeping back into her voice.

"Bet—" Her sudden rage had started tears into my eyes. "I am in bed with you because I want to be."

Her shoulders relaxed in the curve of my arm. "Sorry."

I used my fingers to ease the tangles out of her soft hair, and then brushed it until it shone. My heart filled with a hot, hurting love. Her head rested so heavily

on my shoulder that I might have thought she had fallen
asleep, except that I could see her eyes open. Did she
see the same vision I did? Even if both of us remained
here at Triad, how could love thrive in the midst of
this silence?

"Triad is famous for its healers," I said. She blinked
her eyes back into focus and looked up at me. "Maybe
they can help you."

She said wearily, "So soon? Don't do this to me,
Laril."

"What?"

"Try to fix me."

"I just— All right. I'm sorry."

I helped Bet dress, and we made our way outdoors,
into a bright, cool day filled with the sound and scent
of the sea. A crowd of Walker and Aeyrie children
played a bilingual game of hide-and-run among the
various structures, pieces of farm equipment, and trees
that scattered the yard. A Walker and an Aeyrie worked
together on a rooftop, their staccato hammering slipping in and out of rhythm. In the sun-dappled shade,
an Aeyrie Black reclined, half dozing, giving suck to
a black hatchling held in ids arms. At the sound of the
door closing behind us, id opened one eye and gave a
languid wave of the hand.

"It's Eia," I said in a hushed voice.

"The Ambassador?" As wide-eyed as I, Bet followed me to the shady lawn.

Eia got awkwardly to ids feet, the infant protesting
sleepily, and took our hands in turn. "Laril, Bet." Id
yawned, and then apologized charmingly. "I was up
half the night with the little parasite." When I held
out my arms wordlessly, id obligingly tucked the furry,
fat, sleepy hatchling into my arms.

Bet leaned over my shoulder, and touched a tentative hand to the fluffy fur. The infant yawned, tried an experimental suck or two at my own dry nipple, and fell abruptly asleep. I blinked my burning eyes and said unsteadily, "I never had a l'frer."

I looked up then, wondering if the infant's parent would take offense, but Eia smiled so sweetly my heart jumped in my throat. "Then it's about time," id said. "Sit down, sit down. The lunch bell will ring any moment, none too soon for me." Id dragged over a couple of chairs, but Bet and I sat down in the same one, banging our heads together as we huddled over the infant.

Bet stroked the astonishingly soft fur. I showed her the buds on the infant's back, which would sprout wings some eighteen years in the future. "It's a long time to have to wait," she said.

"It's worth waiting for," I said, just as my elders had used to say to me when I was a child.

"You can keep the little monster," Eia offered generously. I just laughed. After about six months of constant nursing, every Aeyrie parent starts making such offers. I handed the warm bundle of fur to Bet, and she settled back in the chair, looking as broody as an incubating onfrit.

Eia stretched sleek, muscular limbs, and fixed on the two of us a gaze at once friendly and piercingly intelligent. I would have expected a person with so much political power to have more self-importance, but I suppose it is difficult to be self-important while nursing a hatchling. Gray salted id's shining black mane. Ids famous black blade was strapped to ids thigh, secured in the sheath, and looped with astil cord. In the Ulas, to carry a blade anywhere except in the h'shal Quai-du is an act of discourtesy. Here, the people repairing the farm equipment carried weapons, and two Aeyries lounged atop the flight tower, shading their eyes from the sun with their hands as they studied the land below.

"Are you expecting an attack of some sort?" I asked.

"Well," Eia said, "we have learned to be prepared. The supremists and separatists are prone to violence. Did you sleep well?" Id looked at me, eyes dancing. Though Eia obviously knew that Bet and I had not been sleeping all morning, this was the one place in the entire world that I needed not be concerned about concealing the fact. "Delan is painting at the moment. Id told me you flew here in eight days from t'Cwa, against the wind."

"Six, I think."

"Six?" Eia shook ids head in disbelief. "Great winds, to be young again." Id turned to Bet. "Are you feeling all right?"

She nodded silently.

"I apologize on behalf of the healers for treating you like an invalid. We didn't understand what was wrong."

"Do you now?" she asked, half hostile.

After a moment, Eia said thoughtfully, "If you are Ysbet of Canilton."

Bet looked down at the infant sleeping in her arms, and did not speak. But she looked so weary and sad that I took her hand and gripped it tightly, my confused love for her flooding me for a moment with desire to help her. But then I remembered her pride, and let go.

"Did you ever get the letter?" Eia asked.

"You sent me a letter?" Bet said dully.

"I wrote to you that Aeyrie mages do not take apprentices like Walker sorcerers do, but that you could find the nurturing your gift needed at Triad, and you would be welcome here. You never received it?"

She shook her head, staring blindly down at the infant in her arms.

"I guess Raulyn found you first, then. We didn't know until recently that id was scrying our every move—that is probably how id found out about you. Our se'ans keep guard now so it cannot happen without our knowledge . . . though the Mers have left on migration by now. We will see if the Merfriends can maintain the guard."

A bell clanged noisily. The children rushed toward an open door, only to be diverted firmly toward a basin of water on the porch. The people sharpening and painting the farm equipment began packing their tools away. Across the field, the people in bright clothing who clustered around a draf-drawn wagon of straw straightened up stiffly and began to stack their hayforks. But, except for Bet's hand automatically petting the infant's soft fur, none of us moved.

The pieces of the puzzle fit themselves together slowly in my understanding. At last I said uncertainly to Bet, "Delan tells me I'm a mage, too. Isn't it funny, I even suggested to Raulyn that you might be a sorcerer—"

Bet looked at me, her mouth narrow. "Why do you suppose I hated you so much?"

"Because you thought Raulyn was teaching me what id failed to teach you? But I didn't know I was a mage. Raulyn didn't even know."

"The hell id didn't," she said softly.

Eia stood up gracefully, and took the infant from Bet. I helped her to her feet, and we walked together in silence toward the dining room door.

Halfway through the meal, Delan joined our table. "I thought you were supposed to paint the canvas," Eia commented, as Delan set down ids bowl of soup.

Delan looked in vague surprise at the splotches and blots of paint with which ids fur was scattered. "I guess I forgot to wear an apron. Hand me the l'shan, Laril, I'm leaking milk."

"Good," said Eia. "I'm sucked dry."

I handed my miniature l'frer across the table. "You look as if you never went to bed last night."

"Sometimes it takes me like that." Delan tucked the hatchling to ids chest, and ate a few spoonfuls of soup, left handed. Though the long hours of ids sleepless night were written in ids drawn, shadowed face, ids sharp, thoughtful eyes peered at me with tireless energy. "I worried about you, learning so much at once like this."

I shrugged my wings. My relief and my dismay seemed to have balanced themselves out. "Truth be told, my personal problems seem pretty trivial even to me. I want to know when we are going to start talking about Raulyn."

"We have talked daily about Raulyn," Eia said impatiently, "Until our throats were sore and our heads ached."

"And we will talk about idre some more," said Delan.

"Until our tongues fall out of our mouths and our ears turn to stone?"

"Until we have a solution."

"We have a solution. Some of us just refuse to accept it."

"Because some of us are not fools."

"A fool's problem requires a fool's answer, does it not?"

"Eia Stormdancer, continuing to underestimate your old rival will bring you to your grave." Delan turned calmly back to ids meal and finished the bowl of soup, pausing halfway through to switch the infant to the other breast. Eia seemed equally unperturbed by the brief argument. A l'shan of six or seven years old crawled into Eia's lap, a half-eaten slice of bread clutched in one hand. "This is Nasha," said Eia.

I saw the sighing ocean in the child's eyes, the ebbing and flowing of the tides and the ever changing dance of the moons. Such ageless peace in the face of a child unnerved me, and I could not speak.

"Nasha is Merfriend to a male named Dancing."

Nasha said, "The Mers want to meet you." But I could not tell whether it was to me or to Bet that id spoke.

"The Mers haven't begun their migration?" said Eia.

"No. They are waiting."

Delan said quietly, "We will visit them within the hour, then. Now tell me about your bookday."

As if Delan's typical parental question reminded Nasha how to be a child, id chattered happily about ids studies, and then squirmed out of Eia's lap to squeeze in a few more minutes of play before the teachers called idre back to school.

"Dancing and Nasha chose each other over a year ago," Delan explained. "He is just two years old, but the Mers mature far faster than Aeyries or Walkers."

"Nasha is so young," I said.

Delan sighed. "The younger the better, I guess. Not many adults adjust easily to the gestalt. But how to parent a child like our Nasha, a se'an within a community mind . . ."

"Or even how to teach idre, when what one member of the herd knows, they all know, and never forget," said Eia.

"Well, it is a challenge," Delan concluded.

The two sh'mans sat silently for some moments.

"Well," Eia said finally, "I do wonder what the Mers are waiting for."

Delan sat ids spoon heavily into the empty bowl, but did not answer.

Bet and I went with Delan to the Orchth house, while Eia found someone to watch over the hatchling and sought out a Walker named Stilvin. "Is this going to be a sort of conference?" I asked Delan as we crossed the yard to a building that looked like a kip barn.

"Yes," said Delan distractedly.

"Something is wrong, isn't it?"

"Yes. The Mers would not delay their migration lightly."

I looked around myself for Bet, who trudged along behind us, as stolid and steady as a draf. I took her hand tightly in mine, and she did not pull away. "We need to bring pen and paper," I said.

The Orchths shared their barn with a quantity of onfrits, who flew busily in and out of the upper story windows. We cracked a door open and slid through into the warm, gloomy building. The onfrits chattered in the rafters, but in the lower levels of the barn, the silence was broken only by an occasional rustle of straw, or the deep sighing breath of a dream. The great, heavy shapes of the Orchths lay huddled, three or four in a group, on beds of hay.

Delan eased the creaky door closed, and whispered, "Orgulanthgrnm."

The sleeping Orchths shifted and sighed, then settled again into sleep. Delan did not speak again, but leaned against the creaky wall, a pale, ghostly shadow in the gloom. The Orchth materialized out of the darkness, his eyes glowing faintly in the diffuse light that filtered down from overhead.

"We need to share words with the Mers down in the

Gap,'' said Delan. ''They have delayed their migration
and we need to know the reason. And Laril and Bet
need to say what they know about Raulyn.''

''Ah, Raulyn,'' rumbled Orgulanthgrnm. He bowed
his forebody, and Delan tied a black blindfold over his
eyes.

Outside once more, I was able to look at the Orchth
for the first time in full light. At first glance his bulk
and shaggy fur made him look like a draf. But his
flexible forebody, which he could hold erect like a
Walker or Aeyrie, was equipped with forelegs not
much different from my own arms. His forepaws, with
their thick pads and short fingers, could be used as
feet or hands. He looked like a draf that some absent-
minded mage had begun to turn into a Walker, but
never completed the project.

Delan took his forepaw in ids hand, and led him down
the path, to where Eia waited with a Walker male. We
waited in a silent, preoccupied group as Delan fetched
a pen and paper from the house, and then we started
across the field toward the north, two Walkers shading
their eyes from the brilliant sun, three Aeyries beginning to sweat in the unseasonable warmth of the afternoon, and the Orchth, walking steadily and surefootedly
despite the blindfold, finding his way, as far as I could
determine, by sense of smell. I found myself walking
beside him, drawn to something beyond his alienness:
his sturdy judgment, perhaps, and the incredible certainty with which he set down his feet.

''How long have you lived in Triad?'' I asked him.

''Five years now,'' he replied. ''My brother, called
Och, lived many long years in this land. When he returned home to the people, he told us of the land, and
of the friends who entered his heart here. When Delan
called for our help, it was for my brother's sake that

we crossed the water. Now we remain for our own sakes.''

Later, when I had read Delan's written account of Teksan's War, I would recognize this place. Here Delan had walked with Lian of Troyis, the Walker empath who with the Mer called Pilgrim was the first to ever truly cross the boundaries between the races. Delan had walked past these same wind-gnarled, twisted trees, to stand at the edge of this same incredible rift torn into the foundation of the earth, and marvel for the first time at the sight of the sea.

As we started down the steep, winding path, which in places consisted of nothing more than a boardwalk suspended over empty space, Stilvin turned to ask Bet a question. She set her jaw and walked fearlessly forward, as if to say, ''I have crossed the Void; what is a cliff to me?''

I guided the Orchth around the sharp turns, the boardwalk shivering under my feet. When I looked out over the ocean, I saw the Mers. They shot like silver arrows out of the water, spray trailing after their leaping bodies in ephemeral crescents of light. The rough sea foamed and writhed, but they slid back under its restless surface as softly as a song.

By the time we reached the edge of the water, they were waiting for us. Some Mers floated on the rising and falling sea just beyond the breakers, blowing puffs of misty air to glow briefly in the sunshine. Some came in to shore, and lay in the sun on a narrow beach of multicolored sand that glittered and glimmered like jewels.

Stilvin waded into the water to lie down beside one of the Mers. She grasped him by the wrist with one of her hands, and clasped him around the waist with a long, slender fin. The others rolled in the sand like children in a soft bed, until their thick, sleek, wet fur was covered with the glittering glass sand. Only one resting half in the water and half on shore lay quietly. Her fur was speckled with gray, and she peered at those standing on shore with filmed eyes. As the ocean washed over her body, I thought I saw the old scars of terrible wounds in her flesh.

Delan and Eia both waded into the water to squat beside her and lay their hands to her side. "Pilgrim," they said, "Will you not stay in the boat house this winter?"

The Merfolk speak only in the language of water-song, so Stilvin replied on behalf of the aging Mer. "For every Mer there is a last migration. Why defy the tides of time?"

"Because we are a defiant people." said Eia. "Out of the four first Triad-re, you are the last. And you carry Lian in your heart."

"Lian belongs to the sea, Stormdancer, and so do I. Why bid me stay, when my heart longs to go?"

A large wave crashed onto shore, sending the two Aeyries dancing back, holding each other for support against the tugging water, and washing over the Mers and the Walker. When the water slid away once more, the beach, roughened by the play of the Mers, had been smoothed, and the sand had been washed out of their fur. Like the Mers, the Walker unconcernedly puffed a wet breath of air out of his mouth, and then lifted a hand to brush the wet hair out of his eyes.

I found a comfortable stone to sit on. The Orchth had already settled himself among the rocks, his head resting on his crossed forepaws. I could not tell whether he was asleep or awake.

"Tell me why you have not already left on migration," said Delan. "The sea plants will soon die, and you will have nothing to eat. What are you waiting for?''

"Shall we dive to the deep safety of the ocean floor, and leave you alone to face the storm?''

"What storm is this?''

"We have heard idre, crying on the wind. Id speaks with the voice of hate, and carries the power of the hurricane within ids arms.''

"Raulyn?'' said Eia with a disbelieving laugh. "That petty warmonger?''

But the Walker said quietly as the sea washed his feet with sand, "Raulyn.''

Chapter 17

Eia settled idreself heavily onto the rocks, and hitched a battle-scarred wing over the point of a boulder. "I have known Raulyn my entire life," id said. "And though I hate and distrust idre, I have never respected idre even enough to be afraid of ids power. Id is a sneak-thief mage, a weak deceiver of weak, powerless, and disaffected people, an honorless fighter, egotistical, and maybe a little mad. What have we to fear from such an opponent?"

The five of us sat among the rocks, the offshore breakers crashing in our ears so that Eia had to shout to be heard. As the waves washed ashore, some of the Mers lying on the beach allowed themselves to be carried back into the deeps, even as others floated in on the incoming breakers, and hitched themselves up the sloping sand. Stilvin had begun to shiver with cold despite the warmth of the sun, but still he lay with his arms around the Mer. Soon she would be gone, swimming with her herd to the great southern beds of sea plants, far south of the ferocious storms of winter. Stilvin held her tightly, like a lover. Perhaps he was.

Eia continued, "Raulyn and I trained with the same Quai-du master at t'Fon. From the very beginning, we have been rivals. Over time, we became such enemies that our Quai-du master would not permit us to spar with each other, because our anger made a friendly match impossible. But every year in the Quai-du games, sooner or later we ended up fighting each other for a place in the ranking.

"At last, when I had been practicing Quai-du for five years, and Raulyn for seven, we both were admitted into contention for the black blade. I fought match after match, and after each battle won, I asked whether Raulyn had won ids battle as well. After three days of fighting, on the ground and in the air, only one of the five blades had yet to be won, and either Raulyn or I would be the winner of it."

Eia smiled slightly at the memory, but without amusement. "I was young. To lose the black blade to Raulyn seemed a failure so great I could not imagine how I could survive it. But it was Raulyn who decided to win at any cost, even the cost of ids honor. I won the draw, and because I had prevailed against Raulyn more often in the air than on the ground, I chose to fight in the air.

"It was a dirty, angry battle. What with fighting both Raulyn and the evil luck that the winds were giving me, I wearied and began to sacrifice points. But Raulyn fought the best battle of ids life, and the winds that so disserviced me convenienced idre so consistently that I could not help but wonder at it, I could predict that every single one of my attacks would be knocked awry by the wind, and every single one of Raulyn's would be assisted. Even in my preoccupation, I finally recognized the impossibility of such consistency.

"I could not stop the battle to complain that Raulyn was assisted by magic. I did not know until much later that Raulyn idreself was the mage. I could only hope that the judges would realize what was happening and call a halt. But they did not.

"My knowledge of my impending death came into my mind through the back door, and stood there like a stranger in the shadows, waiting for me to notice its presence. Of course, to kill me was Raulyn's only option, so as to prevent the truth of ids dishonor from being made known. I fought defensively, determined to win by survival, holding my guard and refusing to let the wind throw me onto Raulyn's blade, always aware of the sand running in the glass. Soon, time would be called, and the match would be over.

"But Raulyn called a wind against which I could not fly, a fierce downwind which knocked me off my plane, and threatened to dash me into the side of the mountain. I lost my temper then, and rather than fight for my equilibrium, I grabbed hold of Raulyn's foot, and took idre with me."

My attention riveted on Eia's tale, I cringed at the image of two Aeyries, linked together, falling along a steep mountainside. To crash into the glass would be injury or death, but in order to have a chance of surviving unharmed, they would have to break free of each other.

Eia continued matter-of-factly, "I suppose it was fear that cut through my anger enough to convince me to let go of Raulyn. I did, and I managed to break my fall. But Raulyn could not. After many hearings, I was awarded the black blade by judgment, and Raulyn was barred forever from the competition. We did not know for two more days whether or not id would survive ids injuries. Id was only half healed when id left t'Fon in the dark of night, and I never saw idre again."

Eia had told the tale matter of factly, but ids self-blame could not be entirely hidden. Though the competitiveness of the Quai-du games has been fiercely defended by the participants, and though Eia idreself had never missed the games, I heard in ids voice the ambiguity of one who thinks, perhaps, too much. I heard the unspoken question: "If I had not cared so much about winning, perhaps Raulyn would not have cared so much, either. If we could have been friends, then we would not have to be sitting here today, trying to outguess the future."

I glanced at Bet. She stared out to sea, the paper half crumpled under her hand. I said to her, "Somehow, I always knew that Raulyn's reasons would come down to something petty like personal revenge."

"Is it so petty to want your power back? Or to want to remake the past?" Bet's gaze refocused on my face, until I had to look away. How easy it is, sometimes, to start thinking that we are wiser or better than our opponents.

Delan, sitting wearily on a block of glass, watched a wave wash up the sandy beach, cover ids feet briefly, and then slide back toward the sea. Two more Mers had come in with the wave. They hitched themselves up the sand with undulating motions of their bodies, clutching their flippered hands across their chests.

Delan said, "For many long years we have withstood violent attacks. Assasination attempts, assaults on the community, attempts to poison our soil, attacks on the Mers at sea . . . Always we thought, soon it has to stop. This hate cannot continue forever. Yet it continued.

"Not until just a few months ago did we realize that the source of the hatred was not merely political. And it was you who told us, Laril. Do you remember, when Raulyn was spying on us as we visited your parent at t'Cwa? You said, 'Raulyn.' And because you spoke with a mage's tongue, and I heard with a mage's ears, Raulyn's secret was a secret no longer. I think id had hoped to wait for a dramatic moment to reveal ids identity, no doubt at the moment of our defeat.''

"Id has been trying to destroy Triad for years?'' I said in bewilderment. "But why has id failed?''

Eia's face twitched with amusement. "Better to ask, why does id imagine id could succeed? Consider this: why could Raulyn not pull idreself out of the fall? Id was too weary to do so. Bringing up the winds had been more exhausting to idre than flying them was to me. Do you see, every last one of us, mage or not, is governed by the same laws. Whether we are fighting a Quai-du battle, or summoning up a wind, our body pays the cost. Raulyn must work within the same limits that we all must work under.

"But Raulyn is alone, and we have each other: se'ans and em'ans, sh'mans, healers and Quai-du masters, Mers, Walkers, Aeyries, and Orchths, plenty of food and astonishing wealth. We are not the bottoms in this battle, Laril, and never have been. We overpower idre a hundred times.''

I opened my mouth to speak, but heard the scratching of Bet's pen on the paper and held my tongue. She wrote vehemently, angrily, the tip of the pen tearing the page. When she handed the paper to me, I read out loud, "Raulyn is a carnivore.'' That was all, the grossest of insults, written as if in a temper tantrum of hatred.

But it was enough to make Delan's features grow hard and narrow, not with scorn for Bet's childishness, but with anger and worry. "You know this? That id is practicing sorcery?''

Bet nodded once and glared without blinking into Delan's own fiercely angry eyes. I had taken Delan for a gentle person, a reasonable peacemaker. But I found myself remembering suddenly that this quiet-spoken, thoughtful person was credited with single-handedly averting Teksan's War.

"That Raulyn had not one, but two young mages in ids power is no accident, I'm certain," Delan said. "But to force you to use your talents on ids behalf is not—"

Bet had snatched the paper out of my hand, and was writing again. "Ask Laril about sex with Raulyn," she wrote. I hesitated but read it out loud because I could think of nothing else to do. "I'd really rather not talk about it," I added belatedly.

"Was it rape?" Delan asked quietly.

"It was in the end," I said wearily.

"Let us assume, for the sake of argument, that if it was rape in the end, then it was rape in the beginning. You just did not realize it."

I stared blankly at Delan, and then at Bet, both of whom seemed to understand what I did not. It was the Orchth, who had been lying so long in unmoving silence that I had finally decided he must be asleep, who clued my understanding. "The mage was eating you," he said. "Eating you alive. Eating not the meat off your bones, but the life out of your flesh."

After a moment Delan said, "No doubt something similar happened to Bet. What I think she wants us to realize is this: if Raulyn had learned how to drain another's power through sex, then id almost certainly has also learned how to do it more effectively through pain. It is common knowledge that pain is the source for most Walker sorcery. If Raulyn is in fact practicing sorcery, then ids power is not limited at all."

The memory of Alis'te's tortured flesh made me stand up restlessly, and stare grimly out to sea. "Then the moonbane weapon is just a child's toy to idre now."

The Orchth raised his head sharply. "I smell truth. What do you know?"

"I—" I shook my head, feeling utterly confused and exhausted. "I don't know if it means anything. By the night of the attack on Triad, during which Bet escaped and exploded Mairli's powder—never mind, I will tell you the entire story in a moment—by then, Raulyn was utterly exhausted. Bet and I had destroyed ids tower, and I think the stones themselves were some kind of storehouse for ids power."

Delan nodded, murmuring a confirmation that id had heard of such things before.

"The moonbane weapon was a last, desperate attempt to destroy you. If not for Bet, the attack would have succeeded. But when the attack failed, Raulyn did not seem to feel the failure. In fact, id looked twenty years younger the next day. Id must have discovered something that very night which renewed id's power."

I took in a deep breath, and held it. But my memory stared back at me, blank as the sky. "And I don't know what it was," I said desperately. "I just don't know what it was."

By the time we began the climb up the cliff path once more, the day had aged from noon to evening, and we had indeed talked about Raulyn, as Eia had predicted, until my tongue threatened to fall out and my ears felt as if they had turned to stone. But we seemed no closer to knowing what to do about idre.

Eia and Delan argued with each other in hushed voices during the entire climb. The Orchth, to warm Stilvin's chilled flesh, carried him on his back as lightly as if he weighed no more than a piece of paper. At the end of the procession, Bet and I walked hand in hand.

She could not say anything, and I chose silence. I supposed that her thoughts were similar to mine. I thought about the Mers, who had always seemed little more than a child's tale to me, but now moved in my heart, graceful with the ancient mystery of the sea. I thought about Raulyn, for I understood better ids peculiar madness, and I hated that understanding. How much easier it is to simply hate what offends us! And I thought about Bet, whose seven long years of servitude had begun with what she could only describe as the rape of her soul, as Raulyn rummaged through her being, taking what was of use to idre and leaving the rest in shambles.

"I have healed," she had written. "Some of my talents have regenerated. But I can never recover."

"Of course, after what id did to you, you were of little further use to idre," Delan had commented dryly. "I suppose id learned from ids mistakes, and invented a less destructive method to use with Laril."

That was all. My disappointment weighed my steps as we climbed the cliff. I suppose I had been hoping that Delan would know how to help Bet, but id said not a word about it. We walked awkwardly up the narrow path, but I never let go of Bet's hand. Somehow, I knew how important it was.

In the crisp evening air, we could hear chaotic shouting as soon as we reached the top of the cliff, even though the community was still far across the field. Stilvin woke out of his doze to lift his head from the Orchth's shoulder and say to Delan and Eia, "The attack has already begun."

Delan turned to us, and said unnecessarily, "Don't let go of each other. Not for a moment. And stay with Orgulanthgrnm. Do you understand?" Eia was already sprinting across the field, but Delan would not follow after until Bet and I both nodded like bewildered children. The Orchth continued steadily up the path, and Bet and I trailed after, gripping each other's hand so tightly that we cupped a pocket of sweat between our palms.

The yard outside Triad looked like a battleground. As the Orchths, awakened from their sleep by the racket, peered cautiously out of cracked open windows, blinking painfully in the bright light of day, Walker and Aeyrie, young and old, faced off in angry shouting matches. Onfrits swooped and swirled overhead, chittering an anxious cacophony of sound. In the middle of it all, a Walker male and an Aeyrie, dusty and scraped as if they had only recently been rolling in the dirt, writhed angrily in the grips of Delan and Eia, striving to get free. Delan shouted something, but in the commotion I could not understand the words.

A mixed group of Aeyrie and Walker, young Nasha among them, stood apart in a quiet cluster, grasping each other by the hand as tightly as Bet and I clung to each other. Only the Merfriend se'ans and the Orchths seemed immune to whatever poison Raulyn had sent into the hearts of the Triad-re. How easily we Walkers and Aeyries are stirred to hate each other, I thought miserably.

Orgulanthgrnm tossed back his head and uttered an aching, sweet cry. The other Orchths, sheltered in their barn, echoed it, raising their voices like a honed edge to cut through the clamor and silence it. At last, Delan's voice could be heard, shouting, "We are under attack! A clever mage indeed, to turn us against each other, and pull the foundation of our strength out from under us. Look at the Merfriends!"

Heads turned to stare at the quiet cluster. "Take each other's hand," Delan said fiercely. "We are one people!" Aeyrie and Walker groped reluctantly for a hand to hold. "We are one people," they mumbled sullenly, like children forced to recite a creed. But the violent anger which had filled the place like an electrical storm dissipated all in a moment, leaving behind a great crowd of shamefaced Walkers and Aeyries, not the least of whom were the two in the center.

"Raulyn is always underestimating us, isn't id,"I commented dryly to Bet. But my heart defied my tone of voice, expanding in my chest until it scarcely seemed possible that I could contain it. Hate, even the hate between the races, even the ages old, ages bitter hatred of Aeyrie for Walker and Walker for Aeyrie, even this hatred could be banished.

Bet let go of my hand, for just the fraction of a moment, to put her arm around my waist and hug me. I pressed my face into her sweaty shirt. *Oh, Bet,* I cried silently. *If only you were whole! What has Raulyn stolen from us?*

At a hastily-assembled meeting in the Orchths' barn of all people of the Triad, the strength of the community once again displayed itself to me. Even at the one meal I had eaten at their communal table, I had been too preoccupied to pay much attention to my surroundings. Now I noticed the Orchth cubs, awakened prematurely from their day's rest, tumbling about with Aeyrie and Walker children. Now I watched a Walker woman rest her head on the flank of an Orchth, I saw an Orchth call her favorite onfrit from the rafters, I saw an Aeyrie and a Walker hold each other closely in the privacy of a dark corner.

Perhaps it was then that I understood in my heart a truth that few of my people had ever willingly contemplated. I saw the richness and wealth of that gathering, and I understood why my people the Aeyries are a dying race. Long ago, offended by the Walkers that were rapidly populating the land, we had retreated to our isolated mountain communities, to practice our arts, crafts, and sciences in peace. In order to survive, we sold the wealth of our hands, hearts, and minds. But in our contempt we did not learn from the Walkers, and so we stagnated. Because we did not grow, we were dying out. To blame the violent, unschooled, uncouth Walkers for our decline and forget that we had chosen our own solitude, that had been too easy.

In the chaos of activity that followed the meeting, my new understanding fogged my vision and faltered my steps, giving Bet good cause to snap at me impatiently. I have never known anyone so gifted for identifying what needs to be done: she dragged me from place to place, telling me to pack this or carry that, as if she had lived in the community her entire life. The children had been hustled into the main building already, and we followed, laden with extra food stores and the personal belongings of the Orchths. Behind us, some onfrits led the herd of drafs into the shelter of the barn.

On my last trip into the house, I paused outside the door to look at the sky. The heat of the afternoon had dissipated as bank after bank of thick, black clouds moved in. Now the wind had begun to pick up, and I could actually hear the waves crashing into the distant cliffs.

"I fear we will lose the boat house," said Delan. Id had been standing at my side for some time, so quietly that I had not noticed. "It is the oldest building, a landmark in its way. And the two boats at anchor off shore surely will be wrecked. Fortunately, our biggest ship is already at winter anchor in the south."

"It is going to be that bad a storm?"

"A hurricane, the Mers said."

"I thought that was just a metaphor."

Delan tucked a warm hand into the crook of my elbow. "Never say 'just' a metaphor. Have you not seen how the winds of the Void affect the winds of this earth? Which is the metaphor and which the reality? If we change the direction of the wind, as Raulyn seems able to do, are we meddling with the Void, and thereby altering the future?"

I shook my head dizzily.

"When you think of Raulyn's anger, what image do you see?"

"I see—a storm."

"And I—" Delan gestured at the angry sky. "I see a hurricane."

"But why? Raulyn cannot kill us with wind and rain."

"I wish I were so certain of that."

"Eia is convinced that we have nothing to fear from Raulyn. And hasn't the Triad demonstrated again that you—we—are stronger by far than Raulyn's magic?"

"Eia." Delan sighed. "Eia thinks that this whole business is ids personal responsibility. That all we need to do is resolve the old grudge, and Raulyn will be satisfied at last."

"I think so, too," I said honestly. "A blade match, with witnesses, and no magic on either side. You know Eia will win."

"And what would that resolve, unless it were a fight to the death? And how would we stop Raulyn from using magic, once Eia had made idreself vulnerable?"

I began to speak about honor, and then laughed at myself. "Raulyn will do what id wishes to do. You can't protect Eia somehow?"

"My magic lies in my ability to anticipate and prevent. I know that in a match fight with Raulyn, Eia will die. Therefore, there must be no match. That is my magic, Laril."

"And if Eia chooses not to believe you . . . "

Delan shook ids head slowly, staring into the advancing storm. "Then I will be widowed. And who knows what will happen to the h'loa p'rlea, without Eia?"

"Are you telling me that the future of the Aeyrie people depends on what happens here?"

Delan tugged a thin, paint-stained hand through ids tangled mane. "If, if, if," id sighed. "Yes, too much hinges on Eia's survival, and always has. Yes, I am guarding not just ids person, but ids hot-hearted vision. And yes, Raulyn can destroy Eia, and all Eia's work, and all the work of the Triad, with one motion of ids glass blade. I know all of this. But I do not know what to do about it."

Chapter 18

A tortured voice screamed in my dreams. I jerked awake with my heart in my throat, but it was only the wind. The house sighed and groaned with pain, and the shuttered windows rattled hollowly even though the shutters had been nailed shut. What warmth had remained in the room had been sucked away through the walls, and in little puffs and gusts of freezing wind, the storm had entered the very bed, chilling the blankets and turning the sheets to ice.

Bet twisted miserably in her dreams. I wrapped her with my arms and she settled into the warmth of my fur, breathing too quickly to be asleep any longer. Drumbeats of hail rapped sharply on the shutters, and Bet's muscles gave a startled jump. The wind's scream sank to a moan.

"How can anyone sleep?" she whispered. As if in reply, the ceiling creaked overhead, and voices murmured in the hallway.

"Are you cold?" I said. "Let me warm you."

I will say this. Perhaps I had never made love with a Walker before, but I was a fast learner. And Bet— oh, she twisted me like a lump of clay in her hands. "You Aeyries," she said later. "Why are you making me love you, Laril of t'Cwa?"

I replied honestly, "This is the way I can reach you."

"If we could talk with each other would you still want to be my lover?"

"Even more."

"Isn't it hard to love me? Like trying to fill up the Void?"

"You make me rich, Ysbet."

As if to mock our brave tenderness, the building groaned around us. I wondered suddenly what would happen if the winds grew strong enough to take off the roof, or to shift the stones on their foundations. As the wind's sighs escalated to screams, Bet sat up in bed, shivering violently.

"Maybe if you put on some clothes," I suggested reluctantly.

"Listen!" she said. "Don't you hear it?"

"Hear what?"

"Listen."

The wind sobbed and shrieked in my ears. I thought of the Winds of the Void, the Winds of the Future, altered so casually to suit Raulyn's madness. And then I heard the voices, crying with agony, and fear, and desperation, and pain. They shrieked with the voice of the wind, but the agony that chilled my blood and ached my heart was the agony of people. "Hell-winds," I whispered.

"Id must die," Bet said. Her voice fell into the wind-loud room like a stone falling to earth. "Raulyn must die."

We found Delan among the inhabitants of the second floor crowding into the kitchen, folding their bedding into makeshift pallets on the floor, reassuring frightened children in voices tight with worry. In the dining room next door, the Orchths made the walls creak as they brushed past. They told stories in their rumbling, sing-song voices, to distract the restless cubs.

"The roof made such a racket in the wind that no one could sleep," Delan said, pushing us back out into the hallway.

"Will it blow off?" I had to shout so my voice would be heard over the wind.

"The craftsmen say no. But what roof was ever built to withstand a wind like this?" Delan looked worriedly upward at the shadows that hovered in the corners of the ceiling. "The h'shal h'ta is in the attic, full of paintings."

"Couldn't you bring them downstairs?"

"We are so crowded together already that the people in the kitchen could bring only their bedding with them. Why should I receive special privilege?"

I started to argue, but realized it would be fruitless and held my tongue. "This is your second sleepless night in a row," I commented. "How will we stand against Raulyn if you are too tired?"

Delan raised an eyebrow at my presumption, then shrugged. "I can't stand against Raulyn in any case. Not in the way you mean." Id leaned against the wall, a pale shadow with pale wings, weary as a flame in the wind. "I have scried glass, stone, water, and flame. But I see nothing of any use. I have done all I can do, unless you have any suggestions."

We stood a long time in the hallway, just looking at each other.

Then Bet said, "Have you scried the wind?"

Eia found us standing with our ears pressed to a window in the dining hall, surrounded by the warm, fur-scented stillness which always seemed to collect in the presence of the Orchths. "The tower roof has blown away," id said conversationally. "We can assume that few of the trees are left standing. Any of the buildings not made of stone—the barn, the bathhouse, the outbuildings . . ."

Delan straightened heavily. "What am I supposed to say?"

"How long will you allow our land to suffer this destruction? Say that you will challenge Raulyn on my behalf."

"I will not be party to your pointless death."

"Del—" Eia sighed with exasperation. "You are as stubborn as a medog."

"So are you, Malal Tefan Eia. Now leave me alone; I am busy." Delan pressed ids ear once more to the chilly, damp wood. Eia turned angrily away. I looked after idre worriedly, as id walked among the cubs tumbling about on the floor. Then I pressed my ear once more to the shutter. The wind cried with the voices of a torture chamber. I could scarcely bear to listen to it.

Delan finally sighed wearily and straightened, rubbing a sore ear. "I can't understand what they are saying. Can you?"

"No."

"Bet?"

The darkness of the room obscured her in shadows, yet I saw the slight motion of her nod. "Let's get a pen and paper," I said. But her hand on my elbow stopped me. She lifted a hand and with the pen of her finger used the reddish, faint ink of light to write on a paper of darkness the single word, "Lost." For a moment it hovered across the shadows, and then it trailed away in fading sparks.

"Great Winds," Delan muttered. "I wish I had known you before Raulyn got to you."

I lay back into the cradling support of the stone walls, and stared into the darkness. "Lost," I said.

"Lost in the Void. Remember the Walkers that Raulyn left in the Void? Like food in the storeroom. It is their pain that empowers idre. If we could find a way to free them . . ."

Delan hoarsely sighed ids breath out of ids body. "As the Orchths would say, I smell truth."

"Can you do it?"

"I have no talent for the Void. I only found you there because of our kinship. To locate and free utter strangers—maybe I could do it in a lifetime or two." Yet Delan's voice sang peacefully, almost sleepily through the darkness. "I am a fool in my way," id continued. "All night I have been asking a question, the answer to which I already knew. I painted the solution last night, between darkness and dawn. A painting of the two of you, Laril and Bet."

Id took my hand, and reached for Bet's as well. "Laril, you are the one who can free the Walkers from the Void. And Bet . . ." Id hesitated, then concluded in a voice gone soft and gentle. "You know what I do not. I trust you to act wisely."

On the second floor, the wind screamed desperately, its frantic, tortured voice scraping across the stone walls like glass on metal. The raw cold raked icy fingertips through my fur. Wrapped in three blankets, Bet still shuddered with cold like a wraith in wind as we made our way through the deserted corridor.

Ahead of us, Delan opened a door and flicked a tinderstick. One by one, the flames of an air lamp flared, illuminating a patch of hallway and the interior of a cluttered room. A lumpy straw pallet, stripped of its blankets, was supported by ropes stretched on a frame, a bed large enough for two to sleep in comfortably, or three intimately. From the ceiling joist an infant basket hung, dripping a forgotten blanket.

A cluttered desk filled one entire end of the room, and two walls of bookshelves, crammed to overflowing, seemed on the verge of spilling their loads to the floor. A painting, in which mysterious darkness and vivid light conversed together to create a portrait of a younger Eia illuminated by sunrise, graced one wall.

Delan removed the woven covering from the block of pale blue glass which rested on a beautifully carved, age black binewood stand. Such treasured scrying glasses are passed from mage to mage, their clarity and trueness increasing with age. This one looked old enough to have originated in the dawn of time. As Eia, Bet, and I clustered around it, I dared touch its surface with a fingertip.

For a moment I felt as if I had dipped my hand and forearm into snow. But the illusion of cold shifted in the space of a moment to a spreading warmth. Light shimmered in the glass. I guiltily snatched my hand back, but Delan smiled reassuringly. "Calan'a'fa has been used to teach so many young mages how to scry that it all but does the work for you."

Id stroked a finger across the polished surface, light shimmering in the wake of ids touch. "Arta Kindel Raulyn, Ishta Mairli Delan calls you."

In the center of the glass, a star exploded.

Raulyn laughed, a sweet, drunken laugh. I remembered that laugh now. I remembered the sated glow of ids eyes, the intoxicated, easy, satisfied smile of ids face. Oh, I had contented idre with the sweet nourishment of my youthful fire. Such power I had felt, even as I was eaten alive. My stomach twisted with nausea at the memory.

I grasped Bet's cold hand, and clung to it like a guide rope in a storm.

"What is it, Delan, I am busy," said Raulyn.

"You venture where you have no right. I bid you cease."

Raulyn laughed again. "You cozener, such nerve. You have somewhat of mine, how about a trade?"

"Such as?" Delan said remotely.

Raulyn's face peered into the glass, fat and self-satisfied as an infant at suck. "You have my children, one Bet and one Laril. Send them home to me."

"They are not prisoners here. If they wish, they may go."

"They are not prisoners, just as the Aeyries of my household are not prisoners? I love your lies; they have such naive wit."

"The Aeyries of your household are at the Hall of Justice in t'Han. Feel free to seek them there."

"What, will they be exiled again?" Raulyn laughed richly.

"Their fate is out of my hands. Silence the winds, Raulyn."

"Silence the winds? Silence the winds? My dear friend, the winds have not even begun to blow! Your trees are uprooted, your barn is kindling, your drafs are dead and dying, your boats are splinters, your Mers are being butchered on the shoals—"

Delan brushed the glass with a finger. Raulyn talked on, but not a word of it could be heard in the room. Delan yawned and stretched luxuriously. "Is id in the habit of carrying on like this?" id asked me dryly.

"So many have fallen in love with the sound of ids voice. Perhaps id has fallen under ids own spell."

Raulyn's lips suddenly stopped moving. I realized belatedly that though we could not hear idre, id could still hear us. If Delan had meant to fan ids fury, it certainly had worked. Id touched the glass again, and said politely, "I beg your pardon?"

"You play dangerous games, little mage," Raulyn

said, very softly. Delan had succeeded in breaking ids manic, drunken mood, but I preferred it to this cold anger.

"If you are quite done listening to yourself talk, perhaps you would do some serious negotiating."

"You have nothing I want."

"No?" Delan lifted the blade id held in one hand, and held it before the glass. Black as a sliver of night, sparkled about with stars, its fine, sharp edge sang as it moved through the air, and hummed when held still. The cleata skin hilt was traced with rare silver. Its beauty stopped my heart mid-beat, and I ached with wanting, just to touch it, just to hold it for a moment, just to draw a painless drop of my own blood with its impossibly sharp edge. "Not even this?" Delan said.

After a moment Raulyn said indifferently, "The blade has always been mine by right, stolen by trickery. But why should I care any longer?"

Across the glass from me, Eia shifted angrily, but held ids tongue.

Delan said, "Malal Tefan Eia asked me to convey this challenge to you. A fight on foot, at dawn, at the edge of the Gap. To the death."

"Eia always was a fool."

"No magic," Delan added. "And the winds stop now. In exchange, I and all the members of Triad, the Mers and the Merfriends in particular, pledge their noninterference."

"Why should I pin so much on so little? A few more hours of wind, and your children will be dying in the cold."

"You may destroy our house, our land, our animals, ourselves, and our children. But where is the victory in such destruction? No one disputes your mage-power; there is no need for you to prove it. But unless you meet Eia as an equal on the field of combat, you will never know which of you truly deserves the blade.''

"You must think I am a fool," Raulyn said. Ids voice rang through the room, as cold as the wind and as sharp as a knife blade. "I know what you are trying to do. But your few hours of respite will win you nothing. Eia will be dead, and you will still be hostages to the storm.''

"In twenty-five years, Eia has never been defeated. The blood of the best assassins you could send against idre has been spilled on the blade. You cannot win against idre, and you never could, except by dishonesty and duplicity. I am not concerned about the outcome of this battle. But if you do not accept the challenge, I will see to it that you are recognized for the coward you are. That is all I have to say, do you accept?''

Raulyn laughed richly. "Why not, little mage? Why not?''

Before we had finished covering the now-dark glass, the wind's voice had already diminished from a shriek to a moan. Delan collapsed onto the bare mattress. "Get some sleep," id ordered myself and Bet, and shut ids eyes.

Eia led us out. "Never mind, I will get a blanket for idre. Do as you are told," id added ungraciously.

"But there is so much we have to do, and—''

"—And none of it will happen if we don't get some rest.''

"How am I supposed to sleep?" I grumbled as I followed Bet down the steep stairs to the lower floor. But scarcely had I lain down beside Bet when sleep took me like a tide washing a bit of wood out to sea.

Sometimes you have no choice. Sometimes you close your eyes, and trust, and trust, until your body hurts with the effort of it. Sometimes it is the only thing you can do. So I slept deeply, and awoke to a half-singing rumble at the door, and rose up to admit the third or so of Ogulanthgrnm which could fit into the narrow opening. "Not-quite daybreak," he said.

"Where is Delan?"

"In the kitchen."

I bent over to kiss Bet's cheek, and felt her stir under my touch like a streamer in a breeze. Soon, I promised her. But what I was promising I did not know. Calmer than I would have believed possible, I followed the Orchth down the hallway.

In the kitchen, sprawled beside the warm glow of a recently refueled fire, Eia nursed the perpetual hunger of the hatchling, simultaneously eating a c'duni bar from ids free hand. Id scarcely glanced at me as I came in. I looked over ids long. sleek, lightly-muscled limbs, and then let my gaze linger on ids broad, muscular torso. We are a long-lived, slow-aging people. Eia could ride the crest of ids prime condition for years yet before starting the slow decline. Even then, experience would give idre an edge even where the energy of youth failed. If id were going to ids defeat this cold morning, then it would only be because Raulyn once again intended to disregard honor.

Delan sat on the other stool, a sketch pad on ids knees, pen scraping rapidly across the smooth paper. I took a c'duni bar from the basket on the table, and poured myself a cup of tea. I stood behind Delan and watched the swift, loving portrait of Eia and the hatchling take form on the paper. The Orchth settled on the floor and began to play his flute. At last Delan stood up, set down ids pen and paper, and plucked the hatchling out of Eia's arms. "Time"

The Stormdancer took in a deep breath, let it out, and came to ids feet in a quiver of movement. "Well," id said.

Delan put an arm around idre briefly. Their mouths met in a businesslike kiss. "Be careful."

Eia grinned suddenly, cocky as a l'shil. "Why? I want to enjoy myself."

Id slipped out of the back door like a river pouring through its channel, controlled and powerful, graceful as a song. Del watched after idre, then turned to me an expressionless face. Id had gambled the love of ids life, the parent of ids children, and possibly the future of our people on my untried abilities. Still, I felt no fear.

"Take the eggling, l'frer," Delan said to the Orchth.

The infant uttered a protesting gurgle as id was passed from hand to hand, but immediately subsided into peaceful comfort in the furry embrace of the Orchth. "If id hungers, my mate will nurse idre," he said. "Id will grow fat on Orchth milk, and grow up to become a winged Orchth."

"Why not," Delan said. "Id will fit right in."

Hand in hand, we silently climbed the stairs. In Delan and Eia's room, a window hung ajar, and I caught a glimpse of the devastated trees, the flattened barn, and a few drafs standing in a bewildered huddle. Beyond, the ocean was as frothy as a bowl of cream.

Delan uncovered the glass.

A terror washed through my body, unlocking my knees and setting my heart to fluttering. "What difference is this going to make?" I cried.

"We are flying by s'olel, Laril. We will know when we know."

So. The first lesson of flying, the lesson on which the Aeyrie people have always trusted their lives: trust the wind, and it will carry you. So we must believe, even when a moonbane mage twiddles with the weaving of the patterns.

I stepped up to the blue glass. My breath on its cold-misted surface awakened a glow deep in its heart, like the glowing of a coal in ashes. I looked up into the charcoal eyes of my blood parent, and took both of ids hands in mine. "Tell me what to do," I said.

Chapter 19

Did I not know Raulyn's every smell, the intonations of ids voice, the expressions of ids face? Just as I could have followed in ids footsteps through a maze by smelling the scent of ids recent passage, so I could retrace ids passage through the Void. So Delan must have tracked me through that wilderness, tracked me by the smell of ids blood and the blood of ids parents flowing in my veins.

But this track I followed was too recent, too new. I looked behind myself, and saw the glitterdust trail of my life-fire spreading behind me, like vapor in sunshine. This time, I would not be lost here. I had entered, not through a callous rent in the fabric of the Universe, but through the crystalline clarity of the scrying glass. Delan had shown me how to strew my backtrail with stars. Delan had shown me many things.

And suddenly I knew more than my teacher, and I had left idre behind.

Now I cast about, seeking an older, staler scent, seeking the where and when of another time, another passage. I knew that I would find it, and I did. For moments or years I traveled this old trail, flying on wings of my own making when I could not ride the winds of the Void, but always taking care to leave nothing displaced. Here and there I noticed the signs of Raulyn's meddling, and thought I perceived ways in which ids damage could be mended. But not on this journey.

Like a bowstring dipped in the vivid light of sunrise, the thread stretched through the Void, burning with blood-red flame. How long I had been following its guide I did not know, when at last I found what I sought. Raulyn's prisoners hung each in their isolated agony, some burning with blinding white fire, others glowing dully like burnt-out cinders. Their fires were sucked away from them like fibers from a tuft of wool, to spin the eldritch thread of Raulyn's power.

I took my own fire, and made of it a web, frail and fine as expensive lace. With one cast I gathered them in, and as I watched, Raulyn's burning thread frayed away in the rising winds of the Void. With the burden of a hundred lives in my arms, I rode the winds home.

And landed on my knees in a keening, screaming crowd of Walker children, and pressed my face to the rough floorboards, and breathed a deep breath of cold air into my lungs. I felt as if I had flown a hundred days without rest or food. I could have lain where I had landed, and slept.

"Laril." Pale with shock and anger, Delan touched my shoulder.

"I'll be all right," I said weakly.

Aeyries and Walkers, their faces set with horror, filled the room, taking the dazed children away. Before I could turn my face away, I saw what was left when the children were gone. To this day I see them in my memory, the sucked-out husks of people, their bones overlaid by the thin covering of their skin, their eyes staring with dull surprise into the face of death. Healers wandered from one to the next, paused a moment, then shook their heads and moved on.

"It is too late for them. They cannot live," Delan said wearily. "I think they must be Raulyn's followers, the first he used for this purpose. Id has nearly entirely consumed them. So id augmented their numbers with kidnapped children . . ."

I felt sick to my stomach. "Whose children are they?"

"Walkers. We will send them home again, if we can."

For a moment longer I pressed my hands to the solid wood. Then I heard the rising wind rush across the rooftop, and I jerked to my feet. "Raulyn does not realize yet what happened—id is calling forth another storm! But in a moment id will know . . ." I rushed to the scrying glass, stepping heedlessly over the scavenged remains of Raulyn's victims. Delan caught up with me when I had nearly reached the scrying glass. "We have to know what happened to Eia," I said.

"Yes, we must know," Delan replied, ids voice dull and hollow with despair. Ids long-fingered hand resignedly brushed the glass.

A star of light burst across its surface, revealing with strange slowness the choppy sea, the jagged edge of the cliff. My gaze focused on the shattered pieces of Eia's black blade, scattered like trash across the bare earth. Delan breathed, "Great Winds!"

Then I realized what was happening on that cliff's edge, and my heart grew hard and cold as ice in my breast. "Bet. Oh, my Bet!"

* * *

This is how it was when Ysbet ib Ranor awoke from her sleep that cold morning. She sat up in the bed, and filled her nostrils with the bodyscent lingering in the room. For the first time in memory, no weight of de-

pression pressed her earthward, tempting her weary
eyes closed, tempting her with the relief of death.

She smiled grimly. Today the long waiting would be
over, for good or for evil. She got swiftly out from
beneath the covers, ignoring the unpleasant pain of her
broken arm grating up to her shoulder. No doubt those
motherly healers would have fussed over her had she
told them about the pain, but she could spare no time
for them. She would live with a crooked healing if she
had to, if only she could truly live.

The sweetest of lovers, that Laril. Enough to put the
missing heart back into her body, to make her long for
healing, even to make her hope again. But that Delan,
clever as a well-spiced soup, smooth as cream, it was
Delan who had looked at her and known.

Known that while Eia faced the mage in a battle id
could not win, and Laril and Delan ventured into the
pathless wilderness of the Void, seeking something
they might not be able to find, she would not lie late
in her bed, passively awaiting the outcome. With great
precision Delan had chosen the words of ids promise
to Raulyn: No one of the Triad will interfere with the
battle. But, like Laril, Bet belonged nowhere. Delan's
promise did not bind her.

She dressed against the cold, wincing at the sharp
pain of her arm. She tied it up in its sling at last, and
wrapped a blanket around her shoulders for extra
warmth. Even so, as she went outside the cold seeped
through all her layers of clothing, reaching for her very
bones. Shivering, she stood surveying the devastation
of the storm. Pieces of the flattened barn were scattered across the field. Among the broken bodies of the
drafs, a few survivors wandered confusedly. Beyond
the field, a tangle of broken limbs, stripped of leaves,
marked what had once been the grove of trees.

She spoke soundlessly, saying, ''You who raped my

mind and then forced me to serve you, you who mocked me daily and taunted me with death, you who sought only your pitiless revenge for an imagined wrong, careless of the earth, the trees, the mountains, the moons, the creatures of the water, the earth, and the air, you," she said. "Raulyn, the one who taught me to serve despair, the one who with one breath blew out the light burning within me and left me empty and cold as an abandoned house, you, Raulyn."

She held burning hands to the burning sun. "Today you die," she said.

A few Walkers, stumbling with sleep, came out to offer care to the injured and weary drafs. Onfrits fluttered from place to place, crying with surprise at the devastation which had rendered their familiar home all but unrecognizable. But Bet slipped past Walker, draf, and onfrit unseen. After so many years of shrinking herself to fit too small a skin, to be invisible was the easiest of tricks.

She had walked right past Pau's nose the night she disabled the moonbane weapons. He had itched at the place where the breeze of her passing had displaced a few hairs of ids fur. She had disappeared like a ghost the night of the attack on Triad, after someone—of course, it must have been Laril—helped to undo the knots of her bindings. To disappear had been appallingly easy. And to explode the powder keg with just a small spark taken from her stores of anger, that, too, had been easy. But to accept the kindness of this unlikely community, to feel her pain and perhaps heal, to accept and reciprocate Laril's unexpected passion, these things had been much harder.

The world was frosted with ice. Thick ropes of it hung from the trees, and icy ponds filled the plowed furrows. Bet walked steadily, ignoring the burn of cold onto her bare feet. She breathed the frigid air deep into her lungs, and felt it ache there. All the unshed tears. All the lost years of her life. All the dead hopes and dreams. They filled her with an aching, ashyard silence.

She sensed the rousing of power in the building behind her. She paused to look back over her shoulder, and saw the flash of fire in an open window. "May you succeed," she wished Delan and Laril. "May you be well. May fate kiss your hands and unlock all your doors."

Then she turned and continued her long, solitary walk. The sun's edge peered nervously over the edge of the earth, but Ysbet cast no shadow.

As casually as a scholar rips a piece of paper in two, Raulyn rent open earth and sky. She heard the faint sound of ids drunken laughter. Don't you know, crazy mage, that you cannot thrive on a diet of pain? Don't you know that it will only make you mad?

She shifted into an unsteady, slithering lope. At the cliff's edge, Eia danced a quicksilver dance. If a burning flame cast the blackest of shadows, that shadow would be Eia Stormdancer, arrogant and dangerous, thoughtful and gentle, dark and light. Bet saw the stars in the black blade, as Eia and blade danced together.

Someday my Laril will be so beautiful, she thought. Someday ids courage and strength will bring the stars down from the sky, so, to shine like jewels in ids hand.

The laughing Red mage danced fire, the sun flashing in blinding points of light off the jewels in ids wings. But beside Eia, id looked no more graceful than a farmer plowing the field. Bet slowed down her headlong pace. Perhaps Delan had foreseen wrong. This did not look like a fight Eia was destined to lose. But no—three times, she watched them come together, shadow and fire, and each time shadow could have made a deathstroke, and did not.

Bet passed her hands over her eyes, and looked again. A glamour of light overlay Raulyn's flesh, an impregnable barrier. Even as she watched, Eia's blade slashed neatly across Raulyn's heart, but never touched ids flesh.

Raulyn laughed manically, snapping ids fingers in the air. Between one stroke and the next, Eia's black blade shattered in a shower of black stars. "I always said that honor would make a foo' of you, Eia," said Raulyn.

Bet began running again. When she looked up to check her progress, Eia was on ids knees, Raulyn's knifepoint at ids throat. Aeyries do not kneel, or require anyone else to kneel, this was a habit Raulyn had picked up from the Walkers id so detested. "Not yet," Raulyn said, dragging Eia to ids feet. Somehow Eia's hands had been bound together, not by a rope but by something worse, which cast a cold sweat of pain across Eia's face. Yet id turned a calm, proud face to Raulyn, and spoke softly, words which Bet could not hear, but which brought Raulyn's hand out in a bitter, coward's blow across ids face.

Eia fell to one knee, but immediately stood again.

"I want you to watch this," said Raulyn. "Then I will kill you."

Id's arms beckoned in a wild, extravagant gesture. Just a few steps away from idre now, Bet stopped her headlong charge as she felt the energy of the wind turn reluctantly on the spindle of Raulyn's arms. She was too late. She could not touch idre now, with the fullness of ids power upon idre. She dropped her body down to the earth, and hugged it to herself, so that the mage's winds would not topple her into the sea. "Watch," cried Raulyn, laughing hysterically. "Watch this, you sanctimonious, mealy-mouthed monger of—''

Mid-word, Raulyn stopped speaking, slack-mouthed. The rising winds fell suddenly still, still as a midsummer afternoon. In the sky, the clouds boiled away from the sun. In that moment Ysbet rose up out of her invisibility and stood, foot-spread upon the ice-crusted soil.

''You,'' Raulyn said. ''What have you done? What have you—''

''I name you,'' Bet said. ''Moonbane Raulyn, eater of souls. Tell me why you should live.''

''You—'' id said, and began to laugh. ''You, you nothing, you plower of fields . . .''

Id was still laughing as she stepped up to him, empty-handed. With her right hand she reached out and pressed into ids broad chest, dug her fingers into ids hot, soft fur. Still laughing, id slapped ids blade at her arm. But Ysbet had learned from the earth and the stones, and no power of air could move her. Yes, she had plowed, and she had hoed, and she had dug and planted, and built and rebuilt. And so she had found power, power of muscle and bone, power of leg and back, power of earth. Implacable, she pushed idre backward, one step at a time.

'You,'' Raulyn laughed, slashing ids blade playfully at her. ''You empty shell—'' Id was still laughing when she forced idre back, one more step, and ids foot stepped into empty air.

She watched id fall. Watched ids wings open uselessly, the bright jewels flashing in the sunlight. It was Laril who had taught her this, with ids love for the air, with the effortless grace of ids flight. She had never seen Raulyn fly, but why would anyone deny themselves such joy? Raulyn did not fly because id could not; that was why. Id fell like stone, and broke on the cruel rocks below. Almost at once, a crashing wave washed over ids body, and carried it away.

But she did not know for certain that id was dead until she felt Raulyn's chains upon her soul shatter. She, too, was falling over that cliff, but it did not matter to her. It would be quick, she thought, as she teetered on that edge. The Mers would carry her body out to sea, and she would float there on the rising tide, under the distant stars. She heard the waves crashing on the boulders below, and she sighed, and let herself fall.

And soared on white wings.

* * *

From above, the rock looked the size of a piece of paper. Somehow I managed to set Bet down securely, but my own feet slid out from under me as I landed on the water-slick surface. I fell, and the water's icy fingers grabbed me by the ankles. I scrabbled with my fingernails for a handhold, but the water surged hungrily. And then, in a shock of frigid water and irresistible power, a wave crashed over my head. But I felt a hand grip my wrist, and root me to the rock. The sea drew back as if cowed before the mage's power, and Bet dragged me up the rock.

"How could I have let you fall?" I said, when I could speak.

Bet turned her face to me. It scarcely seemed her face, shining with tears and with ocean spray. And those eyes, so deep.

I said, "I don't know how I knew—I brought myself through the Void, right to the edge of the cliff. If I had been wrong by even a fraction . . . Of course, we practice these things," I babbled on. "I cannot fly with something so heavy in my arms, but I can glide,

anyone can, though you are heavier than any Aeyrie—''
At last I fell silent under the steady gaze of her eyes.
Another wave crashed onto the rock, showering us
with spray. No doubt, I thought resignedly, this was a
rising tide.

Overhead, at the edge of the cliff, Eia shouted something. I could not hear ids words over the roar of the
sea. I began to shiver with cold and fear. My hand
gripping the edge of the rock already had gone numb
with cold. ''Bet,'' I said despairingly.

''Don't be afraid,'' she said. ''Laril, I want to ask
you something.''

I gasped as a wave crashed over us, and choked on
a freezing mouthful of salt water. As the water flowed
away, leaving us both plastered with foam and flotsam,
I heard Bet continue, gasping with cold as she spoke.
''You told me that Walkers can attend the University
at t'Cwa. If I am admitted there, would it shame you?''

''Shame me!'' I exclaimed.

''To have it be known that the taiseoch-dre of t'Cwa
is lovers with a Walker.''

''Bet,'' I said as firmly as I could, considering my
chattering teeth. I had noticed that the limitations on
Bet's ability to speak seemed to have been lifted by
Raulyn's death. What else, I wondered, had been
healed in her? But that question could wait. And her
assumption that I would return home—well, I would
have to confront Ishta. . . . Why not? I thought with
a sigh. But that, too, could wait.

''Listen,'' I said, as a wave crashed across my legs.
''I am not, and will not be ashamed. And you will be
more a teacher than a student. You can teach us how
to farm the glasslands, how to nurture a harvest of
caricha—do you know what that will mean to us? If
you and I survive.''

She kissed my mouth, a cold, salty kiss. ''If you

can fly me in the air, then I can swim you in the water. Just hold onto me and don't choke me.''

''But you have a broken arm!''

''I just have to get us beyond the breakers; it's not far. The Mers are waiting for us there. Hold onto me, Laril.''

I held on. The next time a wave washed over us, Bet let it carry us out to sea. But scarcely had we entered water deep enough to drown us, when I felt the bodies of the Mers buoy me up from below. Bet's hand sought out and clasped mine.

I shut my eyes with a sigh, and let the Mers carry me.

Glossary

'achea—a hallucinogen derived from a fungus, which is usually smoked in a pipe.

Aeyrie—a sentient species of winged hermaphrodites who live in remote communities in the mountains. Although they are a creative and ingenious people, their inability to grow their own food makes autonomy impossible.

Ahbi—the lucky moon.

Abki—the dark moon.

alinsa—a starchy white root that grows in swampy areas in the glasslands. A source of food in an emergency.

ast—a blooming sucker plant native to the Glass Mountains, the stems of which are processed to make astil, a tough, silky fiber.

caricha—an edible sea coral.

c'duni—a sweet bar of food eaten in flight for quick energy.

ch'ta—charismatic, having a strong and energetic personality.

cleata—giant sea lizards, whose shed skin is a tough, water-resistant material often used to make shoes.

c'lol-fe—"The wildness which comes after the confinement of winter."

cous—an edible grain.

criya—a rodentlike creature that lives communally, and sings at night.

crich—A powdered, dried fungus, the smoke of which is a mild hallucinogen.

Derksai—one of three lowland areas inhabited by Walkers, where the land is arable.

Digan-lai—a primitive, cave-dwelling Walker people, who make their living primarily by gathering and processing astil.

draf—a six-legged, shaggy beast of burden.

-du—a suffix meaning "having to do with flight."

em'an—an empath, one who has the gift of knowing another's feelings.

Fon—the Sun.

forty-day—the Walkers divide the year into ten periods of forty days each. (The Aeyries think in terms of four seasons, each lasting 100 days, and the Mers think in terms of winter and summer migrations.)

glass—a hard, durable crystal of which most of the world is composed, which occurs in a wide range of colors.

H'ldat—the native language of the Aeyries.

h'lana—a river wind, a strong, high-altitude wind on which Aeyries often travel long distances.

h'loa—a soft wind, a shifting of air.

h'loa p'rlea—the first warm wind of spring, the bearer of plant spores.

h'mil—a crosswind.

h'shal—any common room of an Aeyrie community.

hunterworm—A web-spinning worm which captures and devours flying insects.

h'ta—art.

id, idre, ids—the H'ldat pronouns.

kip—a herd animal raised for wool and milk products.

l'—a prefix indicating that what follows describes a person.

l'din—a gardener, a botanist. Also the name of the community where Teksan lived.

l'frer—a sibling, a nestfellow.

l'per—a parent.

l'shan—an immature Aeyrie, an infant or child.

l'shil—a newly adult Aeyrie, a wingling.

lightwands—a reedlike plant the stalks of which are dried and burned from the end for light.

Lla—the tiny moon.

Magic—unusual talents are considered normal among the Aeyrie population. Those with sufficient intelligence, creativity, and courage may find themselves "growing into" magic (as opposed to learning it). The talents of a particular mage develop as part of the maturation process, and will be unique to them. (However, a few abilities, such as scrying glass, are relatively common.) See "Sorcery."

m'chiste—a traditional Aeyrie card game.

medog—a large, stupid, grazing animal, with prehensile toes, native to the Glass Mountains.

Mer—a sentient, air-breathing species which inhabits the ocean. Mers live in gestalts, or herds, in which their telepathic links with each other result in a highly intelligent group consciousness. However, they normally have little concept of their existence as individuals.

onfrit—sentient, sociable, winged animals, with a facility for languages, the traditional companions of the Aeyries.

panja—a sucker plant with sweet-smelling blossoms.

Quai-du—the traditional Aeyrie martial art.

-re—a suffix indicating association (i.e., a Triad-re is a member of the Triad community).

se'an—a person with the gift for knowing another's thoughts, a telepath.

shadral—a partner in activity.

shadrale l'shil—Beginning sparring practice (in Quai-du).

sh'duni—a milky drink derived from nuts.

sh'man—a title indicating great respect.

s'olel—"The knowing which is feeling," kinesthetic knowledge.

Sorcery—the Walker art of spells and potions, of which acts of sadism are an integral part, which is viewed by most Walkers with superstition and awe. The Aeyries believe that the rituals of sorcery access the sorcerer's inborn talent, but in such a way that the magic and the person are perverted by the process. See "Magic."

t—"of" (prefix)

taiseoch—the hereditary chieftain of an Aeyrie community.

taloica—a meeting, a coming together of disparate directions or objectives.

tela—a sitting room.

Ula—a traditional Aeyrie community, built atop a hollow glass mountain.

waterwyth—An eellike freshwater creature.

DAW

Creatures of Wonder

LAURIE J. MARKS
☐ **DELAN THE MISLAID** (UE2325—$3.95)

A misfit among a people not its own, Delan willingly goes away with the Walker Teksan to the Lowlands. But there, the Walker turns out to be a cruel master, a sorcerer who practices dark magic to keep Delan his slave—and who has diabolical plans to enslave Delan's people, the winged Aeyrie. And unless Delan can free itself from Teksan's spell, it may become the key to the ruin of its entire race.

☐ **MOONBANE MAGE** (UE2415—$3.95)

Here is the story of Delan's child, a spoiled royal progeny, who is kidnapped by an evil magician of its own species, and must tap reserves both personal and magical to save her race from a suicidal sorcerous war.

JACKIE HYMAN
☐ **SHADOWLIGHT** (UE2397—$3.50)

The Radiants have long ruled in the city of Ad-Omaq through their powers as adepts. Yet they are not the only magic wielders in the land. There is an older race, a horned people drawing strength from nature itself. To the Radiants, this race is a menace to be eliminated—but they have not counted on Shadow, born of both races and gifted with the special mind abilities of each. . . .

TAD WILLIAMS
☐ **TAILCHASER'S SONG** (UE2374—$4.95)

This best-selling feline fantasy epic tells the adventures of Fritti Tailchaser, a young ginger cat who sets out, with boundless enthusiasm, on a dangerous quest which leads him into the underground realm of an evil cat-god—a nightmare world from which only his own resources can deliver him.